RAKEHEART

RAKEHEART

RUSTY DAVIS

FIVE STAR
A part of Gale, a Cengage Company

Farmington Hills, Mich • San Francisco • New York • Waterville, Maine
Meriden, Conn • Mason, Ohio • Chicago

LIBRARY OF CONGRESS CATALOGING-IN-PUBLICATION DATA

Names: Davis, Rusty, author.
Title: Rakeheart / Rusty Davis.
Description: First Edition. | Farmington Hills, Mich. : Five Star, a part of Gale, Cengage Learning, 2019.
Identifiers: LCCN 2018044047 (print) | LCCN 2018045919 (ebook) | ISBN 9781432857332 (ebook) | ISBN 9781432857325 (ebook) | ISBN 9781432857318 (hardcover)
Subjects: | GSAFD: Western stories.
Classification: LCC PS3604.A9755 (ebook) | LCC PS3604.A9755 R35 2019 (print) | DDC 813/.6—dc23
LC record available at https://lccn.loc.gov/2018044047

First Edition. First Printing: July 2019
Find us on Facebook—https://www.facebook.com/FiveStarCengage
Visit our website—http://www.gale.cengage.com/fivestar/
Contact Five Star Publishing at FiveStar@cengage.com

Printed in Mexico
1 2 3 4 5 6 7 23 22 21 20 19

RAKEHEART

CHAPTER ONE

Death waited at the crossing.

Through the screen of bushes, he could see twenty men guarding the ford, standing between him and the sparkling water that reflected the Texas sun. Armed. Ready. Confident. They had won the race. Now they were predators hoping for prey. Waiting. Knowing they held the edge.

Death traveled on the road.

The dozen horsemen he had left behind in the darkness would find his trail sooner or later. Likely sooner. This was their part of Texas, not his. Now that the sun was full up, his trail would be visible. All trails led to death. The last turnoff from the main road that took him to the river was miles back. He might make it before his pursuers. Likely not.

Jaws were closing. They had not swallowed him yet.

There were only so many of Colonel Harlan Delacroix's Knights of the Golden Empire in Red Rock County. Maybe if he got upriver, away from the ranches and towns Delacroix controlled—used to control—he'd be safe. Time to find out. Stayin' and dyin' didn't seem like a good plan.

He tied the stolen horse to a tree. He had a Colt and a Winchester, maybe fifty shells extra for the pistol and what felt like less for the rifle when he dug into the saddlebags. He could send the horse into the waiting men. A distraction that might create an opening. No. A death was a death, and there were enough of those already. There were men who needed killing.

Horse didn't ask for this. Only men did fool things like that.

He reached up to stroke the horse's face, scar from the manacles that held his wrist still livid after three days on the run. He hoped the animal would find a better owner. At least it would get a rest.

Death might be waiting up the bank. He paused. There ought to be a thought, a memory—something to recall if it ended here. There wasn't. He moved out.

Two miles later, the trees moved away from the river. He was still. A fly buzzed loudly. Could it be forded? Lazy flow and white ripples meant stones not far beneath. Had to be. No one visible, but the river bent the wrong way for him to see very far. Might be a better chance later. Might not. Lay down the cards. Time.

He limped as fast as he could, knowing from that feeling that had been honed over too many years that once he cleared the safety of the trees he was heading into a trap. Too late! They had beaten him here. Panic rushed through him as he tried to fight it down and think.

He felt the hooves pounding before he saw the men. Men who try to outrun horses die. He turned. Two riders. The Winchester was not the beloved Spencer he carried until they caught up with him, but it was what he had.

They were bouncing in the saddle as they fired. He was rock steady. One bullet slammed the right-hand rider in the chest. As he jerked back, the horse reared. The second rider dismounted as two shots went wide and used his horse as a shield.

"Kane!"

"Connolly."

"Should have shot you."

"Too late now. Give it up. Look at you hidin' behind a horse with your knees knockin' rather than face me."

"Colonel's wife wanted you hung for what you done. Only

reason we didn't kill you already."

"Too late now." A half-drunk guard and a little luck. Or he would have been dead the morning he escaped.

"Delacroix deserved it."

"He was a good man!"

"Says your law. Private army. Hangin' freedmen. Killin' anyone who thought the war was over or just plain got in his way. Nope. He earned what he got. Sorry I didn't get her, too. She killed as much as he did. Never shot a woman, but I'd break that rule for her. Law will make that right."

"Coward. Got the sand to face me straight up?"

"Thought you'd never ask."

Connolly held his own rifle by his side as he swatted the horse away. Kane had lowered his. Waiting. There were rules between men. Even here.

Most of the men who followed Delacroix were cowards, hangers-on who were brave against the defenseless. Connolly was their spine. More brute than brave. No gunman, but an animal whose survival instincts were keen and who had absolute loyalty to his fallen leader. Whatever he was doing, he expected to win.

He sidled toward Kane, watching. Wary.

A distant crow complained as the wind whined. Connolly's head jerked as his eyes flicked away downstream.

Kane realized that Connolly was stalling. Nice game. Almost worked.

He shouldered the rifle and fired before Connolly even had the chance to aim. The man crumpled as he was bringing his rifle to the ready.

Cautiously, he moved closer. Connolly was writhing from the bullet that had smashed his right ankle. Kane had aimed for his gut. Great shooting.

"I'll find you," Connolly seethed at Kane.

Kane kicked the rifle away. He took from Connolly's shirt pocket the small leather-bound notebook Kane had stolen from Delacroix on the night Kane killed him, before Connolly and his fellow goons cornered him. He knew Connolly kept it to gain power now that the colonel was dead.

"Army gets this, you and the rest of your bunch gonna be too busy running to do anything else."

Hate glared back.

"Always liked that stallion of yours. 'Preciate the loan." He walked away toward Connolly's horse. The animal had come to know him in the past few months. That was not why he waited before mounting.

The sound he strained for was barely audible over the wind.

Connolly was sitting with his pistol drawn. Kane still had the rifle in his hands as he turned. He wasn't fast. Just fast enough. Two shots echoed at the same moment, followed by two more that exploded in the same rhythm.

One shot went true.

Kane looked at the lump that had burned and looted until even the army could not ignore the work of him and his fellow cutthroats. Sherman wanted army justice to send a message that the government was in control, complete with trials and hangings.

"Not this time, Cump."

He imagined he heard hooves. He walked over to where the horse, which knew far too well the sound of guns, had walked when Connolly started firing. He swung up in the saddle, wincing at the pain from the leg where he was wounded the night they caught him. He felt worn. A job done, a bad man dead, and ten thousand more like him waiting to take his place. Reconstruction was hard on the ones reconstructing. Made a man wonder why.

Think later, live now.

"C'mon horse, we got ridin' to do."

They rode.

The headquarters clerk was uneasy. Men waiting to see General William Tecumseh Sherman, the commander of the army and ruler of everything he decided to command, which included anything that came to mind, were often uneasy. They were supposed to be nervous. Sherman did that to a man.

Few were this impatient and ill-tempered at being told to wait. Fewer still were so clearly trail-worn they appeared caked in dust and blood and just plain smelled bad. The man's boots had dropped mud on the polished wood of the floor until the man sat and drummed long, tanned fingers on the arm of a worn chair. Everything he wore was patched; much of it had old stains that bespoke violence.

He had stomped over to the silt-stained window and looked out for perhaps a minute before sitting again. Then rising again. He thumped unevenly, mud falling with each boot heel as he limped and paced, staring at the door and tapping his foot in the few moments he was otherwise still.

"He will see you when he can," reminded the clerk as the man sat, then rose and limped back and forth again, reminding the clerk of a prowling wild animal. The glance he got in return made him vow to keep silent.

Kane met Sherman after every mission. Every time there was a new clerk. Kane wondered whether it was Sherman's demanding ways, his eruptions of temper, or the cloud of smoke from the foulest, cheapest cigars on earth that chased them away. He wanted to laugh at the mental image of a pyramid of Sherman's dead secretaries stored in some war department building somewhere.

"Whazzat?" said the man, who pointed to the window and lurched that way and then past the clerk's desk with speed the clerk was sure he did not have, opening the door with its opaque glass and slamming it behind him, making the glass rattle.

Sherman might not have moved in the five months since Kane saw him last. A blue haze around his head; intensity and malice glaring at the world the man fought daily. Sherman's red hair and scruffy beard were moving glacially to gray; his hawk-sharp features adding lines each year, but the vitality and energy in the man had not dimmed.

The bane and core of Kane's existence did not seem to notice the invasion of his office as he scratched something on the piece of paper before him and then tossed the pen on his desk. Kane watched the ink splatter.

"Took long enough," Sherman grumbled. He waved a hand at his desk, where the report Kane had hand delivered two hours ago lay strewn in disorder. Kane knew every word he had written had been read. Sherman was thorough.

"It got complicated."

The assignment had been simple. Infiltrate a gang disrupting the law in east Texas and making Reconstruction a sham. Find proof. Get it to Sherman. Let the army come in, arrest the guilty, and try them all legal-like before hanging them. Then the army would get the credit, so people would believe in law and justice and Reconstruction.

It didn't work out quite that neatly. Kane recounted what Sherman had already read, a ritual that was designed for Sherman to see if the report was close enough to the truth that a man could repeat it. Sherman put his feet on a windowsill as Kane talked and puffed a vast cloud in anxious silence until Kane was done.

"You killed six people." Sherman paused. He knew Kane. "That you listed in this report." He rattled the papers as if dead men would be shaken out of the sheaf of writing.

"You was gonna have to kill 'em anyhow. Saved you the rope

12

and all the time and fuss. You still get to hang the widow. You send for me to complain?"

Sherman lowered his feet from the windowsill and looked out toward the east, toward the despised capital he had fled a year ago to move army headquarters to St. Louis, and whose politicians he hated with a fierce passion. He then faced Kane.

"No." He walked to the door.

"Cooper. Coffee. Now!" The rattling of the glass that followed was even fiercer than Kane's work.

Sherman sat in the chair next to Kane. He inspected the man before him. Kane was still young, twenty-five or something like that, but his face was weathered from outdoor living, with a fresh, livid, pink scar along his left cheek. Kane was lean, with a face that was always almost cavernous. His black hair always looked in need of a haircut, and his brown eyes always had deep, dark circles surrounding them. Kane's nose might have been average before it was broken. Always clean-shaven in a world of men with beards, Kane still managed to look trail worn but also very, very dangerous. With a hundred like him, Sherman thought, he could have marched to the sea and back and then taken Mexico for good measure.

Kane was also loyal. Sherman saved him from a wrongful hanging in '68, and the man had gone to work for him after that. No man in his service had been more faithful in doing what could not be done in public. Kane had no interest in the rights and wrongs of causes and politics. His loyalty was as personal as it was fierce. He rarely spoke. His work screamed volumes.

Something burned deep in Kane—that Sherman knew—but what it could be was as deep a mystery to Sherman as how a man could drink something like tea. If Kane had a life apart from his missions for Sherman, he never spoke of it. Sherman asked once. The answer he got convinced him never to ask again.

Cooper came with the coffee and managed not to spill it, despite his obvious fear of Kane. Sherman watched him leave. Kane, wise in the general's ways, rose and pushed the already-shut door to be sure, then returned to his seat.

Sherman downed most of the cup in a swallow. He puffed, like an engine building up a head of steam before tackling a steep grade.

"No more Texas. Wyoming. Hall County. Town called Rakeheart. At least it is not another named for Lincoln." Kane waited. Sherman was tightly wound. He got to the point in his own way. "Man was murdered. I need to know who. I need justice. Your kind. I need to know why. Not a gang running wild, although there are some out there. Can't chase them all. Plain murder, this was. So I am told. Not a range war or a gunfight. No sense in what they tell me. You tell me straight."

"Wyoming." Kane had never been there. Cold. Way up north. Indians up there, still fighting hard to keep something of their lands. Comanches had mostly accepted that the whites would never leave. Shame in a way. Half his childhood Kane wanted to be one of the wild Comanche riders who rode the skylines on wild horses. But Texas was mostly settled now. Wyoming was a different story. Sioux up there. Montana, maybe there was a reservation. Cheyenne, too. Black Hills? No, that was Dakota, mostly. Crow Indians were somewhere up there. Or was that Colorado? He never could keep the territories straight.

Wyoming. Cow and horse country. That he knew from the men who rode the trails up there. Long way to go. Must be important.

He'd worked for Sherman for about seven years, more or less. Reconstruction was a hard pill for the South to swallow. The army was the law, but the army had rules. Sherman needed a man who got things done, so Kane worked outside them. For Sherman to want the justice Kane preferred meant this was personal. That never happened.

Sherman, having sat for almost a minute, was back on his feet, reminding Kane again of an engine going up a steep grade as clouds of blue emerged with every step. The remaining coffee in the cup sloshed across the floor as Sherman gestured with the hand that held the cup. Words spilled; no, they spewed. The army. Black Hills. Gold. Thieves. Indians. Politicians who didn't give him enough money to guard gold, guard Indians, and stop fools from starting wars. They got an extra dose.

"Thompson has a summary written for you," Sherman said. "Neat man. Too nervous. See him before you go. Maps. He finds good maps. Let me tell you the most important things. Jared Wilkins was a captain on the March to the Sea. Good man. Illinois regiment. Always wanted land. Went to Minnesota for a while; stayed in the army, then left. Moved way out there after the war. Family man. Named his son Sherman. We kept in touch. Widow wrote me once when he was sick . . . oh, a year or more ago. Not much of a letter. Inadequate spelling. I do not know much of her. Rachel. My daughter's name, also."

"This is him." Sherman handed him a small carte de visite-sized image of a man and a young boy. The man was full of face and beard, trying to look important for the camera. Past forty and getting very round. Looked like a big man. Not very distinctive; neither handsome nor ugly, from what could be seen around the bush of dark whiskers. He was wearing an old uniform and trying to look solemn and dignified, which Kane sensed was an effort for the photographer. Much darker complexion than the boy, whose hair looked nearly white in the picture as it spilled out from under an oversize cavalry hat. Clearly a picture meant to curry favor with Sherman.

Sherman now loomed above him.

"Wilkins went to his barn one night. Someone shot him. No accident. Told her I would send someone. The widow. Not sure about her. Something . . . well, it's your job to tell me. Fort Laramie wrote me that they have no idea what happened. Man there who investigates these things had no answer. Didn't think much of him. Commander said he was reliable. Some of them drink too much out there. Flat land. Drives some men mad. You go. I can arrange a special train. You can be in Fort Laramie in four days. Town he lived in is a day west. Thompson has money. Buy anything else you need. Make sure you have money. Not much out there. Train will leave early. Be on it."

"Nope."

The cloud Sherman puffed was a lively expression of his anger at being defied.

"Unless I'm going there as your official representative . . ."

Sherman snorted.

"Don't want no one to know what I'm doin', and I don't want to arrive in this Rakeheart place with everyone knowing you sent me. Only way people talk is if they don't think it matters."

Sherman started to shout him down but abated after a brief war of wills convinced him that Kane would do as he pleased no matter what Sherman ordered him to do.

Kane rose and went to the map behind Sherman's desk. It took a while to find the right place. Then he traced a path from St. Louis westward.

"This place Denver. Rail goes there. Not that far from Wyoming. I'll buy a horse." He paused. "You'll buy a horse. No forts. No soldiers. You got a killer running loose up there, I don't want it advertised I'm looking for him, or I might as well wear a target. There's a telegraph somewhere. I'll let you know."

Sherman puffed on the concept, let it ride. Either trust a man or don't give him the job.

"Kane. Not much out there. Courts. Sheriffs. Territory is stretched thin. Army is what law there is in most places. I want

16

justice. No idea if there are ten judges in the territory. Might be two. Not worried about that. Can't have willful murder. Town jails there might be outhouses from what I hear. Flimsy. This is to be settled. Justice. Final. Understand?"

Kane nodded. He rose.

Sherman puffed repeatedly. "You have done good work, Kane. Might want to look out there for the future."

Kane was puzzled.

"Reconstruction won't last much longer. Grant won't run next year. Not much support for it. Time to end it. Army leaves, no more work there for you. South will reclaim the land, and then we will see what happens. There's an account here with your pay. Never touched. You're what? Twenty-five?"

Kane shrugged. Shy a couple of years, but close enough.

"Near an age to settle down. Might buy land, or whatever you want. Texas might be too hot for you now anyhow. I guess you did your job too well."

The general was right. Six years working for Sherman in Louisiana, Arkansas, and mostly Texas meant a lot of men knew him. He wondered when he killed Delacroix if the man found him out or if all the Klans and Knights knew they were being infiltrated and were on guard. He'd had the feeling he was being watched extra carefully from the start. If Sherman thought it was time, then it was time.

When the army left for good, scores would be settled. He didn't need to be one. The part of Texas that had been Comanche country was the only place he had ever wanted to settle, but maybe that was not a good idea. First, this. Then worry. Sherman might change his mind.

"Wyoming it is," he said at last. "Wire you from Denver, and when there's something to say. Not writing letters. Too many folks read 'em."

"I have money for the widow." He handed Kane a thick envelope.

Kane was puzzled. There had been talk of pensions for men infirm from the war, but not for every soldier who fought. Then he realized what he had been missing. Sherman's real family was the men he marched with. This was Sherman's own money.

"I'll get it to her."

"Make sure she's not involved." Kane's eyes met Sherman's. "I lost a man who thought of me as his friend, Kane. I barely know the woman's name. He rarely wrote of her. He told me about Rakeheart, and its growth, and his plans. He told me about his son. There is a daughter, but she may not be his. Don't recall her name, and he didn't say much about her. If that woman killed her husband, Kane, or she was part of a plot, you must not let the fact that she is a woman dissuade you from justice."

"He send you a picture of all of them?"

Sherman shook his head.

"Not easy to send things through the mail out there, Kane," he said, defending Wilkins.

Kane wondered. Man who keeps half of his family out of a picture is hiding something. He wondered what it was. He thought of telling Sherman what was on his mind. No. Man lost someone. If the man he buried wasn't the man who lived, let it rest. Folks who praised unvarnished honesty never saw it at work.

Sherman stuck out his hand. Kane took it.

It occurred to Kane this might be the last time he saw the red-haired man who had plucked him from prison and made him whatever he was today. He ought to feel something. He didn't.

Beginnings begin with endings. He wondered which awaited in Wyoming.

CHAPTER TWO

Hall County, Wyoming, was a rugged place. He'd ridden the Panhandle a few times. This felt tougher—plateaus that ran for miles; giant tables of rock. Far away there were mountains that poked up purple against the horizon; once he was sure they were white-topped. Panhandle wind was always ready to blow you to kingdom come. Days of nothing to make you forget the days when you could not walk upright against it. Out here, it was a solid, eternal presence. Wind never stopped, but the world wasn't ever giving ground. It was the place you figured would last forever if everything else crumbled. Massive pines in some places where the creeks rushed with water; dry flatland with knee-high bleached grass in others. Cattle country. Horse country. Not much farmland he'd seen so far.

The land had grown rockier as he had gone farther west, and the people harder to match. The train had stopped where it was scheduled, if not when, and a few dozen other places as well. If Kane never took one again, it would be all the same. Noisy. Dirty. Crowded. Drunks. He hated drunks. The friendly ones were the worst. Let a man be.

The West grew rawer as he traveled. Farmers found it hard to pass Kansas by. Men running from something found it easy to drift. Dreamers and skulkers; prophets and thieves. Obsessed with land. With Indians. With losing out on whatever it was everybody was going West to find. Denver tried to be New York when it wasn't a frontier town. All he wanted to do was leave it behind.

He had taken his time after Denver. It had been years since there was time to meander along a trail without wondering who might be on it. This land was bold; sunsets that flamed for hours and a night sky under a dome even bigger than the sky felt in Texas. If you could not talk to God under a sky this big, you never could. Maybe Sherman was right. Maybe this place was big enough for people like him.

He'd ridden six days; met someone only on one of them. At times he knew there were watchers, probably some were red and others were white, but they all kept their distance.

Rakeheart was below him now, along some creek; he'd forgotten the name. They all seemed to have buffalo in them or deer or some such.

He stopped near the edge of a plateau that overlooked the not-too-distant town. He'd stopped at a couple of others. Frost Springs. Gray Flats. Towns seemed insubstantial. They were small, and their rickety buildings that usually lacked much paint, if they had any at all, seemed fragile amid rocks that spoke of looming mountains and rugged hills that must have been carved by the wind.

Windy. It was always windy here. Grit, dust, and cold now and then, even in the middle of summer. It felt every bit as far from civilization as it was. Some days farther.

He ran his fingers through the mane of the horse he'd bought in Denver. They'd had a few days to get to know each other. Horse could run; didn't mind when Kane shot a rifle off of him. Understood what Kane said. Seemed to.

He sat on the horse's back and looked. Town had a main street; ten or twelve blocks of buildings. Street dog-legged a bit. A few small houses to the west. White building set apart. Just about the only thing painted other than a few signs. Had to be a church. Small church. No school. People moving. Seemed like a lot of people for a place that size. He untied the rawhide that tied down his gun in the holster. Lifted it out and set it back. Where there were people, there was trouble. Always.

Railroad moved from the southeast to the northwest along the edge of the town. Pens for stock by the tracks. Trails coming and going. Not roads. Nothing but hard-packed dirt where the repeated travel of horses, wagons, and men had made a mark on the earth.

He approached his task without enthusiasm. He wasn't a detective; Cump Sherman could have called in the Pinkertons, but some reason Sherman did not share made him keep this private. This was beyond his abilities. Usually, the gangs and thieves showed their colors after a while. Other than men who killed because they liked killing, murderers didn't always co-operate. He wondered idly if he simply rode on, let this one go, if ol' Sherman would find him. He knew the answer. Sherman probably had crows reporting back every day.

The horse snorted at something it smelled on the wind that Kane did not. "C'mon, Tecumseh," he called the horse, smiling every time he heard the name. "Guess it's time for us to earn our pay."

The trail from the hill country wound down to the flatland that now seemed to stretch forever to the north. He took it slow. No comings or goings. The flatland was empty. Man trying to not be noticed can't help but be seen unless he keeps to the hills and the patches of trees that popped up for no good reason. He felt uneasy. Exposed. A shiver. Silly notion. It was only another place. Sherman's demand for justice was only another mission. He hadn't shaved on the way, so that anyone looking for a clean-shaven man they knew in Texas would not find him out here in Wyoming.

No one seemed to care that he arrived. No one seemed to be

in town at all, now that he was here. Odd. It had looked bustling from the hilltop.

A mournful looking barefoot girl in overalls was standing outside the stables. She tried to smile at Kane, but there was nothing in it. Young and pretty with long, brown hair falling down behind a face that bore a pert nose and impudent eyes, but miserable about something.

"Stayin' long?" she said listlessly, staring down the street as though she was hoping to see something.

"Not sure." Pause. "Somethin' goin' on down there?"

"Bud Franklin is going to shoot Kevin Morris," she said as though it was the entertainment of a lifetime. "And I can't go."

He grunted in reply. Not his business. Not his form of amusement. He handed her a silver dollar and went to stable Tecumseh.

"Hey, mister, you see anyone out there?" She pointed at the vast expanse of High Plains.

"Nope." He could hear the grumbling.

Kane took off the horse's saddle and blanket. He started to brush Tecumseh, who seemed to like it from the few times Kane had groomed the horse on the ride from Denver. Meant somebody had cared for him.

"Mister, please, can you come with me down there?" she asked from the doorway. "Never seen a man gunned down, and I'm not missing it. Pa's . . . Pa can't be working today, and if I go and leave you here alone he'll get awful mad when he finds out. He thinks everybody steals. He won't ever close this fool place, but if there's no one here and no one coming it won't matter, will it? You'll tell him you wanted to go if he asks? Please?"

A gunfight. He'd seen it. Done it. A girl like her, sixteen or seventeen, she'd never understand.

"Please, mister. Please!"

" 'Spose I can finish later," he said after a moment.

The gunfight must be a spectacle, he thought, as he walked down an empty street. The girl had run ahead as soon as they left the stable. General store had a "Closed" sign. Others were clearly shut tight.

He turned the dog-leg corner he'd seen from the hill. He'd seen gunfight crowds before. Bigger towns. No crowd bigger than this one.

Duckboards filled. Men, women. Lots of kids. Fools must have set a time. He'd have checked his watch if he had one. Townspeople carried watches.

"Hey!" a boy called to him. "They're gonna come out! Better move, mister, or you'll get your head blowed off by Kevin."

"He can't hit nothin!" the boy next to him called. The argument rose in volume.

Kane sauntered to the side. Boy was right. Saloon doors swung as a round young man came out, his smooth, oval face flushed. Big build but running to fat even at his age. The striped shirt bulged over his belt underneath the brown leather vest. Some curls of damp, blond hair from under his hat showed how much he was sweating. Death and liquor. Quite a pair. Men either got drunk and killed each other or got drunk to go kill each other.

A few people called to the young man as he waited by a hitching rail. Awkward. Fussing with his hat; his holster. He licked his lips a lot and looked around the street, as though someone might be coming to end all of this. He had come to a place where he did not want to be and had no idea how to get out of it except by going forward.

The crowd quieted as a sallow-faced man emerged. Dark vest and pants; white shirt. Hat low; gun low. Walking easy. Loose. Relaxed. A man who knew his business. No drink needed; just a man good at guns.

For a moment his eyes focused on Kane, the only other man in the street. Sizing up. As though he could smell on Kane that Kane also knew how a gun was used. But Kane was not in play. The glance ended. He moved into the street. Waiting. Snake-patient. A chore to be done and finished.

The younger man licked his lips one more time as he looked into the center of the street. Kane could see his face glisten with sweat.

This was not a fight. It was murder. San Antonio flashed before his eyes. He could have stopped it. Should have. Didn't.

Drunks and fools. Auntie Amelia said God protected them. Sometimes.

Maybe he could fill in this one time. Penance for when he had not.

"Hello, Bud," he called to the patient man as he walked out to where the man who clearly had to be Bud Franklin was waiting in the bright sunshine of a clear-sky day.

Franklin's head snapped at hearing his name from a stranger. His eyes bored in on Kane, but he made no reply.

The younger man now quickly stepped forward. Pride mattered more than death. The rules. Live by 'em. Die by 'em. He walked up to Kane as though he wanted a round with Kane before taking on the man he had promised to meet. Kane turned to face him.

"Whyn't you tell me what this is about, Kevin?"

The young man was clearly surprised Kane knew who he was. He shot a look at his waiting antagonist as though fearful the man would shoot him as he talked.

"Turning coward?" called Franklin.

"Get out of my way," blustered Morris, shoving Kane.

Mutterings. A restive crowd not getting their show. End it.

Kane drew his own gun and pointed at Franklin. "Lose the gun."

"This is not your business," Franklin said.

"Is now."

"The world's better off without him."

"Might well be, but this is plain and simple murder, friend. The world will be without you if that gun don't hit the ground soon."

Franklin glared. Kane stared back. Kane could tell Franklin had calculated survival before by the way the man placidly reached down and pulled the gun from its holster, making sure Kane wouldn't go off by mistake.

"Toss it here."

Franklin did. It landed in a puff of dust.

"Kevin, the same." The young man was puffing up to fight. Franklin was probably right, Kane thought. Too late now.

"Try not to shoot your foot off doin' it," Kane said as the young man seemed unable to respond. Somebody in the crowd snickered.

The younger man paused, then reached down and dropped the gun in the dirt. He kept eyeing Franklin, as though expecting some trick.

Kane gestured with his gun. Morris stepped toward Franklin, moving closer as the gun kept motioning him toward his antagonist.

"You boys got that bad a grievance, beat each other up if you want. Not the circus the good folks wanted, but it might entertain them a spell." Both faces looked revolted at the idea.

Kane looked at Franklin. "Or keep travelin' if that's how you make your livin'."

"You are making a mistake, mister," Franklin said.

"Nothin' new."

"You don't know what you are doing. This is not over, fella."

Kane nodded. Sooner or later, Franklin would find a man to kill; Morris would bluster into a scrape too deep. By then, Kane hoped he would be long gone from Wyoming.

"Never is," said Kane. "Not watchin' a fool get killed for bein' a fool. Not here. Not now. All there is, fella. Let it ride. Not personal. Just one of them things. Might change my mind when I get to know your friend."

"I could call that bag of fat a lot of things, maybe liar, cheat, or spoiled brat, but friend ain't one of them." Franklin looked disdainfully at Morris. "Don't ever count on being this lucky again." He moved away from the younger man, who seemed to be uncertain whether he had won or lost.

Franklin was studying Kane.

" 'Spose there's a good reason."

"Hope so," said Kane. They were eye to eye, barely two feet apart.

"Do I get my gun?" asked Franklin.

"Not a collector," replied Kane. "Keep it where it belongs, and let the fool boy go. Whatever he did, we both know he's too stupid or too full of cheap liquor to matter. Me 'n you know it would have been nothing short of murder, fella."

Franklin bent down to pick up the revolver. Wiped the dust from the barrel. Slid it back in the holster, watched Kane holster his. Wordlessly, he moved down the street.

Kane picked up the other gun and tossed it out of reach for Morris to fetch, counting as Franklin took the smallest and slowest steps a man could take. Nineteen steps to barely go twenty feet.

Franklin had the gun in his hand as he turned. Kane had silently pulled his as the other man walked. It was no contest. Guns barked. Franklin was good and fast, but it's hard to beat a man who cheats for a living. Kane fired until Franklin was down.

He walked to the gunman, who was all but gone, lying in the halo of dark dirt around his chest.

Franklin wet his lips. Gasped.

"Why?"

Kane didn't bother. Wouldn't matter even if he had an answer. Man was mostly gone when he spoke and finished the journey before Kane could have replied.

The girl from the stable ran over to him.

"That was Bud Franklin. He was a Company Rider. He killed six men!"

"He won't kill no more," said Kane.

He walked the rest of the way alone as the crowd no longer could remain silent. The noise of excitement over someone else's death erupted, fading only as he walked away to the quiet haven of the stable.

He had almost completed brushing Tecumseh when the expected delegation of solid citizens arrived. A couple were young, most old. Most round. All hesitant. Kane hoped if he pretended they were not there, they might go away.

Nope.

A full-bearded older man moved forward, hat off, running it around in his hands. The man had gray hair heading to white, a neat beard, and stood taller than the rest—a big, full man. He wore some kind of black jacket and pants, but both were stained with flour. His white shirt was wrinkled and dirty, but he was eager to make his friendly intentions obvious with a smile that seemed to come naturally in a face that had wide, blue eyes looking at Kane with what was clearly a practiced assessment of the stranger he was meeting.

"Howdy." The man's voice was deep and pleasant; it sounded practiced in the art of being friendly.

"Not plannin' to kill nobody else today, if that's your worry. One's entertainment. Two's bad for business."

"Well, that's fine news," said the man, his cheerfulness seemingly undented. "Jack Conroy. I own the general store."

Store men liked to talk.

"Kane. Wilkins family; you know 'em?"

The smile dimmed a second before words tumbled out. "Fine folks. Terrible, whatever it was out there. Terrible. They owed me money, of course, but I canceled it when I heard. It was the very least that a Christian man could do for the widow, even though . . . I mean, terrible thing."

"They live far?"

"No, no, not at all. About ten miles that way." He pointed north. "Almost due north two miles, then towards Red Butte."

As directions went, it wasn't much help, but Kane figured another question might send the man past his limit.

" 'Bliged." He went back to his work.

"Mr. Kane? There was one thing that we wanted to say, being the town council here of Rakeheart, such as we are."

Kane's thoughts flitted to that Panhandle town where the townsfolk got so sick of gunfights they ordered anyone who shot a man dead on the street to bury him or pay a fine. Grinned. They always got their money, too.

The group seemed to recoil from a man who killed one minute and flashed a carefree grin the next.

"Are you . . . um . . . staying here in Rakeheart?" Conroy got out after no one else in his group spoke up. "Not that you are not free to leave . . . I mean free to stay . . . or you can go, um, of course, we would not detain you because we know that . . . well . . ."

"No idea. Problem?" This was taking time he did not want to spend talking. Sherman was probably already berating his clerk over the lack of progress reports.

"Problem? No, of course not. Not at all," Conroy stammered. "There is no sheriff here, if that's what you were asking about. That is the predicament we face here as we try to make this a God-fearing town."

A younger man with a wide part down the top of his skull

and slicked-down black hair took over, flashing a look of contempt at the stammering older man.

This man had a brown, checked suit with a black vest, a perfect white shirt with one of those ugly little black ties men were wearing these days that looked like a ribbon tied around a man's neck and always made Kane think of hangings.

"Frank Brewer. I own the bank. We wanted to talk to you about that."

Kane was lost. He said so.

"We need a sheriff," Conroy said at last. "You're new here. We all saw you try to stop those fools. Franklin was a . . ." A throat cleared in the bunch. Conroy started over.

"We can't pay much, but there would be a place to sleep and meals. We'd like to talk to you about becoming the sheriff."

The face looked relieved. He had said it.

Kane pursed his lips. As ideas went, he had heard worse. Not many, though. Him, a sheriff?

"Got to see the Wilkins family," he said, not wanting to make too many enemies in case he had to stay around a while. "Them first. Talk to you when I come back."

They agreed that would be fine. Brewer was bursting with something to say.

"Have you been in Wyoming long, Mr. Kane, and, um, did you know Bud from any former acquaintance?"

"The man you shot," Conroy prompted after seeing Kane's baffled look.

He never was good at names. Faces lingered. Names scattered in the wind and were gone. Even those he killed. Especially those.

"Never met him. Been in the territory a few days, if it's your business."

Brewer hastily admitted it was not, and, amid general expressions of shaky goodwill, the delegation left him alone.

"Well, Cump," he said to the horse. "Don't that beat all?"

"You know the Wilkinses?" he asked the girl, who had told him her name was Janie. She had observed the delegation with something that was not quite disgust, but there was not much respect shown, either.

She shook her head.

"Only came to look in on 'em. You don't know 'em at all, small place like this?"

"Not very well. Their kids are little," she said scornfully. "The boy is cute, but his father spoiled him and lets him run wild. The girl is quiet and moody. She is, you know, different, like her mother. Mr. Wilkins came to town a lot—maybe not every week but something like that. Mrs. Wilkins and the girl don't come very often, which is fine, the way things are. He gave me a dollar once for watching his horse extra. I think he was nice, but I didn't really know him."

"Guess you can keep the one I gave you even though I don't think we quite ate a dollar of oats," he said as he saddled Tecumseh.

"I can?"

"Don't figure you'd give it back easy." He smiled.

She grinned back and looked like a different person.

"Guess your pa knows you have a head for business."

"Guess so!" she exclaimed proudly. She stood outside the stable and waved as he rode, after giving him a few landmarks to look for on the way north.

CHAPTER THREE

Such a trail as there was petered out less than a mile from Rakeheart. If anyone ever moved across the rough, rocky ground, it was not evident. Janie's landmarks were a good map, though. He took his time. Working for Sherman, he infiltrated gangs, rode down outlaw groups, and became whoever he needed to be so often he sometimes forgot who he was. He knew there was work to do, but it still felt like a vacation. No one hunting him.

Yet.

He thought about the stack of clippings Sherman's clerk had thoughtfully prepared about how detectives in London worked. Some of it had been amusing to read on the train. Mostly it helped stoke the stove that cold day in Nebraska. He had no idea how to do what he was supposed to do.

It had been about a month. Sherman wanted him to try. He'd try.

Sheriff. He laughed out loud. It intrigued him. He'd already become too noticed to be unseen. Might be the way to stay on. Couldn't be much need for one, if one gunfight drew a crowd like that. Down Texas way, folks would hardly leave the street when two fools wanted to shoot each other.

The tree that looked like proof lightning struck the same place pretty often was now in front of him. Good directions, girl. A mile to go. He hated meeting people. A widow no less.

"Give me a gunfight any day," he said to the horse as the

31

late-afternoon sun began to stream in his eyes while it hovered over a series of stubby, rock-topped hills where the sky-lined trees were the exception. Hard land. Uncompromising.

People the same? He'd find out.

The Wilkins place was small. Long and low. Surer hands built the white-painted center section than the unpainted wings. A knee-high rock fence framed a gateway.

Shadows from the nearest butte covered the place. He didn't like coming in with the sun in his eyes, and now that he was in the shade with the sky above the butte still bright, he could barely see at all. Man could be an easy target this time of day.

Shutters were open. He could see that. He'd smelled smoke for a while, so they had to be home. Too dark to know if anyone was looking back.

"Hello the Wilkins house," he called. "Like to come in."

No answer. Feet moved. They stopped.

"I know you don't know me, but I got sent here by Cump Sherman, General Sherman that is. Here to help."

Silence. The door opened. A short, thin woman came out. Two long, black braids framed her dark-complexioned face. She held a shotgun across her chest. She wore a dark dress and was coatless in the early evening dimness of the shadow that now covered her house. She still did not speak.

"Name's Kane. General Sherman sent me."

"You said that. Any proof?" Her challenging voice was low. The threat was padded, but it was still there.

"None I can show you from the back of a horse." This did not seem the moment to mention the money he carried. He was trying to get a good look. She walked a few steps closer. Gave her a better angle; him a worse one from the dimness where she had the advantage. He could not make out her features, see what was in her eyes.

"I know your name's Rachel," he said as he turned in the saddle to follow her as she inspected him from the side. "Got kids. A boy and girl. Husband served with Sherman on the March to the Sea, stayed in the army a while after the war. Minnesota if I recollect right. Sherman heard about your husband, ma'am, with what happened and all, ma'am, and wanted me to stop by on my way special to see if I could help you, ma'am."

With soldiers, if you said "sir," enough they came 'round. Not sure substituting "ma'am" worked with women. If anything did. He could feel a wall of skepticism. He could feel more than see watchers from the windows.

On impulse, he grinned and waved toward the house. He was rewarded with a noise.

"Enough," she said sharply to the unseen figures. Feet thudded as children ran to prove they had never looked out the window.

"Get down slow. I'll shoot if you touch that gun." She moved to a better spot to watch him, stepping carefully, precisely. Something . . . something familiar in the way she moved . . . toes almost dancing the way they pointed down as she stepped . . . some memory with a pile of Texas dust strewn across it. She was walking barefoot.

He did as he was told. His eyes had adjusted to the dimness as he walked slowly towards her, hands out from his sides.

"You're a long way from Texas." Another challenge. A deliberate warning. She wasn't stupid and wanted him to know it.

"Fact."

He could see her inspection take in everything, from the worn boots to the new everything else. He could see the fireplace behind her. He was sure a small head darted back to the window. Small voices whispered as loudly as only small voices can. He took a step.

"I said slow."

He put his hands wide out as he moved closer but could not hide the grin as he looked for his unseen inspectors. Rachel took a slow, methodical, detailed look. The gun motioned him inside. He passed. For now.

"Can't be too careful. Come in." Then, "Nothing sudden."

There was still a little fire burning, and a candle lit. He tried not to stare as he struggled to sort this out. His eyes were adjusting from riding into the sunset to the shadows outside to the darker shadows inside.

"Sit," she said and moved to the table.

They were good. Kids who could spy and get away with it were better than he ever was.

She set some bread on the table. He took the end of one bench; she sat across. He broke off a piece, offered it to her. She shook her head. He saw some kind of white circle on the end of her braids. It had a decoration on it. Very familiar.

"What does General Sherman want that he sends someone from his very special army all the way out here to Wyoming?" Sarcasm and wariness blended in her tone.

He'd been smiling since she reached across the table and set the bread down, recalling a little bit of a place a long time ago and now a long ways away. Sherman's questions could wait a minute. He had his own investigation to do first.

"You're Comanche." He pointed at her left arm, where the frayed sleeve of her deep-green dress was rolled partway up her left forearm. A tiny bit of ink showed.

A wry smile and a deprecating alto laugh. Her eyes crinkled. The snapping black eyes that watched him turned warm, but no surprise showed.

"Sherman sent you to tell me that?"

"Don't think he knows."

Snort.

"No, I am certain Jared never shared that with him. Wisely. Your general has fixed views on the subject of Indians."

"He does."

"And Jared had very fixed views on telling his hero only what he wanted him to know." The word *hero* had a bit of a sneer that made Kane wonder if Sherman knew more than he was letting on when he cautioned him about the widow.

"Only way to handle the man. Kinda like new powder ready to go off, and you never know in which direction to run."

He waited.

"How did you know a Comanche tattoo? A man came here once who boasted he could smell an Indian at a hundred yards, and he never suspected I was Comanche."

"Like you said. Texas. Ain't seen a tattoo like that in a while since I rode up near to Indian territory. Spent some years as a kid on the Panhandle and all the places kids ain't supposed to go. Some of the Indian kids curious about whites and the white kids curious about Indians had a place we'd all meet and do stuff that probably should have gotten the pack of us killed. Good thing no one told us we was s'posed to be killin' each other, or those rock fights would have turned out a lot worse than I recall. Figgered it out when we got older, more or less. Drifted away and apart by then. Can I see the whole thing?"

She pushed her sleeve up past her elbow and showed him the design. It was a classic Comanche pattern. Wild and free. For a moment he could almost feel that Panhandle wind in his face when he looked at the swirls. He could feel himself relax as if he were there. Men far from home are twice the fools they usually are. And she was pretty. No. Striking. Dark eyes, high cheekbones in a thin face. She was also a member of the broken nose club. A ripped earlobe from earrings or something. No guess on age. Not a kid. Not old. He should not be staring. He had work. He should ask something like whatever a good detective-type fella would ask. Should not have burned those notes!

"How does a Comanche get to Wyoming?"

"Kiowa raid when I was ten or so. They sold me to the Arapaho. They sold me to the Cheyenne. I don't think they thought I would be the calm and quiet slave they wanted."

"Were they right?"

"They were. Kiowa could not get rid of me fast enough. Arapaho man learned Comanches don't like being beaten and know how to get even. Cheyenne weren't bad, but eventually the man who bought me sold me to the Sioux in a trade for horses. I was almost twelve. By then I stopped fighting."

He doubted that.

"You live with Red Cloud or Sitting Bull?"

She shook her head.

"Neither. You hear about the fighting in Minnesota while your war was going on?" He nodded. "My band of Sioux lived there. It was ugly. My—They killed a lot of people. Afterward they sent soldiers to watch us when your war was over. Jared was there, guarding us. He was kind, which was very unusual for soldiers. He had decided to quit the army once all the excitement was over. He took uh . . . me. We moved. First Kansas. Nebraska. Then Dakota. Then here."

"You think that's why your husband was killed? Somebody not approve because you're an Indian?"

She snorted again.

"No one approved. You might ask if I care about that, Kane. Approved! You men say things in funny ways. You want to know if the nice white people got offended by having an Indian in their little town?"

Kane fidgeted and looked at the floor.

"Don't know I ever got invited to make quilts or any of that, but I never really learned how to gossip white woman style, so I never objected. No, no one approved, but no one cared that much, either. Most of the time. Red Cloud spits or Crazy Horse shoots a bear, and they get all het up and Jared would worry, but we lived here six years without anyone getting scalped, so they pretty much forget I am who I am, or even that I am here. I'm that quiet lady who never speaks much. Uppity, someone will call me. I know life can be much worse, Kane, and I do not ask for more than what is due me."

She paused a moment.

"The Black Hills are not all that far, but still it is far enough from the gold and the raids and the robberies and the fighting that it isn't a big fuss. When it explodes, which I know it will from the way that Custer man said there was gold everywhere, and now there are men in the Paha Sapa, they will remember I am Indian, but mostly they forget. I make it easy for them to do so. I go into Rakeheart about twice a year. Nothing there I want. Jared can buy supplies. I mean he did. Jeremiah liked to go along. Libby would go, but she did not really enjoy the town. She thought they looked down on her, the other children. Some of the people in the town are nice to children, but she always felt she did not belong."

"No threats?"

"I don't know what anyone said to Jared, but he never shared anything with me. No one was ever mean to my face. I know that is not the way of white women. The Sioux were more direct."

She paused, going somewhere in her mind.

"I heard what you said about how you felt when you were a boy, but that was a long time ago; I want to know something. Are you one of those men who thinks Indians are guilty of something merely by being Indians? Jared kept me pretty much a secret to protect me as well as curry favor with his hero. I want to know who is under this roof with my children."

Kane shrugged. "Good and bad in everybody. Every race.

Every tribe. Don't spend much time condemning folks because they ain't me. Figger it's their bad luck." He looked her in the eye and let her read what she would.

She gave him a very faint smile. The eyes said he passed a test.

"Do you mind if I ask a question?"

"After so many others, why does it matter now?" Her glare was intimidating. Her tone, ice. He now felt awkward, but it was too late to retreat.

"You speak better English than half the people I know . . ."

"White people, you mean?"

"Well, yes."

"Squaw no use dumb Injun-talk?"

"I didn't mean to offend you."

"You did. Again."

She glared some more as he squirmed.

"Oh, why should you be any better than the rest of them? Jared taught me from the time he met me. He was a good teacher; maybe if he had done that instead of trying to be a rancher and farmer he would have been happier. He would be . . ." She obviously fought down her rising emotion.

"I think it started because he was so awkward with me he did not know what else to do. It was how he showed he cared. He taught me; he taught Libby. Of course he taught Jeremiah but that came later. Libby and I can both speak better than most people. Libby can write well. I can understand numbers, but writing is a chore." She paused. "Jared thought people would treat me as their equal if I talked like one. I don't think he was right about that, but I do like seeing their surprise when I don't live down to their expectations."

For a second, he lost track again. Focus.

"Sherman sent me to find out who killed your husband. Guess they were close. Kept in touch a lot."

"Like brothers. Jared was a lot older than me. He turned forty-four last year. He was an only child. He didn't have any family anywhere. It was him and me and that general from day one. He looked up to Sherman like a big brother, a father, and God all rolled into one. Never wrote a letter but to that man. When Sherman wrote back he looked like a little boy, so excited. There's a box in the bedroom with everything Sherman ever wrote back to him. He saved every last one."

"Went both ways, I guess. Sherman takes it personal when things happen to people he likes. I do work for Sherman. Stray things the army needs done that it can't do on its own 'cuz them rules and the gold braid and the pompous folks get in the way. Never one like this. I need your help to find out who killed your husband. Got any ideas who might have hated him enough to kill him? Range war? That town? Something?"

An indefinable shadow crossed her face. She silently looked into the fire. Maybe you don't ask widows questions like that, he told himself. Maybe livin' way out here she's afraid.

Then he recalled Sherman's caution. Maybe, he realized, she knows something she doesn't want to tell.

The silence lengthened. It dawned upon him that she did not plan to answer.

"Maybe come morning I can look where it happened, maybe you can think of someone he didn't like or some place I can start tryin' to figure all this out to tell Sherman?"

"They all want the land."

"Why? Lot of land out here. All looks the same to me."

"We came here in '69. Got the best water. Never come close to running dry. Jared said we'd be sheltered here from northers. He always figured winter would kill off everyone's herds one year, and he wanted to be the one that survived when it happened. It never did, and now he's gone. Eighty acres isn't much, but it is enough. Everybody wants to get bigger. A couple of them said they would come around to talk when my mourning was over. The rest didn't say it, but they looked around a lot when they came to say they were sorry. Guessing what it would cost to be rid of me."

"Think one of them got impatient?"

"Men are always impatient," she said. "You ask a Comanche woman about white men and land?"

She had been looking away from him and then came back with a sharp-eyed glance.

"You knew before you saw the tattoo. I could see it in your eyes. How? Did someone tell you? You never said. It was more than a childhood memory."

"Nobody said nothing. Spent a lot of years along the Yellow River. Traded with a lot of Comanches. Never had a problem with 'em any more'n with anyone else. Prob'ly don't know a Sioux from a Cheyenne, but there's somethin' in the face with a Comanche."

He moved his right hand toward her face, drawing in the air as he traced her narrow face from her cheeks to her jaw. She pushed the arm down firmly and moved away from the table before turning to sit in a different spot. Her face was now deeper in shadow.

"No offense," he said. "Somethin' in the walk as well. Your voice got Texas in it somewhere same as mine. You was barefoot; never seen white women do that outside of Louisiana by the swamps. The white beads at the end of your braids. I can see the blessings drawn on them now that we are in here. Put it all together, it said Comanche."

"You are more observant than you appear to be," her voice had a bit of an edge. He had clearly crossed a line.

He wanted to tell her that being underestimated was the way he worked. He left that unsaid.

"I do not think there is much to observe. The barn has been

cleaned since it happened," she said. "Kids know he's gone, but they don't know a lot, so don't talk about it in front of them. Clem Ferguson—guess he's the foreman now, since we have about two dozen hands left—he can tell you more. He talked to the soldier who came. The territory sent a solider to investigate the death of a white man with an Indian wife. No, it was the army. He came and looked and left. He talked to Clem, but not much to me. I guess they thought I scalped him. They—"

The flow of bitterness stopped as if a tap was shut off.

"I don't—" She stopped and looked at him. "I'm an Injun woman in a white world who doesn't know a thing about cattle. To my face they call me 'Mrs. Wilkins,' and behind my back I am a 'filthy squaw.' That is how life is in your world." She accented all the words she found hateful.

"Want to know what they call me? Not a lot of folks offering sugar and sympathy out there for anybody, ma'am."

"You live in a hard world, Mr. Kane."

"Only one there is, ma'am. At least you got the ranch. Your men will adjust. Folks usually do."

"For now. Clem told me things weren't good, but they weren't bad yet. Whatever that means. Calves are born. They eat. We sell them. I don't know what can go wrong unless they get sick. I have done the ledgers for Jared because he did not like to do things with writing that were indoors, but I don't know what was behind those numbers. I know that the numbers say we are making money, but there are times it does not feel that way. One day maybe it folds; it ends. I don't know that I care about the ranch enough to run it."

"You got your kids."

"I should tell you now so you will not stare the way most white people do when they try to puzzle out the ancestry of a non-white child. Libby's father was Sioux. She is not Jared's. The soldiers shot her father about a month after I was married.

41

I was barely old enough to have children, and he never got to be a man. He never saw her." Wistful, but not for long. No time for that on the high plains.

"She was Topsannah. That was her name. It means—"

"Prairie flower."

Her eyes met his a long moment. "Very good, Kane."

For a moment, the past claimed her. Then it faded away.

"Jared never cared, though. He was unusual for a white man. The only thing he asked was that Libby have a white name, so I let him pick it. I did not know then it was the same as the Custer man's wife, but by the time I learned that, it no longer mattered."

Kane had a revelation.

"Not the only thing. Your name was not always Rachel. That's Sherman's daughter's name. He made you change your own name?"

"It seemed little enough," she replied.

Seeing no reaction in his eyes, she spoke again, this time with more passion. "Kane, can you imagine being so alone, so desperate, and so frightened that it does not matter to you what someone calls you as long as you can be safe and your child can eat and maybe someone will actually care whether you are even alive?"

Kane shifted from foot to foot. Awkward. There had to be something to say.

"What was your name? Your real one?"

"It does not matter." Her tone said the subject was closed. She compressed her lips as her eyes swept the room. "I have told you what you need to know. Jeremiah is his. All his." The words were stressed. "He wants to be a cowboy. Or a soldier." Bitterness dripped from her words. He wondered why. Little boys want to be what their fathers were until they get old enough to know better. Way of the world.

"Maybe you can hold the ranch for him."

"Maybe."

Then it hit.

"What about Sherman?"

"What about him? Never met him. Jared worshipped him. I suppose he meant well staying in touch with Jared, but that's over now."

"Not him. Your son."

The look she gave him would have frozen a fire.

"You ain't got a son you named after the general?"

Now she was puzzled. She shook her head, braids dancing with the Comanche designs at their tips, and glared back fiercely. "I think I would know that."

"General thinks you got a son named Sherman. Very pale. Very light hair."

"That's Jeremiah."

"Says your husband wrote that he named his son after the general. Boy maybe eight or so now if I recall it right. Pretty sure ol' Uncle Billy mailed your husband money to help his namesake get brought up eatin' regular."

Understanding flared at the word "money." He could see the rage build even as it was contained.

"Jeremiah is nine. And that is his name. Every now and then there were letters Jared brought from Rakeheart that I was never allowed to see. I never saw anything he mailed except for once he was hurt, and I had to write for him. He told this general he named Jeremiah after him? He said we had a son named Sherman?"

"General said so. He don't make up things like that."

She put her face in her hands a moment. Then glared at Kane.

"When I met Jared, he would never have done that. He changed. That place. Rakeheart. It changed him. It drew him and changed him. It was as though he drank from a poison well. The longer we were here, the more he was doing things that were no longer good for him. He wanted to be important. He wanted approval." She paused. "Perhaps in the end, Kane, he wanted more than an Indian wife could give him."

She rose, tight-faced and angry. She had clearly had enough for one night.

"Dawn comes early here. Chores never stop. The barn is yours. Everyone in the crew is out, so no one will disturb you, but I don't know who might ride in. I don't know whose things are where in the bunkhouse, and I know what happens when you cowboys fight over someone moving things that you have not moved in months, so I would prefer to avoid a gunfight by having you sleep in the barn."

He stood also. "Barn's fine. Goodnight, Mrs. Wilkins."

The fire caught a wetness in her eyes.

"Good night, Mr. Kane. Next time we meet, call me Rachel. It is the name I will prefer to hear."

She turned and moved to the wing of the house where he could see a room had been added. A blanket blocked the doorway. He let himself outside. Stabled Tecumseh.

The cool night air was refreshing. Rachel Wilkins was a puzzle. Comanches could bury emotions as deep as a well, but whatever she was burying in relation to Wilkins, it was gone without a trace. It didn't add. There was something off.

Sherman told him that Wilkins doted on the woman. But Sherman had suspicions that sprang from something, and, in a place like this, the most likely people to shoot someone were people already here, not middle-of-the-night riders. Rustlers might use the darkness to steal, but this was different. What had Sherman gotten him into?

Wilkins had lied to Sherman about his son's name. That was clear. Was there a whole different version to the truth beyond that one fact? Rachel seemed surprised. Maybe he was easy to fool. If there was a truth out there, how would he find it?

Doubts and darkness surrounded him, with the light very far away.

There was the smell of coffee when he awoke. She was waiting with a steaming cup as she watched him kick off the blanket and dust off the hay from his clothes. Her hair was loose. She had on a light-brown dress. She looked more like a rancher's wife and less a Comanche. He glanced down. No shoes.

"I do not handle company very well," she said, handing up the cup to his outstretched hands. "I will not live up to your standards for widows, Kane. I have lived life with loss since I was a girl. I was fourteen when I was married, and I was a widow before I was fifteen. I know white women weep and wear black and carry on. This is not my way. If I had done so, there might not be a ranch today. For the children to survive, I must survive."

He could see her better in the light. Her face looked different. Lighter? He did not know he was staring until she spoke with some irritation in her voice.

"I was told my mother's grandfather was part Spanish, so, yes, Kane, I am lighter than many Comanches. Now can you tell me why the exact color of an Indian's skin makes you white men so fascinated?"

Any further conversation was—fortunately for Kane—interrupted by yelling voices. Rachel strode purposefully to the house. Kane gulped down a deep swallow and felt a wave of relief. A man never knows how much trouble he can find simply by being there.

Kane emerged from the barn to see Rachel moving fast out of the house, with her shotgun cradled and ready.

Four young men had reached the gate of the ranch house.

"Hello, Rachel," called one, laughing at his wit as only drunks and the young can do. He leaned severely from side to side as he waved, a sloppy grin on his face.

"Go away, Chad," she called back. "You and your friends are drunk. Again. That's why you got fired."

"You need protection," he said. "We're here to protect you against . . ."

"Against all comers," said a dark-haired young man flashing a sloppy grin.

"Them Injuns might steal you back, missus," said a third young man, as the fourth kept silent, his posture showing he had misgivings about his adventure.

The one called Chad started to dismount.

"Don't," she called out. "You got fired for being drunk, and you and your drunken friends should all go away. You spent the night drinking in Rakeheart, you can spend the morning sobering up there, too. Go. Now!"

Chad continued navigating his way off the horse as though she had not spoken, completing the task with difficulty.

"But you need to be protected," he said with his grin sharp. Then a shadow crossed his face, and he frowned. "Let me show you. I have a gun, and I know how to use it. See?" He started to reach for the weapon.

The bark of a rifle set the young men still mounted back in their saddles as Chad tumbled into the dirt.

Rachel turned on Kane.

The Winchester cocked as Kane walked to the sprawled youth, who was sadly contemplating his right boot, now missing the heel Kane had shot off. He'd been aiming at the dirt by the other foot. Oh well. Ought to shoot the new gun more if he wanted to hit what he aimed at.

"Shouldna done that," Chad scolded.

"Sleep it off, sonny," Kane said. He motioned to the others.

"One of you get him on his horse. Then git."

The two who had spoken to Rachel dismounted. One side glance. Two.

Three.

As they neared Chad, they clumsily reached for their own guns. Before they could fumble them free, Kane had moved the ten feet separating him from them to knock the weapons from their hands and shove the youths hard. They rocked into their horses. One struck out with a hoof, catching the dark-haired one in the left thigh. The other looked on uncertainly, dimly understanding that this lark had gone sour.

"Edward." Rachel spoke sharply to the fourth youth. "Your friends appear to have had an accident. Help Mr. Kane get them mounted and then get out. When they sober up, tell them I will shoot first the next time I see any of them. I hope you learn to choose better company."

"Yes, Miz Wilkins. Sorry."

It was not the first time Kane had piled a drunk atop a horse. Soon, with Edward leading the rest, the young men were heading down the path back from a misadventure gone wrong.

Rachel turned. Kane was gone.

"No man lets good coffee go to waste," he said, beaming with the cup in his hand as she approached him.

"Did you think an Indian woman could not handle four drunk white cowboys who are about as mature as you?" she asked. "I tell Jeremiah that when guns are shot, people can get hurt, and you have to show him the exact opposite. Of course he saw every bit of that. Do you think this is the first time some silly boy drunk out of his mind wanted to protect me?"

"Sensible woman never leaves a loaded gun around little kids," he said. "Noticed it was unloaded last night. Empty barrel got backlit when you cocked it. Thought I'd help. You know how we men are. Got to show off in front of a lady."

"I keep the shells by the door," she said, opening the gun and showing him it was loaded, as she dumped the shells into her hand. "I cannot shoot like you cowboys, but when I am close enough, it does not matter."

Kane, again feeling shallow and stupid, wisely said nothing.

A young boy was in the doorway, as fair of hair and skin as the older girl behind him was dark. The sun was full on their faces, allowing him to pick out the details. The boy looked excited at the commotion. The girl scanned the scene with eyes that knew more, stopping to examine Kane before she focused on her mother, then back to the stranger who had come out of their barn.

"Good morning, Miss Window Spy," Kane said to her, tipping his hat. "I'm Kane."

"You look like a range tramp," she challenged as Rachel tried in vain to interrupt her and Kane grinned. He guessed the girl was about twelve. The Minnesota Sioux uprising had been back in '62. About right. That would make Rachel someplace close to his age if he was adding it right in his head. Then he wondered what was right in his head that he was thinking like that about a woman Sherman thought might have killed her husband.

"Mommy? Mommy?" The boy spoke.

"Mr. Kane is here to visit, Jeremiah. He is a friend of your daddy. He brought some friends to celebrate his new gun. That was the noise. They had to go, but he can stay for a *very* little while longer before he has to go as well."

The boy looked relieved. The expressionless girl knew better.

"That was Chad," she said. "He is disgusting."

"He is gone," Rachel replied firmly.

"So is my coffee," Kane said mournfully, looking at the stain in the dirt.

"You shouldn't spill," Libby told him.

"But menfolk are supposed to make messes, little girl," he

said. "Otherwise the whole rest of the world wouldn't be needed to clean up after them!"

He got a smile from lips that moved as her large, dark, expressionless eyes beheld a world that had inflicted some hurt upon her Kane could not fathom.

"How much of everything did you hear last night, Miss Got-to-Spy?"

Libby looked back silently.

"I know you was there. You still got that cobweb thing on your left ear."

Libby's understanding that Kane was joking her came only after she touched her hand to her ear and saw the wide grin break across his face. She pursed her lips.

"I heard what . . ."

Rachel cleared her throat loudly. The let-me-show-off look on Libby's face was replaced by one promising retribution, which Kane returned with another grin.

"Mr. Kane, even though you have time for childish games, I have children to feed," Rachel said. "We have chores to do and a ranch to run. You may join us if you wish. There is more coffee. There is also, if you are of a mind, plenty of work."

Libby looked smug to see him told off. Her eyes widened when he made a face at her as Rachel turned her back to speak to Jeremiah.

Kane wanted more coffee and a hunk of bread but decided to ride out. The indomitable Widow Wilkins had no room in her life for mysteries or amateur detectives; she was too busy surviving.

"This Clem fella?"

"West pasture." She pointed. "About five miles. Let me know what he tells you I did." She went into the house without looking back, small in stature but large in presence. Libby and Jeremiah trooped behind. The girl gave him one last look as the

49

door closed behind them.

He saddled Tecumseh and walked the horse past the house. No one openly watched him leave or said good-bye. He waved anyhow.

"Bye, Libby!"

No response.

He had come for answers. He left with questions.

"You drank her coffee?" Clem Ferguson laughed from the back of his coal-black stallion. "Had it once and figured I was like to die. Everybody on the ranch tried to tell her one time or another. She ain't the tellin' type."

"Noticed."

Kane could not help but like the young man, not much older in years than the drunks who had marred the morning. Cattle were grazing across fields that seemed less green than varying shades of brown. There were more than Rachel had led him to believe—maybe sixty or so in sight—but they looked like small dots on the vast expanse of the flatlands. The land could have held hundreds and still seemed to go on forever under a sky that was blue as far as the eye could see.

"They could be four good hands," Ferguson said when Kane told him about the incident. "They are all too lazy. Chad's old man, Link Washburn, runs the Double L on the other side of Rakeheart. Says his son has to learn ranchin' from the ground up. Won't let him ride for him, or so he says, but every time a spread fires Chad, he takes the boy back. That boy will be a good man someday if he don't do something stupid to get dead. I think Chad has ridden for every ranch around here and worn out his welcome at all of them. Hear talk Rakeheart wanted a sheriff. Maybe he'll take that on." Ferguson clearly thought the idea of a sheriff was amusing. Kane let it lie.

Ferguson was hesitant to talk about what mattered to Kane.

"Boss had gotten quiet, real quiet. I have worked here three years, like to four. Man was always talking; bring the kids out to see the cows; invite the hands to eat with him and Rachel. Up until that big snow, maybe a little before, this spread was like one family. I do not know what happened, but I know everything started to change. Mostly him. A few times he was in that barn talking to himself a blue streak. Then he'd get all flustered about it. Worried we might have heard what he said, as if on a ranch this small, there's much in the way of secrets."

"Money trouble?"

"The herd keeps growing, and we all keep eating, even if none of us is ever going to be rich. Sale price goes up and down, but that's the business. Every ranch out here is one or two bad years from going under, but it is the way we all live. Never heard him complain."

Kane had to ask the next question.

"They have a problem? Jared and Rachel?"

Clem took his hat off and scratched an imaginary itch on the back of his head. He resettled the hat.

"Rachel's not your usual woman. There was always food, no matter what kind of harvest was had. Never saw her anything but happy to be there. Those kids? She would talk to them all day. You might hear her say about five words a year to the rest of us unless you ask her somethin', but she was always making a fuss over the kids. When she was around the hands, it was smiles and such polite-like, but she mostly never shows a thing. She didn't like his drinkin'."

"He a drunk?"

"He never used to drink at all, but he started drinking heavy over the last few months. He'd drink, and she'd have a look on her face that said she didn't like it. She never spoke up, at least with us around. And he spent more time in town than he used to. Rakeheart."

51

"This Chad," Kane began. "And her . . ."

"Chad thinks every woman ever born is his," Ferguson said, dismissing the idea with a wave of his hand. "Boy thinks he is irresistible to every female in Wyoming. And that's sober. Drunk . . ." He shrugged.

"Think she killed her husband?"

Ferguson looked at Kane as though the man had called his mother a foul name. "Happens. Got to ask."

"Got work to do," said Ferguson icily. "Nice meeting you. I'd watch who you accuse of things. Lady isn't . . . well, like the rest of 'em, but she's decent. You might not want to talk to my crew. They got better things to do than hear talk like that about the woman who is now their boss. Ranch don't have a lot, but we got loyalty."

Ferguson rode quickly away. Never did answer, thought Kane. Never did.

Kane took his time on the ride back to the ranch house. The sun was warm. This Wyoming land could make a man stare. He knew the land wasn't flat, it was uneven. Rocky. Tough. But as the wind blew strong from the west, it looked free, open, and inviting—as though riding across it to some place far, far away from mysteries and murders would be the best thing a man could do with the rest of his life.

He sighed. It was a dream disconnected from reality. If Sherman wanted to find him, Sherman would find him. Somehow.

He looked across the landscape. An antelope emerged from a copse of trees. Three bounds and it was gone. Graceful.

Scared.

The rifle shot sounded as he called Tecumseh's name and kicked the horse's flanks. Nothing whizzed past that he could hear, and soon he and the horse were moving too fast for anyone but the best of shots to hit him.

He rode hard back to the Wilkins ranch. Called Rachel's name. No answer. Colt in hand he prowled. Garden behind the house. Quite a garden. He had not seen it before. Cow barn. Bunkhouse. Stable. No one.

Ferguson had said Wilkins was found in the doorway to the barn. He stood there. Looked out. House was likely, of course. Lot of prairie out there, too. He wondered if anyone heard the shot. Or if there were many shots and only one hit. Or if shooting at the Wilkins house in the middle of the night was common. Guess he had detective learning to do.

There were some gouges in the wood by the stable door that looked new, one for certain he would guess was a bullet, but for all he knew they could have been from a drunk cowboy six months ago. A miss could have gone into the barn.

He drew the hammer of the gun back as he heard the horse; then he saw it. Rachel and her kids, riding triple. She had a rifle in the scabbard of her saddle. Woman would be crazy not to have a gun on the range. Man would be crazy, also, not to wonder, even though he had no reason to believe the gun was aimed at him. Felt that way, though.

The little boy leaped down and came running.

"We saw a bear with babies!"

"Where was that?"

He looked back at Rachel.

"Bears follow the stream," she said. "It winds south and west, and we go there sometimes in the glade where they rest."

Libby, looking intense but staying quiet, came up to stand beside her mother. He was reminded of a pack closing ranks when facing a threat. What was the threat? Him? The truth? All strangers?

"And you, Miss Libby? You get to play with the bear?"

"You don't play with bears."

"I do. Wrestled one in Texas . . ." He went on with every possible misadventure he could think of. He took a deep breath. "Then it made coffee, and I let it go."

"That was awful!"

Kane bowed his head as though she had applauded.

The boy was smiling. Rachel was not. Kane could feel it. She was on edge to guard, whether the threat was real or not. He was trying to imagine her killing her husband. Didn't fit what he knew. Not yet. But her unease was convincing him that her fears were deeper than stray questions from a passing stranger.

The silence became uncomfortable as the flies made more noise than the people.

"Seen what I could see," Kane said at last. "I will be in Rakeheart a spell. Might be back. If you think of something, send for me. Want to get to the truth. Not much I can do to change things, but you need the truth."

He thought again about the money Sherman sent him to give her. Another day.

"Have a safe ride," Rachel said flatly and without enthusiasm. An extra meaning? He wondered.

He rode south, then doubled back to find the creek and follow it. She would have been near where those shots came from, maybe. Maybe not. She never mentioned a shot. Guns on the range weren't unusual events. He'd see.

CHAPTER FOUR

Afternoon was settling upon Rakeheart as he rode in. From the sign he could follow, Rachel and her children did not come home from the trees where the shot was fired. However, there had been horses everywhere, and he was not a skilled tracker.

Janie was still at the stable. She tried to smile, but it died before it formed. Kane did what he could to put it back in place.

"Told him he had to eat extra to make up for the last time," he said as he led Tecumseh to the stall nearest the rear door of the stable. The joke brought no reaction.

"Something wrong?" he asked. The transformation from happy chatterbox to sullen silence was unexpected.

"You should have let Bud shoot him," she said.

"Kevin . . . um . . ."

"Morris. He's one of those men who gets an idea in his head and don't let it go. He thinks I'm his property to grab at any old time he feels like, which is always. Since Bud didn't shoot him, which is what he deserved, he keeps company with the three Colberts. They are as dumb as rocks, but rocks smell better. When they're around, he is even worse, as though he needs to show off so they know he owns me." She imitated a man swaggering.

"Kick him where it hurts."

"Ever kick something that fat?"

55

He started to laugh, but she was too intense. "How about your pa?"

"Mister, he's drunk when he isn't mean. He might kill Kevin by breathin' on him, but that's about it. If I tell him about how Kevin treats me, he might blame me and hit me. I don't want to be hit any more, mister, and certain sure not over Kevin."

Kane took a look at the girl. His first guess had been around sixteen, but maybe she was a year or so older. Brown hair and an outdoor complexion. Face strong more than cute, but he could not help but feel protective. He never had that impulse until he spent too many years trying to remake the world for those people Sherman wanted to protect. It changed a man.

"No husband or man to put him to rights?"

"Pa tried to shoot the last boy," she said bitterly. "I might as well marry a horse."

"Least you'd get a ride to the weddin'."

"It's not funny!"

He supposed it was not. He finished removing the saddle and blankets and arranging everything in the stall. Horse needed proper care, no matter what kind of silly dramatics the human world was going through around it.

He could go to the bank or general store to talk to the town council fellas about this sheriff idea. Or maybe not quite yet. Sheriffin' probably had rules. Buttin' in did not. Maybe do that first, while he could.

The loudest noise in the corner of the Black Dog saloon came from a table of young men. Morris and three others. Almost no one else in the place. Kane ordered a beer, let it sit as he leaned back on the solid wood of the bar and watched the young men play cards. When they are young and drunk, it never takes very long.

One of the three Colbert boys with Morris saw him. Kept staring.

"Too good to drink with us?" called out one of the Colberts, a man with a crop of fuzz on his face and small, beady eyes.

Kane smiled and said nothing in return. One of the other Colberts, the youngest of the three, came to the bar for more beer.

"Oops!" The young Colbert—a smirk on a clean-shaven face—bumped into Kane hard, jostling his arm and sending the beer in Kane's hand sloshing across his boots.

Kane said nothing, wiped his hands, and turned to order another glass.

"Don't spill this one on me," said Colbert.

Kane didn't acknowledge him at all. The less he said, the faster it worked.

"Hey! I'm talkin' to you."

Colbert's hand grabbed Kane's shoulder. Kane pulled the man to him, slammed the side of his head against the hard wood of the bar, twice, then pushed him to the floor.

The first Colbert moved in to defend the family honor. Kane let him swing a few times, then hit him hard under the left arm. Colbert doubled over. Kane hit him alongside the temple, and there were now two Colbert boys on the floor, out cold.

Morris and the third Colbert had started to rise but thought better of it. They sank into their chairs as Kane walked toward their table.

"Hear you grab women in the dark of the stable," he told Morris. "Figure you are some kind of big, important man."

"None of your business," Morris replied.

"It is now. Horse stays there. I stay there. Bad for the horse if the lady's upset."

"Lady!" He spat on the floor. "You don't tell me what to do. She likes me. Women like a man who knows what he wants and takes it." He was trying to bluster while looking up at Kane. It failed.

"Telling you to leave her alone. She don't like it. She don't like you. Neither do I, much. Do not go thinking that 'cuz I didn't let you get murdered and because you got away with having done somethin' stupid, that somehow you was a man who's got privileges. You don't.'"

Morris moved, but, before he could get up, Kane gripped the young man's forearm. Duane Colbert's eyes registered how much he could see Morris was in pain, and his hands went wide to make it clear he was sitting out the dance.

Kane didn't say a word. With one hand on the back of Morris's neck, he slammed the man's head into the table. From the squealing and screaming and the blood, it was clear the young man's nose was damaged, if not broken. Kane let go. Morris covered his nose and moaned.

"Don't make me tell you again. I'll face you in the street like Bud Franklin wanted to whether you want to dance or not."

Kane turned to Duane Colbert. "Brothers?" Colbert nodded. "Got no grudge against you and them. Man backs his friends right or wrong. This time it was wrong. Far as I go, fella, it ends here. You don't like that, leave a note for what to do with the body when you come up against me. Otherwise, nothing personal." The Colbert boy nodded.

He walked back to the bar.

"Any problem?" he asked the bartender, who was putting a wooden club back behind the long wooden bar.

"Nope," said the man. A quick smile. "Sorry there wasn't a full house for the show. Be good for business."

"I'll be around," said Kane, walking slowly out into the street.

Jack Conroy was waiting on a customer, so Kane took his time and looked at the items cramming every inch of Conroy's store. He had no needs, having used the money Sherman gave him to buy new clothes, but there was something about a general store with its disorderly chaos of items piled every which way that made a walk around it seem like the start of a treasure hunt.

About a half hour later, having sold three spools of thread to the matronly woman who seemed hard-pressed to decide which shade of black was best, Conroy walked over to Kane with a face etched in relief and an outstretched hand.

"Mrs. Peters has her ways," he said. "Might weigh a hundred pounds, but she shot a bear last year that was threatening her grandkids. Never know out here, do you? You have some time to think about our offer?"

"Got some thoughts."

Conroy watched the Colbert boys and Morris wobble down the street. Disapproval etched his features.

"I hope you see things our way. Men like that are why we need some law here. There has to be some respect for this town, or it will die."

"Those boys? They won't give you or anyone else any more trouble. Nope." The assurance in his voice made Conroy look a question in his direction. Kane didn't answer it. Conroy let it go.

"Let me talk to the others. We'd like to talk to you . . . um . . . together."

"Horse is at the stable. I stay with him. Come find me. Place to eat here?"

"Last Chance. It was one of the original saloons. Tom Pierce and Mary Ellen run it now. It might not look like much but wait until you eat."

"Obliged."

"Tell them to charge your meal to us."

"Once I take the job." Kane turned to go. Stopped. "If I take the job."

Kane walked down the duckboards. Sheriff. When he was the face of the law, the world was turning itself inside out.

"What did you do?" Janie asked as he reached the stable. She was grinning and almost hopping from foot to foot in her happiness.

"Nothin'."

"Hogwash. They all groveled and crawled as they passed me. Not a peep."

"Good to know." Anything else was choked off when she grabbed him hard and loudly kissed his right cheek.

"Thank you!" she said as she bounced away with a sunrise-wide grin. "Thank you!"

He was in shock, both from the force of the hug from a strong girl about as tall as he was and the smack on the cheek. Tecumseh was staring.

"What are you looking at?" he asked. The horse tossed his head. The horse liked being talked to. Kane always wondered how much of human behavior made sense to a horse. Probably not much. Not much men do makes sense to a horse. Or even to men when they were sane and sober and not off chasin' something that made them miserable so they could be happy.

Stable was a smithy, too. Good thing. Tecumseh had a shoe that was worn. Maybe Janie's pa would show up soon so's he could fix it.

He plunked down at the edge of the stall. Rachel Wilkins. A puzzle. Something off, but she didn't look like a killer. Ferguson? Didn't seem the type. Deeper than he looked, maybe interested in the widow, but not the kind to sneak-shoot a man. That boy, Chad? Hard to imagine him getting the drop on anyone and being sober enough to hit anything. Other ranches? He'd find out. Every town was the same—a solid core of men and women who would whup the wind, the Indians, and one another if they needed to and people who collected around the edges who drifted from place to place looking for whatever was easy to get.

It would sort. In time. Truth was like a bullet in the leg—enough time, enough blood, enough pain, it came out.

The Last Chance still had its bar, and a collection of small tables. Kane sat at the bar on a stool.

"New in town?" sang out a woman's voice. He admitted the fact. "No beer; we only serve food."

"Good."

Whatever she said next had the word steak in it. That was the only word that mattered. And coffee.

An hour later, he was patting a very full stomach as he prepared to walk back to the stable. He thought he'd take a tour of Rakeheart. There were, as Conroy said, four corners that each once held saloons. The original town name, Rakehell, had been fitting for a crossroads that gave cowboys cheap liquor by the barrel. It had been fancified by the territory back before Wyoming became a territory in '68, Conroy said.

Two stores. Conroy's was big and slightly set apart; the other was tiny and looked like it was dresses and ribbons and such things that scared men silly. A place for saddles. One for boots. A few others. Barber shop. Eight saloons. Railroad yard and office. Bank. A small two-story hotel and rooming house. A land office. The church, set apart with graves beyond it. Corrals by the railroad tracks. A printer that claimed he published a newspaper, even though the office looked deserted. Not big, but nothing looked old. Houses up off the main street. Tidy little place. Seemed peaceful enough; the girl Janie said she'd never seen a shoot-out before, so it couldn't be too wild a town—either that or her pa kept a tight rein on her.

As he neared the stable, he saw the banker—Brewer, that's right—with a cigar outside the stable door. He gave Kane the kind of smile Kane figured everybody got when they walked into the bank as long as they weren't asking for a loan.

"We'd like to talk to you now if you have the time," Brewer said.

"Nothin' but time," countered Kane.

Brewer chattered about the town and the men he would meet. Names and descriptions that didn't mean much. Never been introduced to folks who said they were bad people, even when they were. Brewer had probably named everyone worth knowing, but all Kane wanted was a nap after eating too much.

They walked out from the cluster of town buildings to a house. White house. White fence. Neat enough to make Kane straighten his clothes.

There was a Mrs. Brewer who was pretty enough in an Eastern sort of way and who was overly polite but was very nervous and wore too much powder and paint on her face. She worked very hard to make sure Kane knew he was welcome before she vanished to wherever women had to go when men talked business. Silly system. He wondered if all the wives of all the men would compare notes later to see what stupid things their menfolk were doing so they could set them straight. Did Rachel Wilkins disappear meekly to another room? And why was a thought like that interfering?

It was hot inside with a fire and oil lamps. Blue haze from strong cigars. From knowing Sherman, he'd almost forgotten what real ones smelled like. He declined their wine. Watery beer was the price of obtaining information while not making saloon folks suspicious. The rest of it clouded a man's mind.

He missed most of the names. Brewer and Conroy were the leaders. Brewer was talking about the town and how it was growing and would grow more. Sounded like they were trying to persuade themselves as much as him.

"Tell him," softly spoke a youngish man with a fine, blond mustache. "He ought to know about those Riders."

"In time, Gallagher, in time," whispered Conroy.

"Tell me what?" asked Kane. If they didn't want him to know it, he needed to know it. "What riders?"

Uncomfortable glances eventually united on Brewer. Kane had a sudden feeling he could not place that was a warning, but it passed before he could figure out what or who it was warning him about.

"You can't tell a soul," said Brewer.

"Not ten people in Wyoming I know," replied Kane evenly. "Not workin' for men who keep secrets."

He hoped they had no qualms about hiring one who had plenty and would lie.

"Very well, then. The railroad is going to expand, and we want to be part of its expansion."

Railroads did that. Tendrils of iron creeping across the West. Tecumseh didn't like them. Cump Sherman used them to win the war. Kane had ridden them enough to know that once the railroad conquered the West, nothing would ever be the same again.

He waited.

"The railroad barely touches Wyoming," said Brewer. "The line runs through southern Wyoming. Now that the Indians are all but dealt with . . ."

"Whoever thinks that is a fool," said the balding older man at the head of the table with large side whiskers. Buford something or something Buford. He worked at the train depot; Kane remembered that. He almost seemed to have had too much to drink already. He was universally ignored by the younger men.

Brewer continued as though the man had not spoken.

"The railroad will go north in time. Rakeheart is one of the communities that railroad engineers have been looking at as the junction for the line that will head all the way to the border with Canada."

The flourish at the end was supposed to impress Kane. It didn't.

Kane could see why the town leaders were excited. Towns grew where things met. Rail junction would be a big thing. He wondered idly if they had decided where they would put statues of themselves in some town square. He nodded to show he understood even as his mind started chasing down the trail ahead of them.

"The railroad would buy land from the ranchers. Some ranchers see that losing land now will mean big money later. Others do not want to sell. We're working to convince them that we all have a better future if the railroad builds its new northern line out of Rakeheart."

Kane began to wonder if that could have been what happened to Wilkins. Conroy, whom he could see was watching him closely, broke in.

"In the meantime, we have to keep a lid on the wild cowboys," he said. "The railroad can have its junction anywhere. If we cannot show them we are a town where you can walk down the street at any hour without some fools getting in a fight or firing guns off half-drunk, they will not give us another look. What happened the other day has been happening too often, although most of their gunfights are when they are drunk late at night, and only rarely does anyone get hurt. That's why we are talking to you. Rakeheart needs to be a law-abiding town."

Made sense. So did what came next, after there were a lot of shared glances around the table. There was still something unsaid.

"You know about us," said Brewer. "What about you?"

He had never created a past where he obeyed the law instead of breaking it, but that's what this called for. He was aware of the contrast between what he was saying and his real past, but he could see it made sense to them as he talked. He told them all about his old home ranch devastated by the war, the gangs, and the crime during Reconstruction and the last adventure at Red Rock suitably devoid of any mention of General Sherman or the army.

"Met Jared Wilkins in the war," he lied. "Ran into a friend of ours from the war when that last scrape I told you about was windin' down. Wilkins wrote this fella that Wyoming was the best place in the world to be. Got tired of Texas. Thought I would give it a try. Didn't know until I got here what happened. Stopped to see the widow, poor woman. Not really sure how something like that happens out here."

"I suppose that Indian wife of his knows how her man was killed," said the man who said he ran the hotel. Name was Jones. Jacobs. Jeffries!

"Enoch," interjected Brewer.

"After weeks of talking to that man, we had persuaded him to sell and that happens!" Jeffries declared. "Pretty suspicious, I'd say. I knew that she was never on our side in this."

Brewer took over. "Jared was very attached to the land and was trying to bargain for the best he could get. It was business. He was stalling. Everyone wants the best price they can find; that's business. We will see what the widow does. If she wants to sell, we will be ready. If not, we can approach Clem Ferguson, who has been a friend and who will be sure our interests are represented."

Ferguson? Town people always worked on folks to get them to do what they wanted. Ferguson had struck him as honest. Maybe he left his judgment back in Texas.

Kane then wondered: would these men kill a man to get him out of the way of their dreams? The answer followed quickly. It only happened every day.

"I would like to look into what happened out there," said

Kane, making it appear like an unimportant matter. "I'm sure the railroad knows about it. Even if they only know it was a killing, I'm sure they want to know there aren't night riders around here killing ranchers. Feel like I sort of owe it to him, too. Go through the war with someone, you owe them."

He'd heard about such a thing in Kansas where there was some fight over range going on.

"Fine," said Brewer as a circle of glances sent a message Kane did not understand. "But we want the town to be your top concern. That's the most important thing. Can you do that?" For a second Kane thought he saw a smirk. "If you can, then finding out the truth of the Wilkins incident will be fine with us, won't it, gentlemen?"

"Do my best," Kane said to murmurs of assent from the group.

"We can give you thirty dollars a month. You can board at the Last Chance. We will pay for your meals there and stabling your horse."

"You need something, come see me," said Conroy. "I've got more guns than I'm ever gonna sell."

Kane nodded. They were being cheap, but it would suit his purpose to have a reason to stay. "What about a room?"

"Got four. Got three guests," said Jeffries. "Told you I will chip in for his pay, but nothing more."

"Skinflint," grumbled Conroy, almost under his breath.

"Slept at the stable last night. I'll stay there a little longer. That'll do for summer," said Kane. He had one last thought.

"What about whoever owns the saloons. They here?"

"Silas Noonan, he owns the largest. The rest are so small they don't count. He thinks if he has the law to deal with, it will be bad for his business," Brewer said.

"He was also friends with Wilkins, so maybe you can get him to see things different, since you both knew the man," he said after a moment.

Kane searched for some kind of challenge, wondering if Brewer had sensed the lie Kane had fed him about knowing Wilkins. Saw none.

"Friends!" snorted Jeffries. "Anything but!"

"I'll give it a try," said Kane, growing anxious to escape the room. They had avoided any information about these riders Gallagher wanted him to know about. Janie had mentioned something. Maybe she could tell him. For now, he wanted to get out of the stifling room so he could be alone to sift truth and lies.

"Are we all set, gentlemen? I got one more question. If somebody breaks a law, and you want him locked up, where's that going to happen?" he said.

That launched a debate. Kane wanted to offer to go ahead and kill anyone breaking the law if it would get them to shut their mouths so he could get out of there. After the noise crescendoed into chaos, Conroy bellowed for quiet. He got it.

"We can use one of my storerooms, and we'll see about having Pete Haliburton build a room we can use in his stable the next time the man is sober for more than a week. The stable is never full," Conroy said. "Will that work, Sheriff?"

All eyes turned. He didn't recognize the title at first.

"Do just fine," he said. "Gonna get me a good nap and start this sherriffin' in the morning. Good night, gentlemen."

There was general agreement as a bottle of amber liquid had made an appearance and was making the rounds. He guessed they would be a while.

A raucous piano was playing in Noonan's saloon. The Silver Dollar had one, too. Maybe piano playing paid better than sherriffing. Too late now. He slowly walked the street. Felt funny. Like it was his to protect. He shook those thoughts away. He was playing a part so he could do his job and then leave the place behind. Folks who cared about some place sooner or later became part of its dirt forever. He was not making that mistake.

He'd need to ride to Fort Laramie, find out who came to see about Wilkins. Probably need a badge, too. Mostly, he needed quiet. Too much talk. Too much town.

The stable was a welcome refuge. The horse knew him. Might be the only friend he'd make in Wyoming. He spent some time explaining what all this human silliness was all about as he stroked Tecumseh's muzzle. Horse didn't seem to care. He wished for that moment he was a horse so he could not care, either. He gave it one last pat and lay down on a blanket. What had Cump Sherman gotten him into? Set it aside. Worry in the morning.

Chapter Five

The nightmare woke him. The woman had the revolver to his face, cocked and loaded. She said he knew he had to pay. As she pulled the trigger, the world became noise.

Heart-pounding sweat. The stable was suffocating. Sticky. He lurched to the cool air. Gulped it down. He ran his hands over his wet face and through his hair. He had not dreamt of Carolyn in weeks. Her father ran a Louisiana gang that would hire out men to kill farmers who were supporting Reconstruction. Had nothing to do with politics. It was all about buying land. That was in '71. He went in, learned everything. Learned Morris Goodnight had a daughter who was very lonely. Learned she could not forgive a man for betraying her father. Learned that when a woman went bad and started killing, stopping her meant facing someone even more ruthless than a man. Learned that he was a man who would do what had to be done, no matter what. But he hadn't counted on the nightmares.

The doorway of the stable was as good a place as any to sit and watch the dawn come. A couple of the stable's cats gave him a suspicious glance as he sat on the ground by the wall. The stars started to hide, the black turned to gray, and the world began to awake.

One man was up. He waved to Kane as he passed, heading toward the train depot and the stockyards with a cheery wave and an Irish-tinged greeting. Kane wondered what it took to have that simple a life.

There was coffee at the Last Chance and fresh bread. Then he stopped to see Conroy to get his business done.

Conroy agreed to his request to visit Fort Laramie first.

"Want the army to know we're taking care of our own business now," he said, "before the army gets notions of sticking its nose where it does not belong. Brewer will write the territory, too. We want everyone to know Rakeheart is a safe place. Somebody ought to have a badge around here somewhere. What am I saying? I probably do. I take things in trade I never should. If not, Pete can make one easy enough."

As Kane rode east, he could see a well-defined trail turning southeast, roughly running parallel to the way he recalled the railroad. Lot of horses. Lot of riders. He thought about following where curiosity wanted him to go, but decided he already had enough mysteries in his life.

Not much further, about a mile east of town, he saw the shack. Abandoned. Some chinks in the wood, but it could be fixed. He'd see if whoever had built it was still alive. He would need a place to live where he could be alone. Stables and winter might not always be a good combination any more than working for Rakeheart and spending every minute of his time watching his mouth—and his back.

He rode into the morning sun towards Fort Laramie. Rocks and grasslands; then a few stands of evergreens. He knew the plains had other people on them, but he could feel the wind easing the knot inside of him as he rode; elk by the edge of one stand of trees here and antelope running there—hurrying from something. Wyoming. Maybe this was a place to stay. Seemed like enough space for everybody. Then his thoughts turned back to the grasping men of Rakeheart. For some men, everything was never enough.

Fort Laramie was busy. The commander was willing to see the visitor from Rakeheart, but he was very busy.

"Good luck, Marshal," said the bored private.

"Sheriff."

The soldier sighed. "Counties have sheriffs. Rakeheart may think it is a county, but it is a town. Towns have marshals."

Kane shrugged. "Need to use your telegraph."

The private snorted.

"Army only," the private smirked, then jumped as Kane slammed his hand on the table.

"The name is Kane," he yelled. "You got told from army headquarters I was coming. Sherman said I have access, and I want to use the telegraph now!"

An officer with slick, black hair and a massive mustache emerged from behind a door. "I am Captain Mallory. You are the Mr. Kane General Sherman said would appear?"

Kane admitted it and was shown in.

"We expected someone more . . . ahem . . . military," the offi-cer said smoothly. "No offense meant. How can we help you? There is no need to bother the colonel. Back to your duties, Perkins."

"Need a telegram sent to Sherman. Say, 'Complicated. Investigating. Will advise.' Got that?" The officer nodded. "Want to talk with whoever you sent to the Wilkins farm near Rake-heart when the fella there was found dead."

"That was Lt. August Greene," he said. "He is all of the everyone we have to investigate when something out there takes place that might become more than it seems. Would you like to talk to him here? We get very few visitors who have connections to the general, and although I have no idea who you are or why you are close to him, I want no black marks against me. Most of our job is to keep peace with the Indians, and if there is a problem with the settlers, we usually leave that for the terri-tory."

Honest at least. He even agreed to send coffee for his meeting with the lieutenant, who proved to be much older than his captain and not the least interested in whether Sherman was pleased with him or not. Kane told him his twin roles as Sherman's investigator and Rakeheart's new sheriff.

"Territory and us, we make sure when someone gets shot or killed that it's not Indians and not connected to anything that will get bigger," he said, boredom clear in his voice. "Territory wants to be a state, and it would look bad, they tell me. Wilkins was an old soldier; his wife is an Indian. That was why I had to go ask questions I could have answered without leaving here. 'Indian wife kills soldier' would be a terrible headline in one of those awful newspapers they now have. They write something about Rakeheart, then the solid citizens complain to the territory, and the territory scolds the army, and it lands on me. Now it lands on you, at least around Rakeheart. Good luck. Rakeheart had a sheriff for about a week last year before he got sick of them and they got sick of him."

By the time Greene had reached the Wilkins ranch, the body had been moved, but it was clear from the blood the man was killed where the widow said he was. Rachel Wilkins said she thought she heard a shot but told him that, with coyotes prowling the way they did, it could have been her husband protecting the chickens. She told him it was not unusual for him to be up at night and that she did not know until morning, when he never answered her call, that he was the victim.

"Think she killed him?" Kane asked.

Greene's shaggy, gray eyebrows knit together as the man rubbed the gray and brown stubble that spread across his face.

"Gone back and forth. He was dead four days when I got there and buried one day ahead of when I talked to her. Only God knows what she felt when she found him, but if she felt anything the day after he was buried, it was pretty well hidden," he said. "But when I say that I can't help but think it sounds harsh. I got the feeling she was in pain, and not only from the bruises."

"Bruises?"

"She said she was thrown from a horse, but her face was all swollen, and she held her left hand oddly. She walked stiff and held herself funny. All in all, she acted as though she was in more pain than a fall from a horse ought to cause. I chopped some wood for her while I was there and helped with some chores. Yup, she was hurtin' some, and sad. You in the war, Kane?"

"Around the tag end of it."

"There were men who had the look before a battle that said they were resigned to die. Like they knew there was a black cloud with their name on it. She had that look, I guess. Like she was born to lose. Don't see that often in an Indian. Mostly, though, she put up a wall. No expression. Makes you wonder. Did she do it? Kane, she probably is the most likely person, but there's no proof. Not one person can say she ever sent a mean look his way, far as I could tell. Bein' odd ain't a crime. Neither is bein' an Indian. Those Rakeheart folks asked me, and I told them the same thing. Think they wanted her to be it because they want her land for something, but they haven't quite worked themselves up to taking it yet. If she did it to get rid of him, she's gonna end up the loser because she can't run a ranch. Women don't know how; Indians got no idea about more than livin' wild. Sad, but it's life."

"Was there an answer in there?"

Greene smiled thinly. " 'Spose I rode all around it. It could be that it happened that way, but I got nothing to show it did. Nothing to show it didn't, mind. Mostly, I can't see her killin' unless she had her back against the wall defending her kids. Then, anyone would be fair game. She's that kind. Would barely let me look at them, let alone talk to them. But this? Hard to believe."

"So a man got killed that nobody disliked, and the most likely person to have done it had no reason to do it, and there's no proof of anything."

"Good luck telling that to ol' Sherman. Heard he likes things his way and no other." Greene had a wry smile. "Ask you a question?"

"Go ahead."

"There was talk that for years Sherman has had a man—a spy, a ghost no one wanted to admit existed—who spent time down in Texas and some other Reconstruction states. Rode with some outlaws and then put them down so far, so fast, they never saw it coming. That you?"

Kane smiled. "Never heard any profit from telling Cump Sherman's secrets."

"True that. Thought I should say that the Rakeheart bunch . . . well, I spent a couple days there, and I always felt the real men were hiding behind masks. Word to the wise. It's a closed group that is out for themselves, first, last, and only. Not sure I'd want them at my back. Might feel real familiar, if that ol' story was true."

Kane thanked the grizzled lieutenant.

"Forgot. There more towns south and east of Rakeheart?"

"Towns all along the railroad, Kane," Greene said. "Frost Springs is the closest east, maybe thirty miles. Then Grey Flats, about forty miles. West you have Pine Crossing first maybe twenty-five miles away and then Alder's Mill, but that's almost fifty miles. All about the size of Rakeheart; naw, I guess they're probably smaller. All want to have ten thousand people in a week and be somethin' anybody who likes Wyoming the way it is won't want. They all compete."

"For what?"

"Settlers. Railroad. Lot of timber, mines out north. Couple of these places are going to be junctions. The rest will fade away. None of 'em like losin' to one of the others. Like a pack of little kids, and they act about the same, pushin' and shovin'."

Towns. Never understand 'em.

As he and Tecumseh loped back toward Rakeheart, he turned over what he knew, which didn't take long, and what he wondered about, which was a lot.

Men in Eastern suits and flat shoes lied more than men who wore boots and rode the plains. He knew that. But no one had a good reason to kill Jared Wilkins.

The Rakeheart men seemed to get along with him; if anything, his death spoiled their plans, unless they were all play-acting in front of him. Accident? Hard to have accidents in the middle of the night. Rachel? Hard to disagree with the logic, but not one soul could give a reason. He set the mess aside. Sooner or later, no matter how many coats of paint somebody put over it, the truth poked out.

For now, as he made camp about halfway between the fort and the town, there was the last of the real coffee Greene gave him at the fort to drink, bread that was still mostly fresh, and a sky with a dome of stars that made a man feel small, but somehow a part of something greater and grander than towns and ranches. He let all of it go, breathed in Wyoming, and leaned his head back on his saddle staring at it all until the fire died away and sleep overtook him.

Conroy seemed slightly surprised to see him, as though he half expected Kane to ride off and never come back.

The badge he handed Kane had the word *Sheriff* marked into it. Kane wondered. What dead lawman had that before him? Didn't matter. He took it, put it on the coat that would have to be replaced if he was around for a Wyoming winter.

"Talked to the army about Wilkins."

Conroy stopped what he was doing and raised his brows in anticipation.

"No more clue than I have."

Conroy seemed relieved.

"Guess the question I got for you is, with all of you concerned about the railroad and all, does it look bad to have a man killed a few miles away?"

"Not really, son," Conroy replied. "Almost everyone figures the squaw did it, but when folks kill each other out there, there's not a lot we can do about it. Ranch'll go belly up, and maybe then she'll get justice. It takes its time, but it comes around. Could even have been an accident, and she doesn't want to admit it. Wilkins was not very close to any of us here; maybe that's why we don't act as upset as maybe you think we should. Men die out here a lot, you know. Truth is, Kane, folks out here find ways to get themselves killed so often I sometimes wonder there are any of us left."

Kane shrugged. "This sheriff job. Night's the time you want me visible the most or when the cowboys ride in?"

Conroy nodded. "Most times, the town is quiet. You staying in the stable still?"

"Found a cabin. Deserted. A mile east or so. Anybody own it?"

"Ken Tompkins's ranch. No one lives there now. Ken's wife died suddenly last year from the fever, and he left. I think he lives in Cheyenne now. Wherever he went, don't worry. He won't be coming back. There is not much land if you plan to run a lot of stock, but it is all yours far as I know. It's a place to sleep."

"All I want. Stable's nice for now, but I hear winter stories."

Conroy smiled. "Forgot. You're a Texas fella. Something to get used to. The snow is so thick when it falls you can't see the man next to you, and if you go out to travel in it, sometimes it gets flat and white and not a mark on it for as far as you can see. It can be deadly, too, Kane. The winter wind up here can freeze you to death crossing the street if you take your time. Deadly. Beautiful, too. Grew up in Ohio; never tire of seeing this land. Never."

A large-bonneted woman entered, needing Conroy's assistance. Kane left.

He walked Tecumseh to the stable. Clanging said Pete was at work.

"You came back!" Janie. The smile disturbed him even as it enticed him. No one cared when he came and went. That was how the world worked. She was young.

"Janie, my old stall still vacant?"

"Nope, but your horse's is!"

"You are happy this day."

"Pa's back working. He says he won't drink no more."

"He ever promise that before?"

Her face fell.

"That's right! Ride in here and ruin a girl's day!" She stalked off into the far dim reaches of the stable.

Kane stood with Tecumseh's reins in his hand. All he wanted to do was mount the animal and ride as far away from all the things he didn't want to do and all the people he didn't want to see.

The horse shifted. Kane reached up. Stroked the mane. Walked to the end stall he liked. She'd get over it. Or not.

He looked absently out the doorway. A week. He'd give it a week. Then wire Sherman it could not be done and head for Montana. Problem solved.

The smith was busy forging a horseshoe when he saw Kane. "You that gunman?"

"Sheriff Gunman."

"Congratulations."

"Must have known Jared Wilkins."

"I did."

"Want to tell me about him?"

"Why?"

"Ain't sheriffs supposed to find out why people get killed?"

"Let me finish."

Kane watched as the metal went into the fire, back to the anvil for more pounding, and then into a barrel of water. The hissing cloud of steam slowly dissipated as Pete Haliburton set the shoe on the anvil to cool, took off his leather apron and reached out a hand.

"Janie summed you up pretty good," he said.

"Don't figure she misses much. Wilkins?"

"The dead are dead," said Haliburton.

"Somebody living killed him."

"Something off about the man since the fall. Never liked him, understand? Seemed to think because he had an Indian wife, he had to have a chip on his shoulder. Distant one day. Best friends the next. Didn't want to be part of things. Wanted to be important. Who's to care? Felt sorry for her, married to him. Know the type? So noble they want you to know they are noble."

"Who were his friends? Brewer and them?"

"No; he started getting close to Noonan. He's a snake. Nothing in a snake den but snakes. I do not know why they became friends. Back around then, I had to stop Janie from riding off with one of those Company Riders. I do not want her living that life. She didn't forgive me for a long time. I think she understands now that when a man loses his wife, he holds tighter to his daughter."

Haliburton cleared his throat and leaned against a table heaped with tools.

"Wilkins. He started drinking a lot. I drank when I was hurting, Sheriff, after Annie, Janie's ma, passed on. Wilkins was different. He would get mean, like he had to take something out on everyone else. Maybe he pushed somebody too far some night out there, and they pushed back. When we heard, everybody pointed their fingers at his widow, but that's not so much because we know her as there's nobody else who would have cared that much. Nobody really knew him, nobody liked him, and nobody misses him. We might like to know who killed him, but it don't matter as much as whether it rains enough to keep the dirt from turning to dust."

He pushed off of the table.

"That's what I know. I got to get back to work. Janie don't tolerate slackers!" Haliburton smiled, poked the bellows into the fire, and revived the flames.

Kane watched absently as Haliburton's summary of what could be his life echoed. He wondered how well Sherman really knew the man. Everyone knew Cump believed every man on the March to the Sea was somehow better than any other kind of man. Man may have been good. Maybe not. But he was dead, and it was Kane's job to find out how and why. And who. That, too. Sherman would demand that, above all.

Kane spent some time walking Rakeheart. Nod and sort of smile. Some of them seemed to know who he was; others not. In time, all the faces and all the activities would be part of a pattern, but for now he had to learn what that pattern was. Watch and wait. That was the secret to most of life. Sure the secret to survival.

Brewer had told him that since they never had a lawman, they didn't know what the hours were but hinted that Kane ought to know when things would go bad and be sure to be there in time. Kane figured he'd do what he pleased, since his real purpose was to find out who killed Jared Wilkins. If they fired him, they fired him. Rakeheart would have to protect its own self for a while. He had work to do.

CHAPTER SIX

The Wilkins ranch was much the same as it was the last time Kane was there. No one responded when he called. This time it felt empty. Different.

Barn had three horses. Bunkhouse empty. He knocked. Called again. He opened the door to the house, half expecting Rachel to be there with a shotgun. Some wet footprints on the floor. Nothing else. He heard the noise.

Then he caught the smell. Drew the gun. Hammer back. Wait and listen. Softly walking on the soles of his boots but not the heels, he approached the doorway to the big room. He entered aiming at a dead man.

Ferguson was on the floor, a hard red crust across half of his face.

Kane knelt over him. Long gone. Hours dead. There was dried blood on the floor. He swatted the flies. Ferguson had fallen with his feet toward the window. Shutters wide open. Kane's eyes pictured a line from the dead man to the window. Maybe. Dead folks don't drop straight, though. Maybe not.

There were horses approaching hard. Rachel and some hands. No kids. Good.

He went out to meet them.

"How did you know?" she challenged.

"Didn't. How'd it happen?"

She claimed ignorance.

"Clem rode in early. I did not expect him. He wanted to talk about something. I promised Libby I would take her fishing. He said it was important but that he would wait. We were not gone very long, not even an hour if you were using a watch. When we came back, he was there. I got the children out; Libby saw Jared and I don't want her seeing another dead man. The closest men were in the east pasture, so I rode over there and left the children there for now."

Another death. No one to tell the tale but her.

"Whoa up!" he called to the men who were going to move Ferguson's corpse. "Got this badge, so that means I get to figure this out, so don't go movin' nothin' 'til I say so."

Those detective instructions Sherman's clerk sent along said people left clues by dead bodies. He hadn't seen any, but he was going to look.

"What did Ferguson want?" he pressed her.

She shook her teary-eyed head. "It was something about the Company Riders or Jared or that filthy town."

He had heard the term before and would have to find out what it meant.

"He show up often?"

"He was the foreman, and I own the place now. He showed up now and then. Not often, but it was not unusual."

The hands said Ferguson had ridden off from the west pasture a day ago without explanation. With the cattle split in two pastures, one on either side of the ranch house, he would go from one to the other often without much notice or conversation. Kane would have to check the men in the other pasture, but it sounded like what folks on a ranch would do.

Kane looked at Ferguson's body. The man's gun was in his holster. Tied down, the way a man's gun would be if he was going to be around children. No way to tell if he was reaching for it, not with him stone dead. No way to know he was shot from inside or out. House didn't smell like gun smoke, but with the window open and the heat working on a dead man on the floor surrounded by his blood, a smell would have been long gone. There was no obvious bullet hole in the wall, but if the shooter didn't miss, there would not be. The only clear thing was that the man was dead.

Maybe this sheriff thing was a worse mistake than he had been thinking all day. Whatever a clue might have looked like, no one left one.

"Let's get him out of there," Kane grumbled, having no idea what he was supposed to do or how a man did it.

The hands carried Ferguson out to the bunkhouse. Some of the men cleaned up the spot where Ferguson fell. If anything, it looked worse when they were through.

Rachel went to get her kids so they would all be back by dark. He hoped that in the time she was gone he could get some information.

None of the men had much of a bone to pick with Ferguson. Every foreman made men mad from time to time, but Ferguson seemed to be even-handed, and when something went wrong, he faced it. If a hand was in trouble, he knew it.

About as delicately as he could, he tried to find out if Ferguson and Rachel were more than merely the owner's wife and the foreman. Best he could figure was that if they were carrying on, they were the best he'd ever known at finding places in the middle of the night to ride out to where no one saw anything.

The men agreed Ferguson thought Rachel was a very special lady, and a few wondered in time with her man dead if she might think about him as a husband, because a ranch needed a man at the top. He idly wondered if they'd shared that conclusion with her. Would have been a thing to see, he thought.

They talked about Rachel the way so many hands on so many spreads idealized the lady of the ranch. They all agreed her coffee was so strong it could raise the dead, but they all drank it because she made it for them. They could no more picture her shooting a man than they could riding a wild horse.

The picture of Rachel that emerged was that she ran the house, cared for the kids—loved 'em, not merely fed 'em—and if she had anything to say about anything or anyone, she said it to Wilkins in private and maybe to Ferguson as well. Most of the hands were hard-pressed to recall more than a hello, but none of them ever thought she was rude. She was quiet.

What was it the old Mexican woman in San Antonio said? "It is always the quiet ones."

The arrival of Rachel and the children brought an end to questions. Young Jeremiah was interested in the shiny badge. Libby, like her mother, spoke more with her dark, all-seeing eyes. She kept watching him.

Rachel insisted he stay, as if he would have found his way in the dark. He could sense the strain. She chattered. Libby shot her a look a few times; a child knowing something was off but not why.

"Got time to show me this garden I keep hearing about?" he asked the girl. "Not much at growing things myself."

At first, she acted as though she did not want to. She did, explaining distantly but properly what was planted where. He asked about her arm, because she seemed to favor the left. She brushed off the question. He wondered again when he realized that her dress was buttoned tightly on the arms, while everyone else had sleeves pulled up against the heat of the day. He hoped that when he accidentally brushed against her left arm and saw her wince that he was a better actor than she was.

When he asked about the care of various crops, the names of which he was making up as they went along, she at first gave him serious answers, then entered the spirit of the game by telling him she planted some on the moon and others in the trees.

"You know what I am?"

"A cowboy. Mama calls you other things." A little smirk.

"And the sheriff." A shrug. "That means I have to find out what happened when things go wrong."

He wished he knew what her eyes were hiding. He let the silence go until she felt forced to speak.

"You didn't learn who shot my father."

"Not yet. Happened before I got here. Long before. That's why I need your help, because I made a promise that I would find out the truth."

"What do you want me to do?"

"Everybody knows kids on a farm are up all hours, hear everything, see everything, sneak out places. I did. You saw something. Heard something. All inside you, screaming to get out. Tell me."

She was silent. He could feel it—judgment. Risk speaking or carry the burden.

"They were fighting."

"Adults do that."

"They never did. Until lately. They argued a lot. I didn't understand it. I would go there," she pointed to a spot by the creek "where the water flows over the stones, and I would hear less of what they said. I don't know what happened or what I did, but I didn't mean to do anything wrong."

"You didn't do anything wrong, Libby. Tell me. I can keep a secret real good."

She didn't answer right away.

"They yelled a lot. He . . . I didn't want him to see me. I was very careful. Once . . ." She touched her arm, then blinked, then looked him very full in the eyes. "I do not want to talk about that."

"Tell me about the night your dad was shot."

"I was in bed when I heard the shot. I wasn't there a really long time, but I was sleepy. I heard the shot, and I heard

Mommy scream from her room," she said.

Now she was looking Kane very directly in the eye as she repeated the story clearly and succinctly, over and over. He understood she was very intentionally giving her mother an alibi that she would insist was the truth whether it was or not.

Family. The way it worked.

Rachel had said she was asleep. She had said she found Jared the next morning. Did she lie, or did she and Libby never figure out how to make sure they got their stories straight?

Libby was struggling to say something else.

"Is Mommy in trouble?"

"No." A lie? Why not? Everyone else told 'em. "You helped me a lot. A whole lot. And I will keep your secret. And I will come to the moon with you to harvest your garden when it is time."

"Mommy told me that riders come by at night to take Indian girls. She got real mad the last time she caught me hiding."

"I won't tell. Honest. Here." He stuck out his right hand. She took it. A promise he could not keep? He'd made a lot of them. Time would tell. The girl had suffered enough in life. No one bought eyes like hers without paying a high price.

Kane minded his manners through the meal. There was meat in the stew, and the bread was soft. A man could go days with less. Jeremiah and Libby had the chore of cleaning up.

"Will you walk with me, Kane?" said Rachel, who threw a dark-green shawl over the pale-blue dress she was wearing.

"Don't forget my story!" Jeremiah called.

"I will not," Rachel replied. "I will also remember to look to see if you took away whatever it was that was in your room that your sister denies putting there. We do not leave dead animals in the house."

As they walked away from the house, the sound of a sibling debate carried forth.

"They have been through a lot," she said. "I do not know what normal is for children, for white children, but Jared did. They learn some other things, too."

"Love 'em, feed 'em, it usually comes out fine," Kane said. There was probably more to it, but that's all he knew. "Libby. Good girl."

He got a look.

"She seems to respond to your childish ways."

Kane smiled at the comment. Rachel shook her head and exhaled loudly at his reaction.

They walked a while in silence. The evening breeze picked up. She lifted her face to it as they walked into the dipping sun. She turned.

"They will come for me. If you are the sheriff, you are obligated by the law to protect my family."

"Who is 'they'?"

"Rakeheart men."

"Should they?"

He might as well have slapped her.

"You have no mercy in you." She started to walk away. He touched an arm that jerked back.

"Not much of that in this world, Rachel. Not much. Tell me."

"They want the land. Men always want what someone else has. These Rakeheart people have no heart. They have no souls. They are like the rest of them."

"Rest of who?"

"All of those little towns. You don't understand, do you?"

He admitted it.

"The butte behind the house runs for miles, but there is a space of about three miles in our west pasture where the ground is level. The next gap is twenty or thirty miles east. If these people want their railroad, it needs to run through that gap. Sometimes Jared talked about selling that part of the ranch.

Sometimes all of it. Then he would say he was never going to sell."

She shook her head. "I never interfered. It was his world, not mine. I trusted him."

She said that Wilkins had recently encouraged a bidding war for the land.

"He said if they paid enough, it would be worth it. The Rakeheart people came here. Other people came here. I do not know who they were. Soldiers came once. The railroad is their god. They would talk and drink and smoke and glare at me as though I had Red Cloud and a thousand warriors in the barn. I hated them. I told Jared never to sell. This is not dirt, not land. This is home. My home, now. If they come to take it, because whites take land from Indians, I will fight."

She meant it. He was certain. Not his problem. He figured by the time they came, he would be gone. He also felt like he should speak.

"I'm what law there is, and if they break the law trying to take it, they got to deal with me, Rachel. Land's not only yours, it is for your daughter and your boy, there. Like to see your boy run his daddy's ranch."

It was not too dark to see that she was weighing his words.

"Jeremiah is not mine."

He had wondered. More or less assumed, without trying to worry on it too much. Admitted as much.

"It is not just that. He is not Jared's either."

Now she had Kane's full attention.

"I was hurt . . . you only need to know that after Libby I could not have another child. We had to run . . . You do not need to know it all. Jared did not care at first. The longer we were married, the older he got, the more he wanted a son. Men want sons. It is the way of the world. We were living in Dakota when it happened. He came home with the boy one day. He told me Jeremiah was an orphan and that he was about two years old. We gave him a birthday—I think it was Jared's mother's birthday—and we made him our son. Jared said when he brought him home that we had to leave right away, but I was happy to go because it was not a good place to be an Indian. This was true. I did not think then that we left because of where the boy came from," she said.

Her hands tried to shape what came next.

"Here they do not like me, but they leave me alone. I did not ask about him. The boy made him happy, and he was good to me. The boy has been a good boy. I cannot make him my blood, but he is mine to protect. What is in the past does not matter. His story is like mine. Do you understand?"

He did. Sometimes family was made, not born.

"Ferguson got family?"

"He had a brother in the East somewhere. Iowa, I think, or Ohio. I do not know, but there might be letters in his things. You can look."

"You want him buried here?"

She shook her head quickly.

"White people want to be buried together by the church. I went there for Jared, and I will not go again. I will not leave this land for them to take."

He could feel the promise welling up. Fools make promises. That they do.

"No one will push you off your land, Rachel. You want to sell, you can sell. You don't, you don't. Got my word."

She moved her face close to his as she looked up into his eyes. She looked out at the last of the light.

"You do not lie. You are an odd white man. Why are you really here, Kane?"

"Told you. Sherman wanted me to find out who killed your husband. Gonna find that out."

She went back into her shell. "Yes, you did tell me."

The sun was fading fast. A large, dark cloud drifted to the north amid deep yellow that was turning to orange. Far to the east, where the cloudless sky was already dark, there was a star. He pointed to it.

"Way I recall, the Spirit Warrior was running from the Night Warrior, when he fell, wounded. The Night Warrior had chased him, because the Spirit Warrior had stolen a treasure, a vast treasure that the Night Warrior kept hid."

"I have heard this story."

"And the Spirit Warrior, lying wounded, opened the hand in which he had the treasure. And the dark of the sky was never dark again, for from his hand flew all the stars and the moon and all that glowed in the night, so that the People would know the Spirit Warrior would never die, and the Night Warrior would never hold them in darkness again. And in the lights across the sky, the Spirit Warrior lives to this day, watching his children from above and caring for them every day, even those so very far from home."

For the first time since he had met Rachel Wilkins, her face softened.

"I was a little girl when my grandmother told me that story, but it had many voices in it, and it went on forever. The Sioux do not tell the tale this way of the birth of the stars. Only the Comanche."

It was a question.

"There was a trading place not far, when I was a boy. Blind Comanche man would sit there about all day and tell these stories. Don't remember half of 'em. Always liked that one. Thought about it the other night. Something about the sky here. Shouldn't be any different than Texas, but it looked taller and wider."

"You are a strange white man, Kane. You make a promise

90

you don't know if you can keep to someone you do not trust. You tell me a Comanche story to comfort me. My daughter said you played a silly game to make her laugh. Why?"

He shrugged.

"And you dislike being told you are a good man."

"Only a man doing a job, Rachel."

"Tell me, Kane. When you lie to yourself, do you do it better than when you lie to me?"

She laughed as his face registered the impact of her words.

"Let us go back, Kane. Libby does not like to be alone since . . . well, she is nervous without her mother."

Kane did not push for answers but walked silently next to Rachel. Close. He thought about Jared Wilkins. Clem Ferguson. Had they walked next to her, too? Feeling close?

CHAPTER SEVEN

Kane left in the morning. He laid Ferguson out in a wagon, told the hands he would probably be buried in a day, if they wanted to be there, then—with Tecumseh tied behind—they rolled away. Rachel busied herself in the house and did not see him off. Silent Libby watched. Her posture said relief. Her eyes looked a long time at the burden in the bed of the wagon. Her face said nothing.

Preacher Diedrich Siegel shook his head when Kane reached the small frame church with the small steeple that was neither high nor straight. The church bell was mounted on a couple of poles set in the ground.

"Another gunfight!"

"Nope. Someone murdered him, Preacher."

"Another one?"

"Told the Wilkins ranch people they could come by tomorrow to bury him. Hope that was not a mistake."

Siegel waved his hand. "Of course. In Pennsylvania, everything was so formal. Here, there is not the time, and everything is so raw."

The preacher promised to see to a grave and said they would bury him some time late in the day to be sure Wilkins's riders had the chance to get there.

Kane was leading Tecumseh down the main street when Conroy braced him. "Who was that? Who did you bring in?"

"Clem Ferguson. Got murdered at the ranch house out there."

Conroy seemed surprised. "Clem? Good man, not the kind anyone would hate enough to kill. Stayed out of trouble and was always respectful."

"Not a gun fighter?"

"Oh, these riders! They all wear a sixgun, but I think half of them could not hit a barn with one. They all know how to shoot rifles, though." Conroy looked in the direction of the church, where the Wilkins wagon was parked. "Do you know who killed him?"

"Not yet," Kane replied. "I will."

"Yes, yes," said Conroy. "I will tell the others. Two people murdered on a property that . . . well, it should be in more stable hands for the welfare of the community, but we shall give it time. Two people killed is something that the town must investigate. The children must be given proper homes if needed."

He thought about what Rachel said. The ranch. The railroad. Later. Conroy asked a few more questions. Kane gave a few answers; both shared very little. If Ferguson had enemies, or any close friends outside of the ranch, Conroy did not know who they were.

"Clem rode for them for three years. Saving to be a rancher in a few years himself. It's a shame. That's two dead men at one ranch, Sheriff. That woman!"

Kane thought. "Not sure."

"He'd been here six months before *she* ever came into town with him. I'm not a man to pry in another man's business, but I could never put my head on a pillow in the same house with a woman who might lift your hair. Lived here twenty years. The one thing I know is that you never know what they're thinking." Conroy shook his head. "Never knew of any wild ones coming there, but she could have snuck them in. We can pull a posse together if you need one. Army can send soldiers if you think she has a war band hiding out there."

"Not yet," Kane said. Reason. Need a reason they would accept. "Not goin' anywhere. If she thinks she out-foxed us, let her think so. Not sayin' it's her, though. Not sure of that at all. No, sir. Not at all."

"You know best, Sheriff. Whatever you need from me, say the word." Conroy clapped him on the shoulder and left to follow a customer into his store.

Kane was glad to escape.

"You're back!" Janie's grin was welcome. When no reply came, she asked, "Is something wrong?"

"Another man killed at the Wilkins ranch," he said.

"Who?"

"Clem Ferguson. Foreman."

"What about Clem?" Pete Haliburton interrupted. Kane told him.

Haliburton shook his head. "Good man. Wilkins was—Well, don't speak ill of the dead, but never heard of any reason anyone would have cause to shoot Clem. He came 'round here 'bout every time he came to town, didn't he, girl?"

But Janie was no longer there. She had retreated, sobbing, to the part of the stable that served as the house where the family lived.

Haliburton shrugged.

"Guess she was sweeter on him than she let on," he said. "Nobody ever tells me nothing!" He stalked off back to his shop.

Kane stabled Tecumseh and gave him a good brushing. He heard her feet.

"Who shot him?" He was very aware he never said Ferguson was shot. Still, it was the most common way men were killed.

"Not sure, yet, Janie. Sorry if he was your friend."

"He was nice," she said. "He didn't smell bad, and he didn't drink a lot, and he didn't try to . . . well, like Kevin. Nothin' for a girl to do! Nothin' in Rakeheart but town drunks and the Company Riders."

He kept hearing those words. No meaning yet. Not the time. Later. But soon.

"Sheriff!" The young man at the door to the stable was breathless. "You got to come quick!"

The saloon had one word painted over the door. *Noonan's.* No piano jangled now. The hinges squeaked his arrival.

His boots were loud on the wood in the hushed room, where riders and drifters were giving two men at a table all the room they could want while two other men at the table looked scared and trapped.

"Problem, gentlemen?" he asked, sauntering over as though the two men were old friends instead of each poised to pull guns—the cowboy from the holster at his hip, the black-coated gambler from inside his coat.

"He cheated!" the cowboy said.

Kane wondered why a fool cowboy who played cards with a gambler was surprised that the man did what every man knew gamblers did. Either the gambler was having a bad day or the cowboy was cheating, too, and was bested by a more devious opponent. Fools. A world of fools. And he was in charge. For a moment he wondered if he told them to go outside and shoot each other dead for the good of the town if they would do it. Probably they'd miss, and he'd have to clean up the mess anyhow.

"Look at me, both of you," Kane instructed. The cowboy complied.

"Got a name, silver vest?" Kane called.

"Reynolds Parker."

"Then Reynolds Parker, look at me or join the parade to the

churchyard."

The gambler's eyes moved, bird-like, from one foe to the other.

"Git, you two," Kane said to the others. "Grab what was yours that you haven't already lost, then go."

They needed no second invitation.

Kane walked, slowly crossing behind the cowboy, then behind the gambler, as he circled closer until he was about three feet away and between them both. They were both now following his moves. Wonder if this works, he thought. He heard a story about it one time.

Time to find out.

He kicked hard at the leg closest to him and pushed the table over with his right boot, sending cards, coins, and a few greenbacks sailing into the air and onto the floor. Each man leaned away to avoid being hit. By the time they were reaching for their weapons as they rose from their chairs, Kane was on them.

Grabbing the gambler's coat and the cowboy's shirt, he pulled them together. Their hands came up instinctively to block each other as they collided instead of fighting against Kane. As they rebounded from their collision, Kane shifted his grip to the backs of their necks.

It sounded painful. It was. After the second time Kane slammed head into head, there was no resistance. After one more time for luck, he shoved them both down.

Even dazed, they were each interested in continuing the fun as they tried to rise, but Kane was not having any more dancing for the evening.

Their scrambling stopped as they saw the .45 pointing at them.

"By my count, we already got six aces in that deck," Kane said, looking from the cowboy to the gambler. "Figger you got more stashed places I don't want to touch. You both cheated. You both lost. It ends. Either one of you disagree, I can kill you here."

The gambler, who knew his breed were often subject to whims that included hanging when a local cowboy was unwilling to be fleeced, agreed quickly.

"I need to recover my stake," he said.

"You need to recover your horse and go," Kane said. "Moncy goes to the town. Unless you have an objection?"

Living to steal another day beat every other alternative in front of the gambler.

"Let him through, boys," called Kane, who motioned for the gambler to leave.

"And now for you, you fool. Trying to cheat a gambler at his own game? Doesn't end well often, son." Kane raised his voice. "Anybody here with this fella?"

Two riders raised their hands.

"What outfit?"

"Bar Seven."

"Get him back there. Holiday's over, boys. Go!"

With a look of hatred, the cowboy rose from the floor as his two comrades came to walk with him. Kane watched him wobble out.

"Drink up, boys!" called a man in a black frock coat with a white shirt and a small bow tie. "On the house. A cheer for the sheriff!"

Whether they knew what they were cheering or not, there was a round of noise.

"Sheriff!" The man, who from the slicked hair and twirled mustache could only be Silas Noonan himself, held out a hand to Kane.

"Mr. Noonan," said Kane, accepting the warm, fleshy hand. "Did I pass?"

"I beg your pardon?"

"You have been here for years. Your boys, like those four by the bar, could bust up anything. You called me. Is your curiosity satisfied?"

Noonan's smile only widened.

"I confess you have caught me." He chortled. "Clever! Yes. My men tend to be a little hard on the windows, although they get the job done. As you may have noticed the noble and upright leaders of Rakeheart, who are quite happy to make money off of my customers and often are my customers, are less happy with the fact that cowboys come to saloons and towns to run wild and let off a little steam in some rather violent and not very moral ways that towns trying to grow and seem all dandy and proper consider abhorrent."

"What if I had shot them both dead and a few of your customers as well?"

"Ahh, Sheriff, but you did not," replied Noonan. "And so all is well that ends well. I know you have so recently returned with Clem Ferguson's body. He was a good man. You must be busy, but we shall talk again."

Kane watched Noonan walk through his saloon into a back room. Noonan did not try to pretend he was a saint. But is a snake any less dangerous because it likes being a snake? Something to chew upon another time.

Janie was waiting at the stable. Her eyes were no longer red, but her face was still puffy. She tried very hard to hide it with a smile.

"Can you have supper with me and Pa tonight? One of the men paid Pa in steak, and we never get company, and I can make biscuits, and there's real coffee?"

His irritation at the thought of company warred with his reaction to a smile. "Why not?"

"Good! I'll come call you." Off she marched.

Kane took a few minutes to walk down to the far end of Rakeheart, where the pen was built for the stock to wait for the trains. There sat the train station, a small wooden structure that looked like a good wind could blow it down.

A man on the raised wooden platform looked at Kane. Frowned as if he was unsure of Kane's purpose or that Kane was interfering in a daydream. Then a glimmer of amusement flitted across his face as he hooked his thumbs in the waist of his pants.

"Where ye from?" Irish. Even in Wyoming.

"Texas."

"Who ye huntin'?" Kane's blank look inspired another comment. "The badge."

"I'm your new sheriff."

When the man's laughter ended, he looked at the visibly annoyed Kane. "No offense, Friend Badge. You aren't joshing an old man?"

"Like to know the joke."

"Lad, lad, lad. Would not us all?" He appeared to give Kane a close scrutiny.

"New ye are." He paused. "Are ye not the one who sent poor Bud Franklin to his grave? Talk of that was grand."

Kane shrugged.

"They said a friend ye are to the Wilkins clan."

Aware this was turning from a conversation into an interrogation, Kane spoke carefully.

"I knew him in the war. Fine family."

"A family that deserves better," Halloran said grimly before lapsing into brogue once again. "But find ye will that men change, Friend Badge, and not always for good."

Halloran continued his inspection.

"How'd they talk you into this?" he said at last.

"Got my reasons."

99

"Better be good ones, lad. That lot." He spat. "A deep game it is, Friend Badge, and they are the ones with the rules. They use you for their own ends, they do, the lot of them. Those riders . . . Ooh, I could tell you . . ."

A white-shirted man with a black vest emerged from the station. Buford. The old man no one respected at the town council meeting. "Halloran! You were supposed to clean out the baggage room. You won't get a nickel until you do."

The Irishman elaborately winced at the door slamming shut.

"You would think a body would have pity on a man with a head in my condition," he said ruefully. "To work I must go, Friend Badge." He put his right hand over his heart and then raised it high. "Farewell!"

Raving about something, the man toddled off into the station.

Kane asked about the man when he sat with the Haliburtons at supper.

"Seamus Halloran owned a saloon. Drank the profits, they say," said Pete Haliburton. "He never worked much after his wife died, or so I was told. He was one of the early settlers, back in the days they called the town Rakehell. That was long before I came here. Now he does odd jobs. I let him sleep in the stable when it is cold. They all say he's a drunk, but he is not a bad man. He mostly acts like he does not care anymore about anything other than eating when he is hungry and sleeping out of the rain and snow. I have never seen him act hungry, though. He seems pretty content with his lot."

"He's nice to me," piped up Janie. "He has a million stories. I don't know if any are true, but they are good stories. He really does not like Mr. Brewer or Mr. Noonan. I think he knows everyone in town and all of their habits. He is someone you can talk to about everyone in town, and he understands. He knows more about those Company Riders than anyone else. He is awake all hours, so I guess he sees them the most."

"Strange, though," commented Haliburton. "He goes away for weeks at a time now and then. Maybe he goes on a drunk and goes some other place, but I don't know how he gets there. Was a man at the hotel once talking to him about Denver and some fancy hotel there and Halloran acted as though he knew everything the man was saying about the place. Struck me as odd, but I suppose when you have nothing holding you down, there's no law against getting around."

Kane thought that over. Did Halloran hate from an old grudge, or what he saw around him? He would have to ask the older man about Wilkins. Men no one saw were the ones who saw behind the façade. Later.

For now, he was eating very good food, and a young woman was doing her best to make him feel welcome, and her father—unlike fathers Kane could recall from the long-distant days when he had an interest in young women—seemed to tolerate it all.

"You never really said how you came to be here," Janie asked. He hesitated. Only Rachel knew the real reason.

"Thought you knew," he said. "Wilkins. Me 'n him were in the war together."

"Oh. I forgot. You said that when you killed Bud Franklin."

He kept on eating.

"Are you staying?"

"You are direct."

"Kane, here is the way it is out here. When a girl gets to be seventeen she usually has a family, or she is going to be one of those old maids you see. I don't want to be an old maid. A lot of the boys, like Kevin, make me feel dirty just to be near them. You don't."

"I appreciate the compliment."

She swatted his arm.

"I'm not looking to get married next week," she said, "so don't ride out in the morning, but I . . . I don't want to think I am going to die old, alone, and wrinkled."

"Promise, Janie, that I will shoot the first wrinkle I see."

Swat. "Men!" But the smile was real. And it felt good.

Emelia had been gone now eight years. They had never really gotten far in the making of plans when the fever came, and she was gone in two days. At first there had been no room in his mind for anyone. Then came Carolyn, who wanted to kill him when she learned his true identity, and his realization that there was no room for somebody else in a life always lived by pretending to be someone he was not. Now? Time would tell.

Janie had a roan mare saddled and waiting when he got up. She had ridden everywhere, and he still had no sense of the range limits. She had volunteered to show him.

They rode toward the shack he had thought might be habitable.

Her face spoke volumes when she saw the trail to the southeast that showed the traffic of many horses. She was clear that their ride would not take them that way, nor should Kane ride that way alone.

The shack was not far from a stream that trickled along a rocky bed. Not much water, but enough to live on. The roof had a hole that could be patched. Mud that had chinked in the gaps along the walls had fallen out but could be replaced. It was one room with a small fireplace. Nothing had moved in except, Kane could tell, some birds that left the chimney when they arrived. He had lived in worse.

"You should stay with us," Janie said after barely giving the place a look.

"Company Riders?" he guessed.

Dead center.

"What do you know about them?" she challenged, real fear showing.

"Nothing except that I hear about them everywhere. Who are they?"

"They can get you killed."

"Franklin was one."

"Are you from the territory? You know a lot for someone who showed up one day."

"Janie, the same game gets played in lots of places. Franklin used his gun for a living. The way people talk, these Company Riders do the same thing. Tell me."

"Check outside." She got a raised eyebrow. "Please?"

He did.

"Might be a wolf half a mile off with an interest. Nothin' else."

"Don't laugh about them," she said. "They . . . they kill people."

"Tell me."

It took a while, but the story emerged. Rakeheart, like the other towns that were pushing and shoving with each other to get ahead, make a name, and become a place that was important, now and then played tricks on the other towns.

"That's how it started," Janie insisted.

Cowboys would shoot up the other towns now and then. Nobody got hurt, but if they did it when the wagon trains or the immigrant trains were coming, it scared off newcomers. Riders would tell wagon trains how unlawful and dangerous other towns were.

She said Brewer, the banker, and Jeffries, who owned the hotel, were the prime movers in pushing other towns aside, along with Gallagher, who owned the saddle shop. Rakeheart pushed hard, she said.

Then other towns pushed back. Pushing and shoving

103

escalated. By that point, Kane knew where it was going. The towns stopped playing tricks and hired toughs to do real damage. Then toughs to protect against the other toughs.

"They formed what they called the company. The men they pay. They don't come to Rakeheart very often, but when they do, they are the worst of anyone I have ever seen. Pa loads his shotgun and sits in the stable," Janie said. "Sometimes they ride through late and fire at the stores when they get drunk. They don't do much damage, but it gets really scary."

"They can't control them."

She nodded. "They don't have lots of gunfights. That was an excuse because of what happened with Bud and Kevin. The town people want you to be there to stop the Riders the next time they come in. Pa thinks so, too. Mr. Brewer told Pa the Company Riders were 'too big for their britches' a while before you showed up, and they were talking about how to get rid of them without leaving themselves defenseless against the other towns that do what they do."

"And if I live out here, once they figure out the man who killed one of 'em lives out here alone, I'm a target."

"You would not last a week," Janie said. "There are ten or twenty of them. Maybe more; no one really knows. I don't know if they are watching now. The old drunk, Mr. Halloran, used to say they had men in the hills watching every move anyone made. He always made it sound like they could never be beaten."

Janie's words made him wonder. It had been more than a week since he had killed Bud Franklin. No one had sought retribution. Maybe all of Rakeheart was scared over a shadow. Didn't take much to scare town people.

He promised Janie he'd think real hard about moving. She wasn't sure where their hideout was. All she knew was that anyone taking the trail she pointed out was shot at before they could get very far.

A race to town that by some happenstance she won put a smile back on her face. He left her smiling at the stable. It was an image to think on as he walked toward the church to bury a good man whose death was a mystery.

Rachel was not there, but about a dozen Wilkins hands had ridden in. More than a few of the townsfolk joined them. Ferguson had been well liked.

The service was simple. Kane had heard a lot of the words before. They had tried to bury the men they lost when he first worked for Sherman with a group of other men. As the remaining few grew fewer, the words grew fewer as well. When Sonny Carpenter was shot down, there were no words at all, but there were four men left as lumps on top of the ground as payback for one who had been put under it.

Kane was wondering if God understood the way it was for men like him who could only fight the rights and wrongs of this world with the weapons they had around them, when he realized it was silent around him and men were looking his way.

The preacher repeated his question.

Yes, Kane replied, there would be a stone. Noonan had volunteered to pay a man to carve one, something that baffled him when Noonan made the offer.

The hands took turns filling in the grave. One came to Kane with a small, carved, wooden box.

"This was all the papers he had, Sheriff," Ed Jackson said. Jackson, an older man than Ferguson, was foreman for now until the ranch settled itself. "Thought you might see something here we didn't."

There was nothing. Two letters from a year ago from a friend in Colorado. Bills of sale for his horse and saddle. A loop of rawhide. Something . . . he handed the papers to Jackson and dug his finger in the gap between the side and bottom of the box. Jackson dug out his pocket knife and handed it to Kane, who pried out the object.

A flattened, misshapen lump of metal fell to the ground. Kane picked it up. It wasn't a bullet; it was part of one, or something that could have been one.

"He ever get shot?"

"Not on our ranch."

"Mind if I keep this?" he asked, frowning.

"Suit yourself," said Jackson. "Boys and I aren't staying in town. Miz Rachel isn't easy out there with half a crew."

Kane was happy to hear that. Riders nursing their emotions after a burial sounded like nothing but trouble for a sheriff who had other things he wanted to do.

"Tell her I said hello, and I am sorry for her troubles out there."

"She had a message for you," Jackson said. "She said if they send you, she understands. Don't know what it means, but nothing means nothing these days. Me and the boys will be waitin' to hear from you about who gets to pay for killin' Clem and killin' Jared. Sooner or later, a ranch has to take care of its own."

On that note, Jackson collected the rest of the hands, and they were soon riding out. Kane could feel himself relax. It was normal to figure that whoever was threatening the ranch was someone who was an outsider. What he wondered was whether or not that was also true.

CHAPTER EIGHT

The saloons had muted themselves for the funeral. No piano jangled off-key as he walked back down Rakeheart's main street. Death did that. Give it an hour, though, once the dust from the graveyard was off their shoes and the image of the coffin was out of their minds, and they would be louder than ever.

He strolled along, devoid of purpose for the moment. He needed to find out more about the Company Riders. He needed to learn more about all of it. Tomorrow. His missions for Sherman were one thing. There was always the chance he would be discovered. Real life seemed like something other people lived. Now he was living it, and it seemed like he was still an onlooker.

"Sheriff!"

It was Gallagher, the saddle-maker who had wanted him to know more about the Company Riders but had quickly been shushed.

"Mr. Gallagher."

"Gordon," the man said. "No need to be formal. Is it true the Wilkins woman may have murdered another man?"

Kane started to get angry, then realized that would do no good. The men of Rakeheart were what they were.

"Could be, but I don't think so," he replied. "She's not that good a shot to have killed Clem, and it seems hard to believe two different people used rifles to kill men out there."

"Who then?"

"Trying to figure that. Never met a man who didn't step on somebody's toes, but everybody tells me that's who Ferguson was."

"That's because the one he stepped on is dead," said Gallagher. "Come in the shop and we'll talk."

A saddle shop had a wonderful smell of leather. There was about enough room for three people in the place what with all the saddles and other leather goods propped on wooden stands.

Kane inspected the work as Gallagher excused himself, went into the back, and emerged moments later in less formal clothes than he wore to the funeral.

"You are a craftsman, Gordon," Kane said. It was true. The workmanship was as good as anything Kane had seen anywhere, even in San Antonio.

Gordon happily brushed aside the compliment.

"Don't like talking on the street," he said. "Always someone listening."

Kane waited.

"Wilkins was as quiet a man as a man could be until, oh, sometime around snowfall last year. I don't know why, but he started pushing hard to become part of the town council we have. Now, we like to listen to everyone, but when a man suddenly starts thinking the whole town should listen to him, that's not right. He had some different ideas, and he did not like it when anyone disagreed with him."

Gallagher stopped. Footsteps came close, then receded as the figure of a man passed the window of the shop.

"Ferguson and he started drifting apart. No secret Ferguson thought Rachel Wilkins was some kind of queen; maybe that was it. In spring, they all but had a fist fight in the shop here. Wilkins had ordered a fancy, expensive saddle—cost too much even if I say so, but if he wanted it, I was going to make it—and Ferguson was in the shop while we were talking about it. He was mad at Wilkins for spending money and time on things other than the ranch. There was something in their talk, like a threat. They got right up chest to chest arguing, and I was sure it was going to get worse, but then Wilkins came to his senses and realized they weren't alone and stormed out."

"What happened then?"

"Ferguson said something about some man and told me to be sure I forgot the whole thing. Don't think I saw him more than once or twice after. Wilkins, next time he saw me, tried to pass it off that Ferguson was interested in his wife. He was, of course, but not in any wrong way. He was too good a man. He could have made that place hum."

"Was Wilkins a good rancher?"

"Fair," said the saddle-maker. "Did a good job of building the spread, but he didn't seem to be—oh, I don't know the word—didn't seem to care as much about it moving up and growing lately. He acted angry at the world, as though something didn't come out right for him, but he never said what. I know he made the rest think he was going to sell one month, then take it all back the next. No one really knew what he was thinking. The widow? There was no point in even trying to ask her! It could be that he stopped running it properly because he knew he was going to sell. Wish I knew."

The door opened. A lean man, gray in his beard with measuring eyes, walked in the shop. He scanned Kane with particular interest.

"Good afternoon, Mr. Washburn," Gallagher said in his customer-pleasing tone.

"Not sure I've met your friend."

"Sheriff Kane. Link Washburn."

Kane could see Washburn had no intention of offering his hand. The name. The name.

"Chad's pa."

"I am that. You shot at my son."

Gallagher moved away.

"Killed his boot dead. I did that. Boy was a bit full of spirits and bein' young, sir, and it seemed like the best and fastest way to end it before he got himself in trouble. There were four fellas, all a little drunk and all a little wild, sir, and a woman and her kids. Nobody got hurt worth talking about. 'Spose I could have arrested them for being stupid, but ain't a jail big enough to hold everyone charged with that, and I'd be in the cell with them. Bein' a sheriff, that would be embarrassin'. Everybody said he's a good boy who gets too wild. Usually life's the cure for that."

"Ever raise a boy without a mother, Kane?"

"Nope, but from what I see, it's like riding a wild horse with your hands tied—a lot of falls and a lot of surprises. Can't be easy, or it would come out right more than it does."

"A fact. Chad's mother passed when he was nine. Boy was never the same after."

"Sorry there, sir. Nothing personal. Nothing mean in him; he's wild. He comes to town, I have no quarrel with him. Sometimes a man grows up better when he lets all his stupid out when he's young. Maybe your boy is one of those men. Hope for him that's so; only a boy, sir, and I am sorry he lost his mom. A woman does things a man never figures out he was supposed to do."

Kane extended a hand. Washburn took it.

"Now, Sheriff, I might see you later, but this man keeps taking longer to make me a saddle than it did for the cows to live that provided the leather, and I got business to attend to. So, if you will excuse us?"

A visibly relieved Gallagher emerged from wherever he had

fled as Kane left the shop to return to the blazing sun of a Wyoming afternoon in Rakeheart.

"Hope you don't mind eggs," Mary Ellen Pierce said as he sat at the Last Chance for supper. "We had a stash of 'em because the chickens went wild laying, and they were going to go bad soon."

Kane waved off her concern. He was eating every day, more than once a day, and sleeping indoors. Some men had a lot more. Lots of nights he had experienced a lot less. He asked the woman about the two dead men at the Wilkins ranch.

She did not have much sense of Wilkins and Ferguson. Ferguson almost never ate there, and Wilkins came only a few times when he had his wife and children with him.

"I think they had troubles," she said. "I know that Rachel didn't like town. Being an Indian, I guess I can see that because people shot her looks as though she was one of the wild ones, but they tried to be happy with their children. The girl they have, the dark one, she never smiled. In my experience, children like that come from a home where there is nothing to smile about. Tom and I always feed all the ranchers' children when their families come to town. We enjoy the children, and we do not have any of our own. The Wilkins children were well-behaved, Sheriff. There was a shadow on the older girl, though. We could not get her to talk. I expected that she would change with time, but she only came in a few times, and then she stopped coming to town at all. Shame."

When he asked her about the Company Riders, she came closer and spoke with quiet urgency.

"Sheriff, you look like a nice man, and I don't mean to be rude, but that's something I don't ever talk about, and I would thank you never to mention it here again, because there is nothing good that happens to people who make loose talk about those people."

She stepped back, forced a smile, and walked through a doorway to where the cooking was done.

Supper was most clearly over. Kane walked around the street a while to show the town he was as alert as any town could want its sheriff to be, then once the sun was tucked away behind the jagged edge of the far-distant mountains to the west, he went to the stable. He needed a few minutes away from people.

Tecumseh was alone. He saddled the stallion and rode up to the flat-topped hill where he had sat on the day he rode into Rakeheart.

He could see the trail east toward where the Company Riders were supposedly holed up. It was dim enough that he could not see the broken country that would be down that way, but men who lived the way he was told they did always found it. To the southeast was the railroad. There must be badlands between the rails and the flatlands where a gang could hide. He'd have to find them someday, if for no other reason than to get to them before they got to him. If they were everything he was told, that day would come sooner or later.

He looked north toward where the Wilkins ranch sat, far out of sight. Flat enough ground for a long ways if a man wanted to build a railroad or one of those macadamized roads they had back East. To the distant east and far-off west, the ground was broken into hills that would lead to real mountains. Then there was Rakeheart.

The town looked insubstantial on the plains, as though if it blew away in a north wind, the prairie would roll on and never know it had been there. Yet all those folks were willing to put everything they had into that purely because it was the place where they stopped for this reason or that and now invested their hopes and dreams in this little place. Funny thing, towns. Tecumseh's head moved. He'd been speaking out loud to the horse again. Funny thing, people.

He lingered. Land to him had always been a place to stand on. Nothing more. Here, he had a sense of it as something vaster, deeper. Not his; not worth dying for; but bigger and wider and able to fill a man with something that felt like hope.

A gun fired from town. Enough dreaming. He waited. No answering shot. Most likely nothing, but it was time to go.

The tendrils of responsibility were closing in on him, and he admitted the reluctant truth to Tecumseh as—with a glance back at where a long streak of orange was starting to outline the horizon—they rode back to the world where men fumbled and broke all they held dear, bemoaned the loss, and rose the next day to do it again.

Kane was not overly fond of thinking. He'd survived by instinct, reacting to what took place around him. Plans were like fog—they never lasted. But as he walked up and down the streets of Rakeheart upon his return, he knew he needed to map out a strategy that would deal with the two murders he now had to solve.

The town leaders were like gamblers who always kept their hole card hid. Noonan was out for himself. Most of the people of Rakeheart were more focused on survival than anything else. And Rachel? That was a lake of a depth he could not measure. Whatever went on behind her eyes stayed there.

The Company Riders seemed to be the link connecting everything. Maybe when the moon was no longer bright enough to light up the night, it would be time to pay a call and see what there was to know. A little spying was good for a man—especially one who wanted to live.

"Sheriff!" The running barefoot boy burst through the door of the Last Chance, where Kane was having his first coffee of the day. "You got to come quick! It's my ma and pa. He's gonna kill her."

Kane took one huge gulp, picked up his hat, and followed.

The boy ran toward one of the small shacks on the edge of the town. Kane could hear the sounds of the fight. Fight? Mostly a man yelling and a woman screaming.

"Stay here," he told the boy, a thin blond kid of about ten, dressed in a pair of thin, home-made pants and a shirt he'd grow into someday.

The door was slightly ajar. The woman was at one end of the room, cowering behind a rough-hewn table that was on its side. He pushed the door wide.

A wild-haired man's raving condemnation of the woman was checked by Kane's presence.

"What do you want?" he screamed. The shack stunk of liquor; the man was flushed with his hair askew and a day or three's growth of whiskers on his face.

"Sheriff. Got a complaint that someone was disturbing the peace," Kane said, trying to keep his voice flat. "Got to come with me and explain this. Don't mean to interrupt, but I got to do my job."

"She call you?" he said throwing some earthenware object that shattered against the far wall of the shack.

"Nope. I heard you a mile away, and it sounded like a mule in pain," said Kane, swiftly losing patience as the woman whimpered.

"She poured out my liquor!"

"Guess she missed some from the looks of you," remarked Kane. "Sorry. No time to talk. Time to go."

The man was not planning to comply with any suggestion. "She burned my food."

"Well, friend, I burn mine all the time, and you don't see me throwing things at me, now, do you?"

The drunken man was trying to comprehend that remark when Kane stepped fully into the house.

The man reached down and grabbed the shotgun that had been propped against the wall. "You're her man friend, ain't you? You sneak in when I'm not around. One more step and I'll blow you both to pieces."

"There are days when that might be a relief, friend, but for now I got work to do. Put it down and come along. I'll find you a nice place to sleep, and when you wake up and your head stops hurtin', we can talk about it."

"William . . ."

The woman's head briefly poked above the table. Kane had time to see the black puffy bruise on one side of her face before the fool fired.

As the pellets of bird shot rattled off the wall around the hole made by the bulk of the shot, Kane moved swiftly and mercilessly, pulling his gun and raking its barrel across the side of the man's head as he lashed out viciously before the second blast erupted. The man looked more surprised than anything else until the second blow sent him staggering.

Kane knocked the weapon to the dirt floor and waited. Hate to beat up a man with his boy watching, Kane thought.

The man, who topped Kane by three inches and twenty pounds, was not done fighting. He shouted something incoherent as he lurched at Kane before one final blow from the heavy butt of Kane's revolver sent him to the floor.

"Pa!" The boy was at his father's side.

Kane went to the woman, gun still in hand. "Ma'am?"

The table had scars from the shotgun blast. The woman had two fingers hit by shot, but the shot only left small bruises. Her face was another matter. The blackened marks around her left eye were matched by red ones around her left cheek, which were swelling rapidly. Kane called the boy.

"You pa's gonna hurt, but he ain't dead," he explained in between gasps. "Had to hit him hard quick to get this over before he got real hurt." Turning back to the woman, who had told him her name was Mae, he asked, "There anything close to a doctor here?"

"Mr. Pentle, the barber."

"Get him," he told the boy. "Tell him to find ice. Saloon might have it. Hurry."

The boy was gone in a second.

Kane walked to where a knot of people had gathered.

"Nothin' to see folks. Time to move on and let these folks get on with their lives. Bet everybody has somethin' to do."

"What happened, Sheriff?"

"Somebody's life went off half-cocked. Now let's give the folks some room here. Move along!"

Mae was still sitting where he had left her in the wreckage of her life.

"This been happening a lot, ma'am?"

She shook her head. "Bill was supposed to get a job with Frank Tully hauling freight. Frank gave it to his cousin or brother-in-law or something last week, and Bill's been drinking ever since. He's never . . . Donald's ten, Sheriff, and Bill never did this before. He's a good man. Don't lock him up."

Kane considered the size of the man he would have to drag out. He'd need help. He'd need handcuffs he did not have and a jail cell that didn't exist. Maybe instead of trying to lock up the man, the woman and the boy could find a place to stay, although sendin' a woman away for not doing anything wrong sounded wrong.

"Got kin?"

"In Kansas. We have been on our own for years."

Kane thought. Nothing lower than a man taking life out on someone who couldn't hit back. As he looked at Mae, something looked familiar. He had never seen her before, but there was something about the appearance of her face. An inner voice was screaming at him, but he could not make out what it was saying. Later. Later.

"Tell you what, Mae. When Bill wakes up, he and I are gonna have a talk. Part of that talk is that he's gonna see a lot of me the next few days. I see your face isn't healing, he is gonna learn about things I don't tolerate and reasons I think a man can be shot right down. If he's a good man, nothin' more gets said, and life goes on its own way. If you don't think you are going to be safe, then I will find a place to lock him up."

She nodded as Donald and Jim Pentle came in. Pentle made clucking noises as he tended to her face, having been told clearly by Kane that whatever was wrong with Bill Cartwright was the man's problem.

Kane walked outside with the boy.

"Hard when stuff like this happens," he told him. The boy was silent. "Good folks sometimes do bad things. Stupid things. Things to people they love because the world treated 'em so bad, and they feel so alone, and there is no one else there but the folks that love 'em. Understand?"

The boy nodded.

"Didn't want to hurt your dad. Not gonna let your dad hurt your mom. He comes around, he understands he done wrong, he never hurts her again, I got no problem with him. But, son, if you ever see him hurt her, you got to tell me, because in some people it's a sickness, a twisted thing that nobody knows is there until it pops up, and it's not ever gonna get better. Hope that's not what happened with your pa. But if it is, you got to protect your ma. Nobody else gonna do it." The boy nodded again.

Kane stuck out a hand, wondering what was really going on

inside. Settler kids had to grow up fast, like it or not. The boy took it.

"Now you sit with your ma when we go back in. I got to talk to your pa, and he's gonna feel like a fool if he's any good at all, so it's best if you aren't right there."

The man who had been so full of rage a short time ago was now deflated as he sagged against the wall of his shack. He eyed Kane, not quite sober, and not quite recovered from some hard blows to the head, but close enough.

"Done bein' stupid?" Kane began. The man colored deep red.

"Won't make this long. I could take you and find a chain to put you some place where you won't hurt anyone. Your wife don't want that. She's the only reason you don't get chained up or locked up or shot right down dead. Hear this: I see a mark on your son or your woman, I will shoot you dead that minute." He held up his hands as the man began to speak. "Don't make a difference it was the only time or the hunnerth time. It's the last time. One more thing. You find work tomorrow. I don't see you going to every last store, every last place, I'll shoot you dead tomorrow night. Man doesn't hit women when it goes bad. Not her fault. Man acts like a man."

Cartwright nodded.

"Today, you patch that wall. You patch your family. I will be walking by later to see that you did."

He turned and left.

Mae Cartwright was waiting outside.

"Gonna stop later, make sure you are well, ma'am," Kane said, lifting his hat and speaking softly so his words did not carry. "Won't make a big noise about it, and, if everything seems fine, I will keep walking so them nosy neighbors don't get no more entertainment than what's good for them, but I'm gonna do it."

"Thank you, Sheriff. For coming. For not arresting Bill."

"Hope I don't regret it, Mac. Take care of that boy. Kids don't say much when life goes south on a family, but they feel it deeper than they let on."

He kept walking. When folks' lives became a mess and someone saw it, the best thing to do was give them space to fix it, if they could.

On his way back to the stable, he ducked into Conroy's store to ask Conroy if Cartwright was always drunk.

"Good man," said Conroy. "Hard luck lately. He a problem, Sheriff?"

"Nothin' a job won't cure."

"If he comes by, I think I can find something. Hauling stock is getting too much for me anyhow."

Kane nodded and left. He supposed he had done his job.

As he walked, he was trying to reassemble a thought that shattered like a dropped plate while he was watching the Cartwrights ruin their lives. Gone. It would come back. He hoped.

For a moment he had a stray thought of Rachel Wilkins, but there was no reason to ride out there. Maybe one would come.

But not yet.

CHAPTER NINE

It was the kind of morning Kane agreed with the people who thought alcohol should be outlawed.

The Double J boys had been in town the day before and wrapped up their time after buying supplies by making sure they would have a night to remember. Kane figured most would forget everything after about the middle of the evening, except the ones who had new cuts and bruises from adventures and misadventures that led Kane to increase his collection of knives and guns taken from cowboys who were as likely to cause themselves harm as anyone else.

Not bad. Not evil. They were young, and they were wild, with some of them not very smart to begin with. Boys in the bodies of men. In a few hours, once they all woke up from wherever they had collapsed, they would ride whooping out of town as though life could not get any better. Four were in the stable. One snored loud enough to make Tecumseh's ears twitch now and then.

Kane walked toward the Last Chance. It was early, but Mary Ellen knew he was an early riser and often made coffee before anything else got started. He could hope.

"Sheriff!"

That was a word he had come to dread. Coming at him across the street was Frank Brewer, the banker and the man who was, in fact if not in title, the leader of the town council of men that hired him and ran things around Rakeheart.

"Mr. Brewer."

"I was hoping to catch you before the bank opened. They told me you are an early riser. I believe starting the day early is a habit of successful men."

"Yup. On my way for breakfast."

"Ah. I had mine at home. Domestic pleasures are important to a man's routine. I will only keep you a few minutes. Let me unlock the bank, and we can talk in private."

Kane had no choice but to follow along.

The bank was small. There was room for three teller windows. A door that Kane assumed led to the vault where money was kept was behind them. The door was protected by a gate made of metal bars.

Brewer had a big, fancy rolltop desk that filled some of the space between the teller windows and the door. A smaller desk was across the room. The banker moved behind his desk and pointed to a chair by the wall that Kane then dragged over.

Kane could smell something, like some scent from a woman, and then realized that it was coming from Brewer. He had read in some newspaper advertisement once that there was some kind of water that men put on their hair to make it smell, but he never had known a real person to use it. Why would a man want hair to smell like something awful? As much a mystery as why men wore flat shoes instead of boots.

The banker was in his late thirties or so, built strong, with long fingers Kane assumed were used to wrapping themselves around a fountain pen more than a .45. His black hair was perfectly in place with a part down the middle that was straight and broad. He was not handsome, but commanding, with a prominent nose, aggressive chin, and thin lips. The man's brown eyes were trying to project warmth, but Kane had the feeling that whatever face Brewer showed to the world, it was not the one inside.

"Allow me to be to the point with you, Sheriff. There are some concerns that have been raised about the extent of your activity at the Wilkins ranch."

"Two men shot dead sounds like something that ought to concern the folks in the nearest town," Kane countered.

"I can see your point," Brewer said in the smooth tone men used when they were preparing to talk someone into doing what they wanted. "I think that any good sheriff trying to do his duty would feel bound to look into those. Do you have any idea who killed either Jared Wilkins or Clem Ferguson?"

Kane was instantly irked at the question for a reason he could not explain, other than the pure contrariness of a man who likes to be his own boss pushing back against anyone trying to tell him what to do.

"Haven't found much yet," he admitted.

"Exactly. Whatever has happened, or might be happening, at the Wilkins ranch is not a grave concern to those of us who are trying to make Rakeheart a growing and thriving town. I completely understand that you believe it is your job to look into these killings, and if it is possible to apprehend the person or persons responsible, the town council and I would fully support you," Brewer said.

Kane waited for the rest.

"However, we believe that, given the history of this valley, in which the Wilkins family was not very connected to Rakeheart and had very little to do with anyone here in the town, any time spent there or trying to unravel whatever has been going on at that ranch should only come when the needs of the town are fully met."

"You tellin' me not to figger who killed them?"

"Not at all," said Brewer. "We want to be sure that you understand our intention in hiring you was to provide protection for the town and its citizens and not to go off looking at what might have happened on some ranch that is miles away. If you are able to bring to justice someone who kills in the way those men were murdered, it is for everyone's good, but I and the town council would expect you will spend most of your time here in town to be ready for any eventuality that should occur. We do not want you to leave the town unguarded for any significant length of time. I commend your motives, Sheriff, but as your employer, we are trying to direct you to focus your time on the job we have hired you to do."

Kane wanted to argue. He also wanted to know what he could have learned at the Wilkins ranch that was so important he was now being told to leave it alone. If he knew something, it would have been nice if someone told him, because he had no idea what happened. He put his best subservient face on, though, because over time he had learned that when men gave pretty speeches, they were hiding what they really meant. The worst thing to do was let them know they had been seen through.

If Brewer wanted to lie to Kane about why they were having this little conversation, Kane felt fine lying back about whether he would listen to what was as plain an order as ever delivered in any army.

"Understood, Mr. Brewer."

"Frank. We are all friends here, Kane."

"Might need to go out and make sure the old Wilkins hands understand there's not vigilante justice out there, Frank, because when they came to town there was some loose talk, but I understand what you want. I'll protect the town. Probably a dead end out there anyhow."

"Good," Brewer said. He started to wave Kane off in a cursory dismissal now that their meeting was over but cut the gesture short. Kane still noticed. "I will let you go about your business, Sheriff."

Kane offered a pleasantry that was as insincere as anything

Brewer had told him and headed quickly for the Last Chance. Man needed a good cup of strong coffee to wash the taste of that meeting out of his throat.

As he walked the short distance, he could see the man from the depot, Halloran, moving at far too fast a pace for a man all reports claimed was a drunk who dove into a bottle years back and never came out.

"Halloran!" he called.

The man stopped.

"Ah, Friend Badge," he called, Irish brogue so thick it would need a knife. Kane wondered how much of a front Halloran was putting on.

"You seem urgent in your business, Halloran."

"Ah, 'tis urgent business, Friend Badge, or I would have time to talk. Sarah Lewis's cat is having kittens, and I have been called to supervise the process."

"Halloran, are you drunk? How does a man supervise a cat having kittens?"

"With great care, Friend Badge. With great care!" Cackling at his joke, Halloran sauntered away, leaving Kane feeling—again—that Rakeheart had played a joke on him.

There were times Kane did not know which was worse—the stupidity of the wild cowboys or the boredom of the hours when the little town looked so peaceful and drowsy, it was hard to imagine it had another side.

The day passed uneventfully. Mae Cartwright had no new injuries. Bill had a job with Conroy, as promised. Not much money, but he could rebuild his pride. Cartwright avoided his glance. Kane did not press it.

His stroll took him down to the church. He walked to the rows of headstones. Ferguson had a wad of lead. Lead that looked like it had come out of something or gone through something—most likely a man.

The preacher was soon beside him.

"Did you want to see Mr. Wilkins?"

"Nope."

"I thought you were his friend?" Word travels fast.

"In a minute. Who was the last person killed before him?"

"Lester Boneharvest," replied Siegel. "He fell off a roof."

"Last person shot."

"Ahh. Frank Kruger. Very odd. Came in to town about oh, let's see, September, and he was found shot dead around the end of October. No, November. About first snow time. An unpleasant man. I don't think anyone was ever found to have shot him. The town was particularly callous about that, but he was not a very nice man, and it came right before we were buried in a foot or more of snow."

"Where did he get shot?"

"In the chest. It was quite a wound, from what I was told. Some massive round, not like the bullets in a normal gun, or so they kept saying."

"No, Preacher, where around here?"

"They found him not far from Noonan's. There's a small ravine about fifty yards behind the place. He was in it. Some boys found him. At first, they claimed they did it as if it was something to be proud about. Terrible influence, the guns and the liquor . . ."

"Nobody knows why or who?"

"This is a raw and violent place, Mr. Kane. He was not a nice man. I recall that he asked a lot of questions and seemed to want everyone to get a different idea of what he was doing. He may have been one of those Pinkerton men. He offended someone who was drunk or said or did the wrong thing. The boys who bragged would not have done so if they thought they would be condemned for saying that."

Siegel looked over the graves.

"Life is so cheap here, Sheriff. So cheap."

They came to Wilkins's stone. Kane thought about a spent slug and wondered where—and who—it came from. He walked as he thought. The cemetery was still small. There was one communal stone for tiny ones who died young of disease. One name he did not see. He asked.

"Halloran? I think I heard he had a wife, but I don't know anything about it. I have only been here for four years, so if she died, it might have been before my time."

Kane thought about that. Stones had dates on them going back a lot farther than that. But if talk was right and the woman's death made the man fall apart, who knows what he did? It was Wyoming. It was the frontier. Nothing was as common as death.

Conroy looked displeased at the interruption. He was talking to a pretty young woman about flour and did not want to be taken away from his conversation.

"Got a question, sir," Kane asked. Groveling always helped.

"Glad to help, Sheriff."

"Most boys around here use Colts, don't they? I was thinking if we need ammunition for a posse, you understand."

"Oh, yes. Cowboys and Colts! Now Mr. Brewer. He has a LeMat, you know. So does Silas Noonan. I think they both have them for show, you know. Terrible for accuracy. But they were both Virginia-born, even if they made their money out here. You know, Jeb Stuart? They both want to be the dashing cavalier. It takes me forever to get their ammunition, so I stock well ahead. Some of those new Smith & Wesson guns are out here. I have one of those new Remington pistols for sale, but no takers yet. I think it may be too expensive. Rifles are different, though. We have a lot of the boys with old Sharps rifles and Remingtons as well as the Winchesters, and every so often someone comes in with a relic from the War between the States, so I have some musket shot and powder. I tried once to keep up with what everyone needed for their shotguns, but now I have given up. There are too many of those."

Conroy went on for about fifteen more minutes describing who shot what. Kane wanted to leave, but the shopkeeper had rarely been this talkative. When the flow of words hit a pause, Kane excused himself, smiling as he realized Conroy, who might never have fired a gun, was fascinated by them. He also realized the young woman watching appeared enthralled at Conroy's knowledge. What a pretty face does to a man at any age.

"Sheriff!" He stifled a groan as Conroy emerged from the shop, excited.

"Forgot. Jared Wilkins had one of those, too. Those LeMats. I had one more once; somebody gave it to me in trade for something. That was a few years back." Kane thanked Conroy. He turned the lump of metal over in his fingers after pulling it from his jacket pocket. He'd seen a few in the years after the war, but not much since. They fired a lump of lead not unlike what he held in his hand.

He ran back to the store and pulled the door open, hard. Yes, a surprised Conroy said, he could fire the one he had, but why? Was it related to Jared Wilkins's murder? Or something else?

Conroy was put off for the moment by being told he could not share it right now, but Kane knew that soon it would be all over town within a day that the sheriff was looking for a man with a LeMat pistol.

He walked over to a tree. Loaded the cumbersome thing, wondering why anyone would use a gun that used powder and shot when there were simpler, better guns available. But they were, he thought as he looked at the intricate metalwork and wood grip, a thing of beauty. All meant to kill.

The LeMat bucked and boomed. The ball lodged in the trunk of the elm. Kane dug it out with his knife. Not exact, but close. If the ball Ferguson had set aside for safe keeping had been shot into a person, it would have different damage than the one Kane fired into a tree. He wondered what would happen if he asked to shoot a volunteer to test an idea.

He thought about Rakeheart's LeMat owners. Noonan? Fancy man. Fancy gun. He did not look like a man who ever did his own dirty work. Brewer? Maybe. The man was pushy. Wanted to be respectable and respected and bluster his way to importance. He could probably shoot someone. Jared Wilkins? The man was still lost to Kane, but Kane had a picture of a man whose moral veneer was cracking, who was no stranger to guns, and who had started acting differently, if he was told the straight of it, when Kruger was killed.

Questions. Questions needed answers. He wondered how profound the look of disgust would be on Rachel Wilkins's face if he asked more questions about something she truly wished to simply put behind her, regardless of what Sherman wanted.

Enoch Jeffries had dried up years back, Kane decided. The man's skin looked like leather, and in the first five minutes of their conversation, he did not have one good word to say about anyone or anything. His entire world revolved around money, something he worked zealously to acquire and rued ever having to spend.

"Kruger? Of course. That's why everyone pays in advance," Jeffries said. The man was tall with a thick crop of sandy hair that had mostly turned to gray. He always wore black Eastern suits. Kane had never seen anything resembling a smile on the man's face. Ever. He was pasty from living indoors, wrinkled and dried.

Kane wondered if there was anything Jeffries remembered about the man, or if he had left any belongings behind.

The hotel owner took his time replying and looked Kane over, as if he could discern the purpose of the questions from an inventory of Kane's features.

"Big man. Not tall. Burly. I think he was some sort of private detective. He carried a gun but not the way cowboys do; he kept it in his jacket pocket. He asked a lot of questions about all kinds of people. Some of them were personal and offensive, about families and their children, and I recall telling him I was not at his convenience to gossip about my neighbors. He asked who was wealthy and who was not. He asked questions that I regarded as offensive."

"Young, old?"

"Neither. Experienced. Younger than I am, older than you. He knew what he was about, which is what made him so annoying. It was as though he knew someone's secret and was going to dig it up. But what made him so hard to fathom was that he asked questions about all sorts of people. I could never determine who he was here to investigate."

Kane turned that tidbit over in his mind. Man comes to a small town with a target, knows that town will repeat every word if he only asks about one man. Instead, he asks about many people to mask his intentions. Clever way to operate. A man who did that had experience dealing with towns and looking for people who were trying to hide from the past.

"He only ask you?"

"I thought so at the time, but he asked everybody the same kinds of questions. I think everyone hoped he would leave, but he was never rude, never violent, only infernally and eternally asking very personal questions about the private business of families."

"How private?"

"Which families had children, and were the parents married and living in Rakeheart when the children were born? Families that had become wealthy recently. Those kinds of things. I have no idea what he was seeking to learn, but I doubt he learned much of anything."

"Then he was killed."

"Correct. One day in the fall, November or December; I know it was before our first big snow, they found him. He said he was from St. Louis but gave no address. And I know we did look for one."

"What about his belongings?"

"He must have had some belongings, but I recall he traveled light. I will look to see if they were stored, but right after he died and they buried him we had a massive, early blizzard, and he was forgotten very quickly."

That rang false. A man who clearly kept himself a secret would have had whatever he left behind pored over to learn his secret. The lie didn't disturb him. People lied for the same reason they breathed—because they always did. But the reason for it puzzled him.

Kane thanked the hotel owner and left. If Kruger was asking questions about children, there was one family he knew of where the kids didn't look alike, and the boy didn't look like anybody at all. Sooner or later, Kruger would have seen them or heard about them. More questions Rachel Wilkins would not want to hear.

Janie told him more of the same. Kruger rented a horse a few times, having come in on the train.

"No cowboy that one," she said, adding that Kruger looked ill at ease on any horse he rode. She did not know where he went. He could guess.

"I asked him once if he was looking for someone who had been kidnapped, and he didn't deny it, but he never said what he was doing," she said. "Then he would ask who had big wagons like the homesteaders have. Maybe it made sense to him, but it never did to me. How about supper again with me and Pa tonight? I got a pie recipe I want to try."

So young. So earnest. There was only one answer.

Halloran added one bit of hearsay to his picture of Kruger's brief time in Rakeheart.

"The man was aggressive, Friend Badge. Rubbed everyone the wrong way and never seemed to care. He and Wilkins— more than everyone else. Yes, he and Wilkins, a man who seemed happy to throw away a family that he did not deserve." Halloran seemed to want to say more, but changed tack, leaving Kane again frustrated at never getting the details he needed.

"It was around the time Wilkins was becoming important in his own mind, and it could have been just that. It could have been more. Then yon Kruger was dead, planted and buried by two feet of snow, and everyone had more important things to worry about."

"What do you mean?"

"Wyoming is buried in snow for the winter, Friend Badge, and men prepare for it. An early blizzard means a lot of work for hands to drive the cattle or horses into safer, more sheltered places, have hay for them, and bring the young and sick ones into barns. A bad winter that kills stock would put most of the ranches out of business. The blizzard caught everyone unprepared, and by the time everyone dug out, Kruger was old news from weeks past. Yon poor army man made his trip only a day or so before the snow. That one they send to tell them when someone gets killed that it doesn't matter much. I do not know why they send the poor man, but they do."

Greene.

For a moment he thought about Brewer's warning about staying close to town. He went to see Conroy, invented an excuse to see Greene about wild riders and Indians. Conroy told him to take his time. Cartwright was hauling goods. He flushed a bit when Kane saw him, nodded, and went on with his work.

Kane could have made the ride faster, but he had come to prize his solitude riding across the landscape. In his weeks in Wyoming, he had come to understand that the roughness of the land held promise. The wind was bending the tall grasses dotted with wildflowers here and there. July would be ending soon, and then would come the time, he was told, when the creeks slowed to barely a trickle.

He rode past one of the great contradictions of the land. After riding across a table of high, rocky land, the ground then turned into hills, with some of the tallest pine trees Kane could recall seeing, before turning back into hard rock again. The only constant, he knew, was the wind. It gusted up dust devils and seemed to moan in the branches of the trees, a mournful song that understood what life was like for those trying to eke out survival.

"Closed bunch, aren't they?" chortled Lt. August Greene as he leaned dangerously back in his chair.

As he sat in Greene's quarters at Fort Laramie, Kane had to agree.

"Kruger was a funny situation. Late last year. November or October. Gets cold early up here, Texas." He grinned. "Nobody likes to be out in a storm, and it was getting low and dark and cold like the first one of the early ones. Early for snow, but it starts when it does. That Conroy fellow had sent some farm kid to inform us that a man was murdered. Not shot the way those cowboys do when they get drunk. They know we don't care about those unless it gets something started, and they sent me."

"Was it anything?" asked Kane. "Who was he?"

"They lied about who he was. Sure of it. The man was three

days dead when I saw him, but he was about frozen. Not a young rider; older. Better dressed. Nothing on him but his clothes when they found him, or so they said. Ever meet a Pinkerton?"

"The detectives? A few."

"Figgered. He reminded me of them. Heavyset; looked like a man who could have taken care of himself. Gun was gone, but the inside holster he wore under his coat was expensive. His effects had nothing in them. No pictures. Nothing with his name. Nothing. Most folks have something with them that says who they are, even if is a lucky piece or an old picture or some letter with a name on it. This man brought nothing. His name probably wasn't Kruger, but that's the one they buried him with," Greene said.

"Nobody said much?"

"You know that bunch by now. Had to say he was killed by some unknown person, but unlike your Wilkins fella there, nobody made a fuss. Nobody ever asked us or anyone else about a man like that. Like he never existed. I wondered if he was looking for someone and found him, or one of them had some shady past. But, in the end, it was clear he was dead, somebody shot him, and nobody was ever going to know. Day I got back, it snowed a foot or two, and then when spring came we had the usual round of boys going crazy after a winter. Can't say I forgot him as much as there was too much to do."

"You saw his body."

"Said so."

"Big hole in him? Bigger than most?"

The front legs of the chair crashed to the floor. "How'd you know?"

"Like one of those LeMat guns from the war?"

Silence. Greene's voice was now heavily tinged with curiosity with more than a touch of suspicion.

133

"A lot like. You find somethin'?"

"Clem Ferguson, foreman at Wilkins's ranch, had a lump of a lead shot he'd saved. 'Bout the size of a LeMat ball. Wilkins was one of three or four men with one. Makes me wonder about the connection."

Greene chewed the information. "Not sure what it means. If it came from Kruger, might be somethin' Ferguson held over his boss's head. But how can anyone prove one certain bullet came out of a man? From what you say, Ferguson could have been hiding that lump of lead for Wilkins, or he tucked it away to use against somebody, which could have been Wilkins or Geronimo for all I know. If Wilkins was the only one with that kind of gun, it might mean something. Might still if you can find out which LeMat it came from, but I don't know how you do that. Might be the others keep them as keepsakes of the war and never fired them. Not many in Rakeheart were in it, but it's hard to know. Most men want to leave that behind. Wilkins was one of the few who never wanted to let it go."

Greene's mouth worked as he thought. He shook his head.

"You got something to be curious about, but neither the territory nor the army is going to get much excited over it, 'specially since it was a long time ago now."

"That's why I came to see you. Figgered you'd know whether anyone would care and what anyone might do."

"It's like having one piece of wood that you think looks like a leg, son. It's a long way from being a chair."

"Rakeheart got killers in it?"

Greene laughed.

"Wish I knew. All those towns fight each other, you know that. Rakeheart . . . they take it more serious than most, but those towns play hard with one another. You know about those riders?"

"Company Riders?"

"Them. Cause of all the mischief, I think, but, far as I know, you're the only local law for fifty, sixty miles, and nobody says a word against them, because, for one, there's more of them than there is you, and if you ain't in Rakeheart, the law is whoever has the edge. That's them." He held his hands palm upward. "Army investigates complaints, not hunches. Lot of smoke about the Riders, but no fire. No complaints filed. Everybody tells tales, but nobody brings in anything solid. No reason to go off half-cocked. The citizens of Rakeheart want the army to come in, all they have to do is show up and explain themselves."

"And what's your hunch?"

"Rakeheart is like one big string in a huge knot, and you got pieces of that knot loose. Don't know what pieces, but I know one thing."

"What's that?"

"You got those Riders, Rakeheart, even the Wilkins ranch and that woman—she don't say much, but she's a lot smarter than most of the men around her—don't let her fool you. Not a lot of folks there I'd turn my back on."

Kane rose. It was the truth. He thanked Greene, who followed him out the door.

"Not sending Sherman a note this time?"

"Way with Sherman," replied Kane, "he don't care about it being worked on. He cares when it's done. Riles him when I tell him too much for his own good. Then he riles me. Wouldn't be surprised if you hear from him real soon."

Greene laughed and wished Kane luck. Kane guessed he would need it.

CHAPTER TEN

Kane had spent two frustrating days asking questions without getting much in the way of answers. Noonan and Brewer were each very quick to know exactly where their LeMats were kept. Both were clear they were for show; Brewer's—polished to shine—was on the wall by his desk. Kane was sure it had not been there when they met a few days ago. Noonan's gun was also similarly cleaned and polished as if it was an item for display. Kane was hardly surprised. He never told Conroy not to talk about what he asked, and, even if he had, the results would have been the same. A small town was a small town, even if it thought it was going to be something else one day.

Janie was now openly flirting. He wondered if he should move to that shack. She wanted to have a husband, a home, and a family. All good things. He still could not imagine a life beyond figuring out this puzzle, or abandoning the hunt, and moving on. But she was pretty and was certainly the only smiling face he could count on seeing as he wandered about the town. He set trying to tell her what he wanted in life down the road until, at least, he could figure it out well enough to say it.

Mae Cartwright's face was healing nicely. She had done something with it—some combination of flour and some colored stuff—to mask the worst of the bruises while they were at their most livid. Her husband was working, not drinking, and maybe there was hope that one family would walk away from its brush with disaster.

For all that, he was failing at his main purpose. He had no idea who killed Jared Wilkins, Clem Ferguson, or Frank Kruger—whatever and whoever he might have been. He had done everything he knew how to do. Wasn't he past the time he said he was going to spend on this? Sherman couldn't expect results every time. Only a fool stayed when it was time to go.

He was walking along the main street when he could see faces looking past him with the look that said something was coming that put fear in their hearts.

It was.

Six riders, slowly walking their horses forward, were entering the straight portion of Rakeheart's main street, like the slow and confident way a rattler slithers up on its unsuspecting prey.

For a moment, he wondered why the Company Riders had come to him instead of waiting for him to go to them. Had he found something, said something, done something to make himself a threat? Or was this nothing more than a long-overdue visit prompted by their timetable, not his actions?

Their posture was clear. This was intimidation.

He was always bad at that. Real bad.

For a second, the thrill of doing what was downright foolish jolted up and down his spine. As his heart picked up its pace, he could feel his nerves steady. Pulling clues out of thin air was not the kind of work he knew how to do.

This was.

He moved from one side of the street to the other as though the riders were not coming closer. That these were men to be feared was clear on the faces of the women who were emphatic in their haste to get away from where he was walking.

Men who usually were prone to lounge along the street and talk endlessly about the weather or nothing at all now seemed to have urgent errands that seemed to involve moving very quickly into the relative protection of the nearest doorway or whatever shop was closest.

The riders were thirty feet away when he called to Janie, who was keeping pace with the riders as they moved. He wondered idly if one of them was also being considered as husband material. Probably. He was certain he heard a friendly tone in her voice and a man's response in kind.

He started to move across to her as though there was no line of menace creeping closer. He called her name and waved with his left hand. Her face was a study in conflicted misery. She wanted to say hello, did not dare say hello, but could not pretend he did not exist. The compromise was a wretched smile and timid flop of the hand that could pass as a wave.

They were maybe twenty feet away. He was now in the middle of the street.

Then he stopped.

Drew. Cocked. Fired.

He had fired high. Nobody's horse deserved to be shot. Luck was with him. He bagged a hat that went sailing from its rider's head and bounced down the street. Maybe he did better not aiming.

As that man reached back to grab what was already far gone, others were reaching into their holsters when Kane's second shot went high over the group.

"No weapons in town, boys."

Surprise was complete and total.

"Not very hospitable," said the third man from the right. The leader. Thin beard. A little older than Kane. Medium build—didn't look impressive sitting in the saddle, but a man who radiated authority. Wind-worn, sun-darkened face. Knocked off balance but trying to find his way back, sure that he would.

"Made me sheriff. Sheriff has got to keep the peace."

"Not planning to violate the peace, Sheriff. Never had a problem before. My men and I only want a drink at Noonan's."

"Have all you want. Drop them guns there, and you can get 'em back when you leave. Safer for everybody."

"Sheriff, I don't know where you get your notions from, but this one is a mite odd. Never heard of such a thing as leavin' our guns behind. Could be you don't know who we are and why this town should be giving us a welcome and not a slap in the face like this. Some folks won't like this when they hear about it."

"Don't mean to make folks run cryin' to mommy." Even if Halloran was right and he was the town cat's paw, he was enjoying the role for the moment.

The man regarded Kane from his horse. Kane figured the life he pretended to live while he worked for Sherman was a lot like the one this man lived for real.

"Name's Wood. Brent Wood. These men here are part of the Company Riders. Name mean anything?"

"Nothing good."

"You are not being a reasonable man, Sheriff."

"Trying to protect my town, Wood. Can't be no harm in that. Not like this is personal. Same rule for every gang that rides in. Not my fault if you are the only one to ride in so far."

Both men let the lie stir about and mix with the dust whipping around in small circles. Time to push this, Kane thought.

"Not askin' again, Wood. I can hit men even better than hats. Guns or git."

"You are making a big mistake."

"Feel free to make your own."

Wood waited a little longer. If anyone in the town was talking, walking, or spitting tobacco, it was not evident from the silence. Kane felt that wind tug at the hair he had never remembered to trim. He was ready to fight, ready to fire at any man's movement. Then he could feel Wood settle back in the saddle.

"You win this round, Sheriff. Price might be higher than you want to pay, but you win it."

Wood slowly unbuckled his gun belt from around his waist, buckled it again, and slowly placed it over the pommel of his saddle. The other riders with him followed suit, some with glares at Kane.

"That's a good first step," Kane said. "Now drop them on the ground, and I'll pile them at the stable, and nobody will shoot off nothin' they'd miss while they enjoy that drink."

"Got a name, Sheriff?"

"Bet you already know it, Wood, so whyn't we not play games?"

"Kane would be a short name on a gravestone."

"So's Wood."

Two poker faces locked wills. Only one came out on top.

"Let the sheriff play his game, boys," called out Wood.

Soon, the riders' gun belts, with the weapons still in the holsters, lay in a pile of leather and metal. There were still rifles in the scabbards of every saddle, and Kane guessed at least one had another gun tucked somewhere, but he knew he could push this too far, if he had not done so already.

"Well then," said Kane, bowing slightly, doffing his hat in a sweeping gesture and moving out of their way. "Welcome, boys, to Rakeheart, and enjoy your time here. Drink up and spend your money."

They dismounted.

Kane continued to cross the street in the way he had begun. As Janie, who had come to collect the horses and take them to the stable, began collecting the guns and putting them over the saddles of the appropriate horses, he tipped his hat to her. He never looked back.

Halloran was lounging in a doorway.

"They all go into Noonan's?" Kane asked.

"Every mother's son of them," the old man replied.

Kane felt the knot relax.

"You know that this is not over, for all that the spectacle was as grand as a parade?" said Halloran. There seemed to be a glint in his eye. Kane had not seen him on the street earlier. "It is enemies you have made this day, Friend Badge."

"It's never over," commented Kane, resuming his leisurely walk through Rakeheart.

If the riders had wanted to see what he was made of, they got a taste. He got their measure, too. An animal that knew when not to attack was wilier and deadlier than one that knew only to strike.

But why? That *why* always nagged him. Some men were simple. They were brutes stomping anyone in their way. Others were greedy. These men were disciplined, not like so many of the men he chased for Sherman who were violent for the thrill of looting, burning, and killing. There was purpose in them. What was that purpose?

The thought came. It could backfire. Probably would. Then why not? He was going to pay anyhow; might as well make it worth it.

The piano jangled loudly against the silence as he walked into Noonan's, where Wood and the owner were in an animated discussion at the far end of the bar. He walked slowly towards them, keeping his right hand visible and hooked in the buckle of the gun belt.

Noonan slithered off as Kane approached, the oil of his smile sliding past Kane as he moved away to deal with what Kane was sure was a nonexistent problem. Either that or arranging who would shoot Kane if things went wrong.

Wood had a glass of beer in front of him.

"Another?"

Eyes locked.

"Why not?"

Kane tossed a nickel on the bar.

"How well you know Jared Wilkins?"

Wood looked at him over the rim of his glass of beer as he sipped. His face showed that was not the question he anticipated.

"Rancher. Shame. Some accident or other."

"Not your work?"

Wood recoiled as if slapped. He was turning purple in the face as his hand gripped the glass so hard Kane thought it would break.

"There's a lot you don't understand, Sheriff. A lot you might want to think about before you say things."

"Honest question. One hand we got a man who gets shot. Other hand we got men who shoot men for a living. Man taking an honest look at the situation might see how those might be connected. Saves time to ask."

"No connection, Sheriff. We're honest men."

"Clem Ferguson."

"What of him? He say something?"

"Not much now. He's dead."

"Lot of hard luck out there."

"Not much a believer in luck striking twice in the same place when it happens to folks who live in a place other folks covet. Could be that men good with guns are intimidating a widow to force her to sell."

"You ride a wide trail, Sheriff, and you say some things that could offend a man's pride. Never heard that's good for a man."

"Man named Kruger? Ring any bells? Found with a big hole in him last fall right before the snow."

"Sounds like being around this town is hazardous to the good health of a lot of men, Sheriff. Might be something you want to think about. More time here might not be so good for you, either."

"Prob'ly not. This sheriffing business, though . . . all these questions . . . like poison ivy. Get an itch, and you scratch it and another and another. And every scratch brings another itch. It don't end until you scratch all the way down and draw blood."

"Painful."

"Might end that way," Kane admitted. "For somebody."

"That a threat, Sheriff?"

"Call it an observation, Wood." Kane pushed himself away from the bar. "Enjoy your beer. 'Spect I'll see you around."

"You will, Sheriff. Keep them ears open. Might learn something you need to know before going off half-cocked."

Kane gave a thin smile and tipped his hat. "Mighty fine advice."

He turned his back and slowly left the saloon, hearing the sounds of voices begin to rise with each step he took away from Noonan's and into the darkness of Rakeheart.

Boys stirred up the nests of hornets and bees because it was what boys did. Boys that lived to be men also knew that staying in one place when the bees were riled would often result in an unpleasant response. There was a line between cowardice and common sense. Kane figured he was right up to it, but not quite over it.

Tecumseh had company in the stable. Probably not the place Kane wanted to sleep right then and there. Might be too tempting a target. Night riding wasn't ideal, and staying out of range felt a lot like running away, but there was nothing like causing trouble to make a man suddenly feel the need to embrace caution. Then again, what he had in mind might seem like foolishness to anyone else.

He saddled the horse, wondering what it might be like for an animal to have some fool person come along and wake you up in the middle of the night for no good reason. He kept a hand near his gun as he led Tecumseh, then unlatched the big door of the stable. No one either way. He closed it after him, mounted, and slowly rode out of town, one direction in mind.

An itch had to be scratched.

The shack he was starting to wonder if he would ever move into emerged from the dimness. He had missed the road that turned southeast but backtracked and found it. He took his time, uncertain whether he would face a welcoming committee. Six riders were in Rakeheart. He wanted to know how many more there might be. Greene made it seem like the riders might be more talk than reality; the town council, as though they were an army. He needed to know.

Smoke.

Three stubby trees were nearby. He tied Tecumseh, left his hat with the horse, grabbed his rifle, and walked the rest of the way on foot, moving slowly. He had time.

He could see that the wide-open horizon was now filled with the edge of a plateau that ran toward what he knew were the high table of flat lands to the south and small hills to the north. They had found a place that was cozy and easy to defend.

The flattened trail left by innumerable hoofprints led up a rise. The trail was lighter against the darkness of the waving grass along its edges. The waist-high grass was not much for cover, but it was all there was.

Slowly. Step and look. Step and look. Men who prowl by night have keen senses. He did. They would.

A gully opened up below him. To his right, a campfire glowed. He kept to the higher ground for now. The gully was a cul-de-sac with almost sheer drops from where he was to the camp. One way in, one way out.

What he saw was trouble. Almost two dozen men lounging. Card players laughing. Add them to the ones in Rakeheart, and the Company Riders might have thirty men all told. Probably more, if there were more sentries like the one to his left briefly skylined.

In a place where the towns were puny and where cowboys were better at shooting critters than one another, this was almost like having a small private army. These men didn't play little tricks the way Janie said. This was a gang of toughs that was too big to live off what Rakeheart could provide. Had to be.

There were at last two buildings he had seen. They might be rough bunkhouses, but they were a sign that the Company Riders were not planning to leave when winter stalked the plains.

He looked down, trying to see details in the dimness away from the fire. There had been no reports of rustling or robbery. If thirty-some men were making a living stealing, he could not imagine what it was if no one was reporting anything missing. He came to scratch an itch, but all he got was more itch.

He was so lost in thought he almost got careless. He had moved too fast and lost track of the sentry, who was now twenty-five yards away. Kane could hear the man's rifle cock in the wake of the loose dirt that rolled out from under Kane's right boot as he stepped back from the edge of the gully to melt into the brush.

Still. He hunkered down in the grass as best he could.

Crunch. A step closer. Crunch. One further away. Another.

His breath was too loud. He was certain he would be visible to a man walking in darkness all night, even on a night like this without a moon. There was no way the man could not see or hear him. He licked dry lips. The steps moved away.

Kane shifted. A little longer.

Crunch-crunch-crunch. Kane was sure he had been discovered. The steps stopped. Twenty feet? Maybe.

A small gust wafted the scent of tobacco his way. The man was standing, wolf-patient, waiting for the prey he knew was there to move. The rifle in Kane's hand would be too loud, unless he wanted to face all of them. The noise of reaching for a knife would give the man a target.

"Know you're there," came the voice. "Give it up."

Kane could feel his leg muscles cramping. The words did not mean for certain he had been found. The game was played this way. But as the man loudly exhaled, Kane feared that the game was nearing an end.

Noise. Shifting.

"Gonna start shooting."

One shot would stir the riders below. Hit or miss would doom him sooner or later.

The rifle fired toward tall grass twenty-five feet to his left.

Kane gripped the rifle. Maybe he could kill the sentry and get to his horse before the men below him responded, as long as none of them mounted quickly.

Unexpectedly, hoots of derision came from the camp below.

"Killin' a shadow, Porter?" called one.

"Gonna shoot off your foot!" mocked another.

"That rabbit come back that drew down on you last week?" called out one voice, as more voices joined in the laughter.

"Somebody is up here!" called the sentry.

That got even more mockery.

"Help me look!" called the sentry. "There's somebody here, I tell you!"

"That's what you told us last week! Might be that big rabbit with big teeth and a big gun coming back to get even!" a voice yelled.

"Enough! Both of you!" called out an exasperated voice that expected to be obeyed. The man ordered two men to go up to the sentry "in case."

The sentry muttered as he walked a few steps farther away. While the banter had been taking place, the man had moved further to Kane's left. He would not have much time. He slowly tried to move out of his hiding place. The sentry was now walking straight towards him. Kane heard the steps. He could hear the voices of the men who were begrudging the fact that they were plucked from their card game to chase shadows. He would be caught between them.

The sentry stepped next to Kane. "I know you're here," he was saying softly, looking well past Kane. Kane could see the figure looming dark above him. "I know it." The man shouldered a rifle and was aiming over Kane's left shoulder.

"Frank! Where are you?" called one of the riders sent up to appease the sentry.

"Over here!" he called. He moved toward the voices.

"Where?"

"Here, you fools!"

He fired twice.

Kane used the distraction of the second shot to move. He was now fifteen feet away. The sentry and his relief were moving away, toward the edge of the cliff. Keeping as low a profile as he could, while trying to be both quick and quiet, Kane moved to give them a wide berth until the volume of the noise made it clear that he was out of danger.

But where was he? For a minute, Kane could not orient himself. There. That tree.

He moved as fast as he could in the dimness, knowing that to fall on a rock could end his misadventure the wrong way. There was one shot. Nothing after it but guffaws.

Soon he was down the rise and back to Tecumseh. Slowly, to not attract the attention of any eyes he might not know were looking, he led the horse by the reins for most of the way back to the shack. To wait. If the riders were suspicious enough, they would be pursuing. The worst thing that could happen was that he could get caught between a group looking for an intruder and Wood and his men coming back from Rakeheart. For now, he needed to be patient and stay hidden where he knew he was safe.

It was nearly dawn when the riders who had gone to Rakeheart rode back, the pounding of their racing hooves only sounds in the night. When they were gone, Kane mounted and rode hard for Rakeheart as the world grew from blue-black to gray.

CHAPTER ELEVEN

Janie was waiting when he arrived. Angry.

"They want to get you for what you did last night."

"How did you know?"

"You humiliated them in front of the whole town!" She was yelling.

"Oh. That." He had been turning over the puzzle of the riders in his mind and had all but forgotten bracing them.

She regarded him as though for the first time she was realizing he might be different from other men.

"Don't you care?"

"At the moment, not so much. They found out what they wanted to know. Ladies find stuff out over tea and when they talk polite daggers at each other. Menfolk don't do the polite part. I need a nap. Maybe later."

"They're hard men. Didn't I tell you that?"

"Maybe I'm just like 'em."

She looked at him with what for her was a long time of quietness. "No," she said softly. "You might do hard things, but you're somebody else under. There are things a woman knows that a man never sees."

Whatever it might be that he was, it was not for her to know. In fact, that was a question he was not sure even he could answer very well.

"Got to get me some food," he said.

"Already made it," she said. "Bacon got done a few minutes

149

ago. Coffee's hot."

She took his arm, taking the lead. "Pa won't eat it all, and it would be a waste." She smiled.

He let her lead him to their kitchen. She smiled again. His need for sleep, and the larger question of worrying about the Company Riders, became unimportant for at least a small span of time.

Maybe this sheriffing wasn't so bad after all.

While Janie went to help her pa run the stable, Kane turned over what she had said: *A woman knows.*

He had avoided Tillie Witherspoon's dress shop for the very good reason that no man goes in a dress shop unless he had to. Kane figured he had to, if he wanted to know the real story of Rakeheart.

Tillie Witherspoon was about four feet ten inches tall, at best, weighed next to nothing, and probably had more energy than any train. She spoke rapid-fire with pins in her mouth as she worked on a dress for Brewer's wife. Kane kept expecting her to spit one across the room at him.

"Hmmph," she snorted. "Jared Wilkins. Men do change when they want to be important. I was planning to give her some nice tea when she came to town next, but now, with all of that, I suppose we won't ever see her. Not that we did much. Cat's eyes. That's what she has. I would think of her as a cat that saw everything, said nothing, judged everything, and no one was ever the wiser about where they stood. Can't say I like her. Not that I couldn't; never talked to her enough to know her. Him? Well. At first, he seemed like a good man. Every one of us wondered, of course, with those children, but he put a good face on it. He changed like the weather in the fall. It was not a woman. Certainly not. They always call it business. Was it him you wanted to know about or her? I do not dislike her, but she is very distant. She watched more than she talked. It can't be easy being an Indian with the way people talk in a town like this."

For the sake of filling out his knowledge, he threw out some other names.

"Oh, that Kruger man. He was so rude and always interrupted me. Don't you believe it is a shame when a body can't get in a word edgewise because someone will not let her speak? I am certain you do. Rude, he was, although that does not justify being shot that way . . ."

"What way?"

"I heard he was shot in the back, but I did not go to see because I have my work. I am not one of those who talks and talks endlessly as if I were idle. Talk. Talk. Talk. I mind my business. I talk to my customers for their comfort. You should understand, sheriff, that there are very few places in a town out here a woman can talk without men around. We have our secrets."

Her peppery summations of the town's leaders were uniformly scanty about good qualities and laden with commentary about their deficiencies in manners, morals, and clothing, although she admitted they "tried."

"They stopped this from being a wide-open town and changed its name to something more proper than Rake—Well, I cannot say the word. You are at the stable. Is that Haliburton girl still flitting about from man to man? Shameless. One of these days . . ."

The only man who came in for praise was Halloran.

"Seamus loves children; shame it is that he never had any. He can play the fiddle, Sheriff. Of course, I do not look kindly upon some things that go on when they have these dances—and I hope you will be vigilant when they have one at the harvest time—but I go to hear Seamus play. Sometimes those young men think they can keep up, but he can play faster than their feet can move. He is the only person I have known to make the Wilkins girl smile. Poor thing always looks lost. No . . . that is not the right word at all. Miserable. No; that's the poor Brewer woman, and I do not know how she tolerates that, but I cannot talk about that. Brute of a man. Yes. The Wilkins girl. Sad. That is what she is—sad!"

She also decided Kane needed advice.

"You don't dress like a sheriff, Mr. Kane. You always wear those dark things, and you look more like an outlaw than those rude Company Riders," she said. "Buy one of those horrible checked shirts the cowboys buy at Mr. Conroy's store if you want anyone to ever look at you and smile. Are you really a sheriff? From the way you act, when you walk through town, you seem more worried about someone following you than whatever might be taking place in the town. You look more ready to shoot someone than talk to them."

He told her he would consider buying a shirt after she told him she would be more than willing to make one. Before he could escape, having received far more information than he wanted, she had more to say.

"You know I hate gossips. Terrible the way folks talk. You know he's not hers?"

"Ma'am?"

"That little Jeremiah Wilkins boy. She's dark, and he was . . . well, not really dark like Indian dark but sort of with his dark hair, and that boy is as light as the sunshine. Everybody in town agrees that two parents with dark skin and dark hair cannot have a fair-skinned, blond child like that. There are things you learn breeding horses that are the same as in people, Sheriff. My uncle bred stallions in Kansas before the war. I wanted to tell her we understood, of course, because she must have felt terrible about it, but I don't really know her well enough. The whole town knew the moment we saw them all, but she tried. Very brave in that way, even if she is odd. And Apache."

"Comanche."

"Pardon me?"

"Rachel Wilkins is a Comanche, ma'am."

"How can you be sure?"

"Knew them from Texas, ma'am. Know a Comanche when I see one."

"Oh, Texas. Well, I am sure you do know them. Well, we had a few Texas cowboys come through a few years ago when they misread the trail to the fort. I thought Wyoming cowboys were wild."

Some time later, after a discussion about Texans that was amusing for its inaccuracies and with injunctions to avoid ever drinking at the Lucky Dollar, commentary about the boring nature of Preacher Siegel's sermons and the need to find a wife if he wanted to remain free of gossip, coupled with a vivid determination that most of the marriageable females were not worth his time because one smoked a pipe and three had chewed tobacco to her very certain knowledge, he emerged with a vastly more vivid picture of the residents of Rakeheart and a slight ringing in his ears.

Conroy came out of his shop to grab Kane's hand and pump it vigorously.

"I heard about it. Wished I'd'a seen it! Thought for a while we were like that man in the story with a tiger by the tail but you showed 'em. 'Bout time those Riders learned they don't run everything and everyone around here."

"Is that what you really wanted?" asked Kane. "Because if it is, the way I see it, there is one of me and a lot of them, and, when one man goes up against a lot of men, that one man usually loses. I think they might come back."

"No, my lad," chortled Conroy. "Tails between their legs.

That's how I heard they left. We can't have folks thinking they can ride in and do anything they please while they are here. Got to have law for Rakeheart to grow. Law is more than guns. Been wild out here so long people forget there's another way. Well done, Sheriff. Well done."

He returned to his shop as Kane made his rounds to find that, if anything had happened overnight while he was being foolish, it did not leave any evidence visible in the light of day. That, he knew, meant that a certain sheriff could take a nap in a certain spot.

It was not to be.

"Sheriff!"

Preacher Siegel was moving quickly. "May I speak to you in confidence?"

Having barely finished a session with Tillie Wilkerson, he wondered whether she already knew what Siegel was about to say. He decided it would be wrong to tell the preacher to wait a minute so he could ask, but he wanted to.

There was, of course, only one answer. They walked to the small church and sat on the last row of its rough-hewn benches.

"If somebody broke a law or killed somebody, I can't make promises," Kane said.

"No. Well, not yet," Siegel said. "It's about Pete Haliburton."

Janie's pa. Wonderful sober; Kane had seen that. Dangerous drunk; Kane had heard that more than once.

"What did he do?"

"The talk is he plans to join the Company Riders."

"Little old, isn't he?"

"They've been down in Bear Canyon for the summer, now that there are so many of them, but I think they want some place closer. I think Haliburton wants to get out of his business, and there is talk that his daughter is keeping very close company with some Rider who comes to see her at night."

Kane had seen Janie talk to about every man who came by, but he'd never noticed anyone who seemed special. Folks were usually good at sneaking around when they figured there was something worth sneaking for. He felt a slight twinge, because he had thought Janie was interested in him, but he knew that was not rational. Although she cooked great meals and had a great smile, he had no thoughts of settling down. He still wondered why he had stayed as long as he had.

"Pete is not a bad man, Sheriff, but if he does this, he won't last long. He thinks the riders will be his protection, but they will only use him and throw him away. Can you talk to him? Maybe he will listen to you."

"I thought he hated the Riders. Thought I heard him say so."

"Pete Haliburton hates almost everyone, Sheriff. Sometimes, I think he hates himself, too. Can you talk to him?"

"I'll talk, but if a man wants to do something stupid, Preacher, there's usually not much a man can say to stop it."

"Well, it is my duty, Sheriff Kane. It may not be much of a flock, but it is mine. There are times when I think that their re-action is to tell me *no* even before I get the words out. I left the East because I thought I could bring God's word to this wild country. I wonder sometimes if I was wrong. Death is so common, almost casual, that the way I looked at the world in the East seems like the outlook of a stranger to me now."

"Preacher, it ain't never a waste of time to remind folks that there's wrong and there's right, and a man has the power to choose. That don't change, whether it's Texas or that New York City place or out here in Wyoming."

"No, it does not. Thank you, Sheriff."

"Don't thank me; didn't do anything yet."

He heard the church doors open right after they shut behind him.

"Sheriff?"

There was always one more thing.

"Whatever Tillie might say, my sermons are hardly dry. Come by this Sunday and see for yourself." Siegel was smiling as he turned back into the church.

As he left, Kane caught sight of a figure moving by the graves. Halloran. The man started moving away, but Kane called his name.

"Come often?"

"No, Friend Badge, not often. There are days the world is full of her and days when she is very far. Think ye the dead walk where they will and stop by now and then for a whiskey?"

For once, Halloran seemed to be without his veneer. Kane pressed.

"The living occupy my time, Halloran. Straight answer. You play at being a drunk. Am I right? Haliburton is a drunk. You are a man who does what you please to get by, nothing more, and it is easier to let the world see you as a man poured in a bottle than one who simply gave up on living because it all seems pointless."

" 'Tis a poet ye are, Friend Badge. A philosopher."

"What I am is a sheriff waiting for an answer."

"And why does it matter? A criminal do I seem to be, Friend Badge? A dangerous desperado feared for his savage ways?"

"You know a lot, Halloran."

"I see a lot, Friend Badge. I hear a lot. If I were to work at it, I might know a lot, but I came to a point several years ago where I was trapped, Friend Badge. For suicide is a mortal sin, Friend Badge, and a waste of the life God gives us. But if live I must, care I need not." He held up a hand. "Better with words than you have given pretty speeches. I stay because I have no reason to go, for life will not be infused with meaning because of where I am. If meaning is sent to me, it will be sent. Until that day, I will eat when I am hungry, stay warm in the cold, and drink when I am dry. I ask for nothing more and want nothing more."

Kane could feel the frustration within him. If he could know all Halloran saw and heard, Rakeheart would be as plain as a mapped valley. So close, and so far.

"But, Friend Badge, if it be a bit of balm to your soul, the world is no worse for the loss of Wilkins and Kruger. Ferguson I saw so little I knew not, but when no one speaks ill of a man, one does wonder what he did when none were looking."

Kane muttered something.

"I shall further share that nothing foul happens in and around Rakeheart but Silas Noonan is at the bottom of it, and that the poor Wilkins family has suffered enough for the sins of others and should not be disturbed even if there are sins to be laid at their door, and that any soul who should disturb them should face a deserved punishment."

"That a threat?"

"A pledge, if you will, Friend Badge. And, Friend Badge, best of all, since I am no longer a man who cares, there is no one with whom I will share my very sincere and heartfelt certainty that you are as much a sheriff by trade as I am an eagle." Halloran bowed. "Until we meet again, Friend Badge."

Kane wanted that nap, but he had a duty. He wanted to know why Halloran was in a cemetery when he knew there was no wife of his buried there. Halloran was playing some deep game, but Kane could not imagine what it was. He caught himself talking to the air as he walked to the stable. Maybe Rakeheart was getting the better of him.

Pete Haliburton was alone in the smithy. Janie was wherever she often went during the day. He had promised. He also had a vision of Janie as one of the women he saw at the Riders' camp. Every woman who rode that hard trail knew it was going to be something different. Every woman was wrong.

"Hear you're throwin' in with those Company Riders," Kane said without preamble.

Haliburton's head snapped as though Kane had struck him. "Sez who?"

"Don't matter. That the right of it?"

"Riders protect this town, Kane. Ought to be heroes here, not treated the way those uppity friends of yours like Brewer want them treated."

"Not about the town, Haliburton. What about your daughter? Want her to have that kind of life? Those boys might not have crossed the line yet, or maybe nobody was looking when they did, or maybe everybody is too scared to talk, but when they cross that line and someone has to make 'em pay, it's the women who pay the hardest."

"Jealous are you? Janie likes one of them better'n you?"

"Tryin' to save you a world of hurt and her a life of misery," Kane said. "Known men like the Riders before. It always ends bad, Pete."

"High and mighty because you think you faced them down the other night," Haliburton retorted. "You don't know nothin'. Once they get the word . . ."

"The word from who?" Kane pounced. He knew someone else was the brains of the Company Riders, and this was his chance to find out.

"Said too much," grumbled Haliburton. "Horseshoes don't grow on trees. Got work to do. Maybe you better find yourself a place to stay, Kane. Hear there's a place you were lookin' at. Not sure you're welcome under my roof. Gone by tomorrow would be good." Haliburton walked away towards his tools.

There would be no nap now. Kane had the frustrating feeling that he had the chance to grab hold of whatever was going on in Rakeheart, but that, in the end, he was chasing smoke. Going in circles. One man left he'd never really spoken to, because who and what he was appeared to be so obvious.

Silas Noonan laughed aside Kane's questions. Patience exhausted, he put Kane in his place.

"Sheriff, the Riders are the only way Rakeheart protects itself from the toughs that other towns hire. Ask anyone and you will hear the same story over and over. I would not suggest they are men of great worth or that anyone should hold them in high esteem, but they are a necessity out here on the frontier. You have been here a month or so, Sheriff. Mind your business and keep the wild and stupid from shooting holes in one another and ruining the work of those of us who have built businesses, and you will be doing your job. Now run along and do that," he said dismissively.

He had one more twist to drive home.

"If I am correct, you have been trying to solve the murders of three men and have absolutely no understanding of what happened. Given that success, Sheriff, perhaps you might want to think of considering a different line of work or moving to some other part of Wyoming. Being a sheriff is a dangerous and thankless job in a town like Rakeheart where you do not know whom you can trust."

Noonan palmed the silver-headed cane he was holding as he sat behind his desk.

"Rakeheart neither needs nor really wants you, Sheriff Kane, as much as those who hired you think you can save them from themselves. Do you really think that, when the day comes, there will be anyone at your back? Good day, Sheriff."

Black rage accompanied Kane to the stable. The worst of it was that Noonan was right. He had been worrying away at three murders and accomplished nothing. He also knew that with maybe thirty men, if it was a showdown between him and the Riders, he would be joining Jared Wilkins in the graveyard.

As Haliburton pounded a horseshoe on his anvil, Kane saddled Tecumseh and thundered out of town.

The old Tompkins place was before him. He had never filed whatever paper was needed to legally move in and wanted to give it one last look before he did so.

His past impression was confirmed. Not badly built but neglected. His eyes inspected what needed to be repaired as his head argued over whether to even bother.

Part of him recognized that there was some truth in what Noonan and Halloran said. He was not likely to have much in the way of support from men who hired him to make problems go away, not become one. If he could bring the Riders to heel, well and good. If not, they lost little. But there was the stubborn side that did not like to be pushed. Anyhow, he did not want to be pushed until he wanted to go, which might come out to the same thing in terms of when he left Rakeheart but did not feel the same inside.

He thought about Wilkins, whom no one liked, and realized that, although he started with the man's death, the beginning might have come earlier, with Kruger's murder—the one nobody seemed to want solved and that they were all very happy to forget.

That lump of metal had meaning. It also had mystery. Would Rachel Wilkins help him solve it? Or was she hiding something else?

Either way, he had to know.

Chapter Twelve

"Maybe you should set your office up here since you come out here so often," Rachel Wilkins challenged as Kane sat atop Tecumseh in the ranch yard.

She was dressed for riding. Pants, boots, hair in a braid, and a flat-crowned hat, like his, atop her head. The horse she preferred was waiting by the ranch yard's biggest oak. She was clearly impatient to be gone and annoyed with his questions. No one else was home. There was no need for company manners.

"Got questions," replied Kane. "Need answers."

"And I have a ranch to run with cowboys who do not seem to understand whose ranch it is and children who think their mother should be their mother and father. The sun refuses to stand still so I can get all my chores done, and now you come around asking about guns and silly things I have no time to attend to. Right now, we are driving back the stock from the west pasture that have wandered too far, and I do not have time to spend talking. The children are there, the hands are there, and there is work to be done, Mr. Kane."

"Miz Wilkins, a man was killed with a rare kind of a gun, and I need to look here for that gun because your husband . . ."

"Then look! If you want to look for a gun, go look for it. There are enough of them thrown all over the place. You cowboys and your guns! I would not know one kind from another. Go. Look until you are done looking. Turn the place upside down until you are so convinced that you will understand I have not been on a one-Indian crime wave of killing. If you find anything, so be it. I believe Jeremiah lost a piece of an orange top. One of Libby's shoes vanished years ago that you might find as well. The cats hide things as well. Enjoy encountering those! If you are gone when I get back, and you should be, remember to shut the door."

She mounted her gray mare and was soon galloping away in fury, having again accomplished the task of making him feel both guilty and stupid for doing a simple thing that was only his job.

Felt odd, he thought, to prowl someone's house alone. Wrong. She said to. He had to. This waiting had gone on long enough. He went inside.

The house was sparsely furnished, and most of it looked made by hands that did something else for a living other than build tables and chairs.

The house had two rifles he could find. A small one that looked used and a larger one with dust all over it. He had not looked to see what kind of gun Rachel had when she left. A great detective he was turning out to be.

One chest held things Rachel wore under dresses. Felt wrong to look. One small leather pouch on a loop of leather was at the bottom. A medicine bundle. Very faded. Comanche. Something else. A carved piece of wood. Rough-done. A bear. He guessed it was from her first husband. White men carved animals to look like animals. Indians carved them to depict gods and spirits they represented.

Four broken, hand-carved wooden flutes were piled with the things on Libby's side of the tiny room she shared with her brother. Charcoal markings were here and there on Jeremiah's side. On the floor. On the backside of tree bark. On some wood. One might have been him, or his father, or maybe it was a tree.

A small desk had a ledger. The writing was very tiny and very skewed. Had to be hers. Wilkins was a big man, or that's how his picture made him appear. He could not have made numbers that small. That made Rachel most likely a liar when she said she didn't know how the ranch was doing. He sighed. He could have been done and gone if everyone had told the truth.

Wilkins had hired nine men since the fall. A puzzle. The ranch didn't appear to be growing. The ledger showed a couple of men had left around that time, but Wilkins added far more than he lost. If Kane didn't know better, he'd think Wilkins was bracing for a fight. But who with?

He also noticed that there were some items that did not have explanations, and they all were money coming in. Every month there was something: fifty dollars, a hundred dollars, twenty . . . For a small ranch living on the edge the way they all did, that was something important.

The money started coming in the fall of '74. Nothing recent had been added. He leafed back quickly. If there was something of interest in the items purchased at Conroy's and the monthly payments of wages, it escaped Kane. Numbers did not tell stories; people did. He made careful note of the amounts and times, then put the ledger back, eyes sore from the strain of looking at the tiny, neat rows of numbers.

The bunkhouse had guns aplenty, but most were old Colts and rifles. There was a crate of .45 shells in a corner. A lot of shells. Gangs in Texas would steal those when they could. Odd to find so many on a ranch that was supposedly a place no one bothered, but with that and the increase in men hired, it made him wonder if either Wilkins or Ferguson knew something was coming and wanted to be prepared.

He crossed to the stable. The cow barn had been, well, a cow barn. Anything hidden there was gone for the ages, as far as he was concerned.

Last stop. He stopped as he reached the stable's open doors. He looked out across the plains. He looked behind up the slope. He understood. The best place to shoot was not the most obvious. Anyone who had been to the Wilkins place in the daylight very much could get back there, have a horse not far, and get away. Or maybe it was all his imagination trying to make simple things hard.

He looked at the doorway again. One gouge was smaller than the rest. The wood around it was lighter, as well. Did it happen last month? How could he tell, and who would tell him if it did?

Barns were the world's best hiding places. He found where Libby hid; it was a little spot where she could hear everything and be invisible. There were two corn dolls and a makeshift house from scrap lumber. There were some bandages just right for a very small arm. He found two hiding places where Jared Wilkins had stashed dust-covered jugs of liquor beneath the hay. Eventually, not far from the jugs, he found what he was looking for.

The LeMat had been tossed in a pile of hay. Not carefully buried; merely tossed and eventually covered. Months ago. No way to know if it was deliberate or accidental. Dirt and grime covered the weapon. The barrel smelled like old, wet powder.

Now that he had found what he was looking for, what did it mean? The wall of defiance Rachel erected to keep outsiders out was not likely to be breached by a simple question. A man like Ferguson saved a lump of metal because it meant something, or it could prove something. Or someone else thought it could prove something. Did Ferguson keep it for Wilkins or to use against Wilkins? Conroy said there was bad blood. No one else had that to say, though.

A man hid a gun because he didn't want it found. Obvious. Why not dump it twenty miles from anywhere? Because it needed to be hidden quickly, and the person who hid it was not riding the range, but at the ranch. But if he had shot Kruger with the gun and shot him in town where the man's body was found, he could have thrown it away anywhere between Rakeheart and the ranch, not brought it back to his own barn.

Kane was wishing one thing in all of Wyoming would start making sense as he stood outside the barn, looking idly around the Wilkins place as though something was going to jump up and solve his problems for him.

He finished searching everywhere. It took longer than he thought. The place was small, but there was a house, bunkhouse, barn for horses and a shed for cows, as well as some other outbuildings. For some reason the Tompkins place entered his head. That had been one shack, with no evidence of any other buildings. No working ranch, no matter how small, had only one building. It was a real ranch as much as he was a real sheriff.

It was early afternoon. If he pushed Tecumseh, they could make it to Rakeheart before dark, and he might be able to get a question answered from the one person who would know.

At least Rachel would have her wish; he would be gone when she returned.

"Of course I remember Ken Tompkins," Tillie Witherspoon said emphatically, gesturing with scissors that came far too close to Kane's nose for his own comfort. "He died last summer. Or vanished, really. Strange man."

"Was his wife a customer?"

She laughed uproariously. "Wife? If there was a self-respecting woman that would have come within a mile of that filthy man I would have been surprised. Never saw him without tobacco in his mouth. Filthy habit. Mrs. Pemberthy would come in the store to avoid him if he was in town."

No wife. Another Rakeheart lie.

"What exactly did Ken Tompkins do?" Kane asked. "I've

seen the shack. I was looking for a place for the winter and was thinking about staying there."

"Haunted, the fools say," she snorted. "Lights and goings-on. Ken Tompkins was a no-good who may well have done an honest day's work at one time, but he did not do it here. Now I am not one for gossip, Sheriff . . ."

"Perish the thought."

She eyed him a moment for traces of sarcasm. She either found none or decided it did not matter.

"They say he was one of the men who helped move stolen goods through the valley. You know they won't let anyone sell liquor to the Indians, or guns, but they get them anyhow. I heard he was involved. Wagons out there. Then one day he was gone. I always figured he came to a bad end. Preacher Siegel said a prayer for him one week instead of a funeral, but that was about all. One less bad apple, as far as I am concerned."

He thanked her profusely.

"I hope I was a help, Sheriff. I was never able to understand how they got along!"

"Who, ma'am?"

"Why Tompkins and that Wilkins man. I would have thought that someone like Jared Wilkins would never have dirtied himself with that man, but perhaps he was useful for something. Far be it for me to judge. I am only a woman in a man's world and a helpless one at that. I know once Tompkins tried to be too friendly with Rachel Wilkins, and you don't do that to an Indian, Sheriff, without being prepared to pay the price. She left him in the street doubled over. I thought she did the right thing. I heard her husband afterward . . . well, you know how men are in private when they think their wife has made them appear 'less of a man.' Whatever that is supposed to mean. The poor woman. Seamus Halloran said it took weeks for her to heal. He could not abide that Wilkins man and how he neglected his family."

He understood. At last, he understood. At least, he thought he did.

Rachel's face changed colors because, when she knew he was there, she put some powder over a bruise her husband had given her. Mae's face reminded him of Rachel's because there was swelling around the eye no makeup could hide.

Kane held his tongue and offered Tillie Witherspoon his thanks. More lies. More mysteries. Maybe it was time to let the whole mess go and let Rakeheart and the Company Riders fight it out and let Rachel Wilkins deal with the ghosts haunting her family. Maybe, maybe. But first there was something he had to do. He had to know.

CHAPTER THIRTEEN

There was smoke coming from the Wilkins chimney as he rode up to it in the dimming of the day. Kane took a long, deep breath and exhaled it slowly. He'd thought about turning around fifty times. It was what it was. Once he had the truth, he could ride away. This time, he told himself, he really would ride away. Really.

"Hello, the house," he called.

The door opened, and he could see her, backlit with the shotgun by her side.

"You gonna go away if I tell you to?"

"Nope. Probably not if you shoot me, either."

"Stable the horse and wipe your feet. I mean it about the feet. You tracked dirt all over the other day."

The door slammed.

A place with bread and a little stew was set for him. He could smell coffee.

"Sit and eat. I feed everything that rolls up at my door, so don't think you're special," she growled. "There's always coffee. Don't know what you cowboys see in it. Drank it once. Awful stuff, but the boys keep asking for it, so I always have a pot ready. Sometimes it sets on the fire for hours, but the boys drink it up no matter what." She shot him a look that was a challenge. "White people have strange habits."

He never got to reply.

"Hello, Mister Sheriff." Sad-eyed Libby had a little smile. He

168

had thought of her before he left Rakeheart. This visit mattered.

He gave her instructions to find his saddle and bring something in from one of the saddlebags. Rachel, although puzzled, nodded permission, and Libby set off, Jeremiah at her heels like a puppy who didn't know what was going on but was game for it if it meant running.

The brown paper package was soft. Libby set it on the table and looked at her mother.

"Sheriff Kane brought it, Libby. Ask him."

He nodded.

Tillie Witherspoon had clucked and clucked as she flitted from pile to pile until she made the selections. Now, Libby's eyes popped as bright red cloth, yellow, green, and several shades of blue appeared.

She could not stifle an exclamation when a small wooden flute emerged and fell to the floor. Conroy had the toy in his shop, and Kane had seen it while pacing one day as the shopkeeper waited on a customer.

"Don't know what girls like to make but figgered you need something to make it from," he said. "Maybe you got a doll needs a dress. Figgered making noise is good. Bet your mom likes lots of noise."

Libby was watching Rachel, who was not only surprised, but clearly pleased. One Wilkins was not, however.

Jeremiah looked on, unsure of what, if anything, came next.

Kane dug into his jacket pocket and handed the package to Jeremiah. The boy fumbled with the extra loops of string Conroy had used, then an object within landed with a thunk on the table. It was a small penknife—not too useful in the hands of a man, but not too dangerous, either, in the hands of a young boy.

He finished unwrapping. A few pencils and some pieces of paper emerged.

"I know you like to draw. Boys need to whittle things," Kane said. "That's what they tell me."

Jeremiah squealed and held everything up for his mother's approval.

"Not my table and chairs!" Rachel commanded before she sent the children to their room; they ran off excitedly, with the volume increasing as they left the world of adults behind.

"You are a mysterious man, Sheriff Kane."

Kane looked into the fire, as if it would give him the courage to say what he wanted to say. He kept his voice low and then looked her full in the face.

"I know, Rachel. I know what happened."

She was good. Her face never moved, even her hand on the table never twitched. Stray thought. Teach her poker, they could be rich in a year. Or dead. Or both.

"I know," he repeated.

"Not here," she said. "Give me a minute. We will talk outside, alone." He finished his food, nodded.

"Libby! Sheriff Kane doesn't know how to find the Protector in the sky. I have to show him. You behave with your brother."

"Yes, Mama!"

"She's a good girl," Kane said. "Good mother protects her children. Never doubted you were a good mother, Rachel."

Rachel's eyes reminded him of a cornered animal.

"Not here."

They were out in the night. Cool after the heat of the fire. Endless stars in the black and blue depth of heaven. Rachel wore her dark-brown shawl over her green dress. She blended with the night as if each were part of the other.

"Who was Frank Kruger?" he asked, not looking at her.

"Who?"

"Older man. Square set. Rough-and-tumble look. Came to see your husband right before the snow. Never came back."

"Many people came to see Jared. He might have been one. I do not know the name." He could hear the tension in her voice.

"Pinkerton man. Hunting something. Found it, I'd bet."

He could hear her bare intake of breath.

"Him. Yes."

"Somebody murdered him in Rakeheart last year. Right before the big snow. Right after he was asking about children. Somebody used an old LeMat gun like the one I have in my saddlebag that I found in your barn, where it had been tossed under the hay."

No response. He turned. She was nodding in response to something unsaid.

"Jared stole Jeremiah. He lied to me about it at first. The parents died, he had said. There were emigrants going past our terrible farm all the time, and so many of them did die. Then I found out the truth. I did not know until after we left to come here. The boy—he was small for his age—could not go back. Jared loved him. Jared thought we were safe here. That man showed up, but only once, but he never came back. Jared said the man was hunting the child, but that he convinced the man Jeremiah was ours."

"Would he have told you if he killed him?"

Silence.

"I do not know," she said with regret shading her soft voice. "He spoke less as time flowed and carried him past me. Last autumn he was very silent often. I do not know why that was or how that I failed him."

He'd save the rest. Skip to what mattered.

"But he started hitting you."

He could see her face in the dimness, but not her expression. Just as well.

"Indian men hit their women. Not hard, not often, but it happens. When dinner gets burned. Not what I am talking about. More like a sickness that never ends."

No reply. He gave it time.

"It got worse," she said in a dull, flat monotone. "Not constant, but it never stopped. Bad this spring. Real bad. He was hurting, and that was how it came out; as though there were devils in the man."

Kane reached out and briefly touched her right temple.

"Hurt you bad here."

She did not push his hand away.

"You put powder over the bruise for weeks so Libby would not know. Or maybe not. But I know you had it on when you needed to hide it that first time I showed up. Didn't have it on that night, because it was fading. You did in the morning. Didn't catch it then, when you called me out for starin'. Figured it later."

"Aren't you clever?" Her self-assured tone was shaky.

"Think it scared him. Men who hit women usually hate it when they see what they did. Then something happened. Something big. Something I don't understand with Rakeheart. Might have been the land, the Company Riders, Noonan . . . don't know. Maybe this Kruger man. Did Jared kill him?"

"He never said. He drank instead. Darkness overcame him and owned him, Kane. The man who cared for me died, or maybe I should say he walked away day by day until at last he was too far for me to ever reach."

"What did he use to break Libby's left arm?"

"How did you know?"

"You wrapped it tight. I barely touched it that day she showed me the garden. It was too hard to use her arm without wrappings. Still hurt. She tried not to show it, but she could not quite hide it. Found one old wrapping in the barn the day you let me search. Animal fat on it. Lot of markings on the inside. Indian medicine. If it was an accident, she would have said something. Kids brag about injuries in an adventure. When she didn't, I figured it was something worse."

Her eyes looked like vast, dark pools looking up at him.

"He said it was an accident. He said she surprised him in the barn, and he thought she was an intruder. I know he was lying. He was hiding something out there," she said.

"Liquor."

"You found it?"

He nodded.

"You find well, Kane."

"And that night he spotted her outside, where she saw things he didn't want her to see, and he was going to punish her? What did she see?"

"No one will hurt her again. Ever."

"Put the knife away. I'm not here to hurt her. You were supposed to figger that out by now."

"How do you know I have one?"

"You killed your husband to defend your daughter. Right? Figure one more ain't that hard."

There was a silence. He expected a denial. It did not come.

"And why should I not do everything I am able to do to protect those who are mine to protect?"

"Not going to do anything."

There was silence as she considered his words. Then came the verdict.

"I do not believe you," she said. "Your general sent you to find out how he died. You are working for him. You will tell him."

"He sent me to tell him a reason. He'll get one. Ferguson killed him; then got killed. It ends there. Got no interest in making life worse. Daughter has enough shadows on her spirit. No more. It ends, Rachel. It ends."

She was quiet. He could almost hear her sort risks.

"If I wanted to arrest you, Rachel, I could have brought fifty men. I am sick of it all, Rachel. All the lies of those men. All the things they do. I got sent here by Cump Sherman to do a job for him. Job's done. You don't like my version? Give me a better one. Enough dead men around that I can blame one of them. I only have one condition, and I let this go."

"And what is that?" Sharp. Suspicious.

"What did Libby hear or see? She is so busy trying to lie to protect you she hides everything."

"Clem and Jared argued. They argued often in the last few weeks. They did it when I was not around. Clem had something on Jared. Something bad Jared had done. I don't know what it was. It could have been this Kruger man. I don't know, Kane. Libby didn't understand a lot of it. They talked crazy things. She said they talked about gold . . . about the Black Hills. They are days away. There was something about the Company Riders. Either one of them or both of them was dealing with those men. There was another man involved who she thought they had killed, or who had killed someone. Libby could never understand it."

"Any names? Brewer, Noonan?" Pause. "Tompkins?"

"I don't think so. I don't know. The names of those Rakeheart people mean nothing to her. She knows the hands and her brother and me. She knows the names of the stars that guide the Comanche and the Sioux. No one else matters. There is sadness upon her, Kane, and one reason you will live is that you have pierced it."

Kane sighed deeply. He had done what he came for. He'd wire Sherman something. He wondered if he'd held off reporting the foreman's death so he could lay the blame on him. Ferguson had cared about Rachel. He wondered if the dead man would accept that taking the blame for her crime would be the final kindness he could do for her.

As for Wilkins, the man Sherman recalled died long ago, if he ever lived outside of Sherman's fantasy that all the men on his march were somehow better than real people. Cump could keep his fantasy intact, Rachel could get on with life, and he could see if there was a place maybe up Montana way where he could live a quiet life, if such a miracle were possible. Best it was going to get.

He looked at Rachel's shadowy figure in the dimness. Life was a fight from the start. She didn't need any more. His conscience was clear.

"I'll ride out after we go back," he said.

"Afraid I may kill you in your sleep?"

"Thought crossed my mind."

"You are right. There has been enough," she said. "Libby says you are a good man. She may be wiser than her mother. I can only hope that she will forget. Jeremiah may learn things I do not want him to know, but the truth would hurt him, for he was proud to be the son of his father. He must be protected."

"You are leaving."

"This is a place I thought would be safe. It was not. There is no safe place, Kane. I do not know where we will go. I fear one day, the men of Rakeheart will come to take it, so I may as well sell it to them."

"Where will you go?"

"North. It is wilder there, I think. I do not know. I have no people and no place. I would not be welcome with a white child on a reservation and not welcome with an Indian one in a white town. I have been waiting for a sign from the Great Spirit. I still wait. You should stay here tonight. You will be safe here—safer than riding alone. I fear you have disturbed too many people in your search for the truth, Kane. I know you do not mean harm. Yet, I still do not fully trust. I do not think you lie, but promises rarely come true with whites, even when they mean to keep them. Only when you are gone and the moon after you is gone will I not expect a man with a gun to appear."

Staying on the ranch made no sense. It was a risk. He agreed.

"We should go back to the house," he told her.

She was like a stone.

"He called her an Indian brat," she said, head turned away. The hurt in her voice was as raw as though it had happened yesterday. "I will never know how long he had that bottled up in him. And still I cried when he died. I warned him. I did warn him, Kane. He told me I should know my place. I do not know what he became, but he was not the man who for so long was so kind. I try to hold that man close and never let him go. That is why I think now that we must leave. There is poison here. Those people. Rakeheart. Something from that terrible place crawled into him and infected him, and it changed him, and I am so afraid it will get Jeremiah and Libby and me."

He understood.

He was thinking of not even going back to Rakeheart after sending a telegram to Sherman, or maybe tossing them his badge from the back of Tecumseh and riding some place where either there was a town that didn't hate, or, better yet, no town at all—if there still was such a place anywhere in the West.

Rachel had gripped his arms intensely as she spoke. She still grasped him in silence. It hurt. He disengaged his arms from hers and put his around her. She wept on his shoulder as it all broke inside of her. And the stars looked down.

After false promises he knew he would break to ride back soon to see Libby, Kane loped towards Rakeheart with the full of the morning before him.

Rachel had tried to talk more than she usually did. He could see Libby sizing up her mother, knowing something was off.

They would work it out. Jeremiah gave Kane a stick with no bark on it.

"I made sure he didn't cut his hand off," Libby said in the time-honored denigration of a younger sibling's accomplishment that was as much a part of life as the sky.

Rachel was quiet as he left. He was, too. Nothing was left to say.

The waving grasslands were turning brown as the August heat began to show its force. For all that Wyoming people talked about winter, Kane could not imagine it.

One lone horseman meant little to the herds of deer and the bears with young along trickling creeks. The wind blew fresh and clean.

The night had been a time of decision.

First Rakeheart, to tell them he was leaving. Then Laramie, to telegraph Sherman a lie he hoped the general would accept. He told himself he was being straight with the people of the town by going there first, but his inner self told him he was putting off that message to Sherman as long as possible.

Then Montana. Or maybe farther out in Wyoming—he had no idea where boundaries ran. Some place where there would not be a telegraph that could connect Sherman to him. Some place where the railroad did not pollute minds with ambition—if there was such a place. He doubted it, but, on a morning like this, there was always the hope that he could ride on and on and not worry about the details.

CHAPTER FOURTEEN

The day was more than halfway gone by the time he arrived in Rakeheart. Didn't matter. It would be a short stay. He would find Conroy, hand back the badge with some explanation that would be all lies, then light out for Laramie, blame everything on dead men, and head out.

North. Rachel was going north. Maybe. Montana territory was a big place. Cold, too. Maybe Texas boys belonged home. Might be different without having Sherman's work to do. Might be like having a life of his own.

Maybe he could ride herd and let all of it go by. There were ranches enough that hired without many questions other than what name to call a man. Sounded like a drunkard's dream, but it would hold for the day.

He led Tecumseh to the stable. Didn't unsaddle him but loosened the cinch before finding him fresh hay. They'd both gotten used to eating too much and too often, but one last good feed would be fine for the animal.

"Kane!" Janie ran to see him as he was stepping out into the street and gave him a hug.

Being hugged by a young, pretty girl was a fine thing, but it was a puzzle.

"Where have you been?"

"Business at the fort." She seemed very intense or anxious. Something. Her pa was working in the smithy. Bang-bang. Bang-bang. *Bang! Bang!* Then he was quiet a while before resuming the steady rhythm of a man working.

"Come with me." She grabbed his hand, started to lead him out behind the stable.

"Something wrong?"

"No, why? Aren't you glad to see me? Don't you like me?" She smiled at him and ran her hand up his arm.

"I got to go see Conroy, um, Janie."

"Can't it wait? Please? Please?" She was pulling him.

"Janie . . ."

She turned, wrapped her arms around him, and kissed him hard on very surprised lips—though not too surprised to respond.

"There!" she said. "Now come along. There's no privacy here."

He did not want to explain then and there about heading someplace. And wasn't she keeping step with some Company Rider?

He let her lead him to the more private back side of the stable. Whatever she was up to, he could explain to her here.

The look in her eyes puzzled him. Fear? Concern? Guilt?

Then her eyes grew very wide and looked past him.

He turned.

Trap!

Wood and six men with drawn guns were walking. She had set him up.

"Git, girl," Wood said. She stayed there, rooted.

"Wood."

"Hello, Sheriff. Got business we didn't finish."

Kane was still dumbfounded he had let himself be betrayed and fooled so easily. Man deserves it when he forgets where he is.

Janie was still standing next to him as the Company Riders closed in.

"I told you to git," Wood said to her.

"Why you need them guns?" Janie asked. "You said you needed to talk private-like when them other folks wasn't lookin'."

Wood laughed scornfully. "Oh, I do, girl. Got a lot to say to Mr. Sheriff here. Don't think you want to see it, girl. Git!"

"Kane . . ." she began.

"Told you to git, you stupid girl." Wood shoved her to the ground. Another man held her as she scrambled to her feet and tossed her like a rag doll back into the stable. Her father emerged from the smithy and grabbed her, screaming and kicking. He began yelling at her, and she was yelling back as they disappeared farther from view.

Wood was now a few feet from Kane.

"Karl." The big man who had tossed Janie around moved closer. Other Riders moved around from the side.

Kane got in one punch that hit Wood before they pinioned his arms.

"Don't know you, Texas. Don't care. You landed on the wrong side. Your hard luck. This is business. It ain't personal."

Kane got in one kick that came close to where it hurts.

"Now it's a little more personal."

The first punch doubled Kane over. The next ones jarred his head. One caught his right eye. He could feel the wave of dizziness.

"Let's go," he heard Wood say. Something about a lesson or a show.

He was being led. Sunshine. Not dead yet. Focus on what was positive. There would be worse to come. Of that, he was certain. His sight was adapting, but there was something in his eyes. Probably blood. They were in the main street of Rakeheart. The piano was jangling. They must be near Noonan's.

Kane all but jumped when Wood's gun fired at his ear. The

rest he started hearing as though he were far underwater and someone was yelling at him.

"Out here!" the lead Rider called. "Out here now! Every one of you."

Hazy faces. The sun hurt when it hit his eyes. He could hear the buzz. If they wanted an audience, they were planning a show. He knew who was going to be the main attraction. He tried to struggle, but it did no good.

"Get the rest," Wood ordered. Kane heard murmurs growing louder.

"Got a lesson you need to learn," Wood called out after a time. "You got to know who your friends are. You got to know who you don't never want to have as your enemies."

Wood came nearer. He was grinning at Kane. "Karl."

The big man came over. Kane saw the work gloves, with hard, leather seams. This was going to hurt.

It did.

When Karl paused, Kane could feel blood flowing down his face. One eye was swollen shut; the other getting there. His mouth was bleeding. If his nose wasn't broken, it was a miracle. At least one rib had to be busted. The gut punches had him retch past what a man could hold. Kane was still alive, but nothing more than a mass of hurt. Breathing hurt. He'd have been limp on the ground if they were not holding him up.

Somebody was pulling his hair back.

"Not so tough now, are you?" It was Wood. He let go. Kane's head lolled.

Wood's voice pitched louder. "All of you. This is what happens when you cross anyone you ought to think of as your friend. Don't forget it. Don't want any of your men to end up like this, do you?"

Maybe the show was over. The hands holding him relaxed. Kane head-butted Wood, unknowingly catching his nose. Fresh blood flowed, but for once it was not his. Wood roared anger, punching Kane hard in the ribs and the gut, bending the victim over further as Kane moaned uncontrollably.

"You might live past this day, Texas, but you ain't never gonna forget it." He turned to his men. "Find me a piece of lumber."

Kane breathed and bled. Distantly there was a thought that he might die, but it had too many miles of pain to overcome to be real. He had never stopped fighting and was not going to do that now. Growing fear gave him strength, but it was not enough.

"Bring him."

He was jerked forward. His head was dunked in a trough. The water startled him. For a moment he thought he could see. Now he was awake. Now he was scared.

"You asked for this. Hold him!"

Kane didn't know what was coming, but he fought to avoid it to no avail. Soon he was laid on the duckboards, face up. He could feel the sun on his face. It was a hazy ball. Then a shadow. Wood.

"Remember this, because you ain't never going for your gun with this arm ever again."

Kane struggled.

Then all the pain of the past hours was as nothing compared to the agony that filled him as Wood brought down a piece of lumber hard on Kane's right forearm. The crack of breaking bone was as loud as a gunshot.

Someone was screaming as he hung on to the edge of consciousness. It was him.

"You get one more for being good."

The gunshot and the breaking of the glass in Noonan's large window came together. Another shot. His right leg danced and stung.

Kane was aware of the noise but could do no more than listen.

Janie's voice echoed as she strode from the crowd forward.

"You used me! You made me a Judas goat! You said . . ."

"Haliburton, get your daughter under control!" Wood called. "Janie, you drop that gun or I will slap your fool head so silly you won't know which end is up, fool girl. You and your pa want to be part of the Company Riders, this is how we do our business. Now shut your mouth and go home, girl!"

"Drop dead!" she screamed.

One gunshot came first, then several more, and then loud screams.

"Janie!"

"You shot her!" Kane heard.

"They shot a woman!" someone said near him.

Wood was now raging. A rapid series of shots rang out as he fired into the air.

"Bring them both."

Kane almost passed out from the pain as he was dragged to the middle of the town's street and dumped. He was aware someone was dumped next to him.

"Now all of you, listen," called out Wood. "Boys and I have a thirst. A powerful thirst. May take a while to settle. Anybody want to move either of these two before we're done, you can git what they did."

He tossed the board he had been holding to the ground and stalked into Noonan's.

Kane could hear noises. Talking. The buzz lingered but faded. He tried to move, but the second his arm flexed, the pain overwhelmed him.

Rakeheart was melting away, not wanting to see what was in the street. Anger flared briefly as it mingled with the pain. Wonderful folks to have at your back. The sun felt hot on his congealing face.

"Kane?"

He made a response. It didn't sound like a word to his ears.

"They said . . . said they had a job for you . . . didn't mean . . . Oh, Kane!"

Kane's battered mouth was beyond words. They did not form. He only heard noises from his mouth.

An icy hand grabbed his.

"You cold, Kane? I'm cold. Don't . . . let go."

That he could do. He could squeeze her cold hand with his usable left one.

Now she, too, was only making noises. The hand quivered. He tried to say something. He tried to move his head, to lift himself up to see how badly she was hurt. White light flooded him, and Rakeheart vanished.

When he awoke, the sun had left his face. Dark. Too dark for his eyes anyhow. Janie's hand was in his. It was cold. Stiff. He tried to move his hand, but her arm would not budge. He pulled his hand free. Pain flared. He reached it toward where he thought she was. Felt something damp and sticky by her body. Girl must be dead. He'd meet her there soon. Wherever "there" was. He tried to raise himself up. He fell down a dark hole.

A moment later. Hours maybe? It was pitch black out. Or his eyes were failing. Someone was near. He tried to move. Nothing. He could sense that Janie was gone. They must have taken her. Dead. The thought ran through his head. He failed. He made a noise.

"Shh!" was all that was said. Pain rippled white hot as he was lifted like a sack and tossed on a saddle. He tried to say something. A hand that smelled of dirt and tar covered his mouth. A smell of lilac came, too.

The horse started to move. He tried to protest. He was not ready to be buried yet!

If any sound came out, it produced no response. The horse

kept moving slowly.

The sounds changed. No more town. They stopped. His hands and feet were now bound under the horse. The horse lurched, faster now. Not a gallop but moving faster.

Kane pulled hard to free his hands, but the pain in his right arm sent him down into a deep, black pit that had no end.

"Mama!"

The word came clearly to Kane. For longer than he knew, he had been floating and drifting, like a small rowboat on the wide parts of the old Red River. When his eyes opened here and there, he had no idea what he was seeing. Sometimes light. Sometimes darkness. Once there was a storm, and he knew he was indoors somewhere.

White flashes of pain surged in the dark now and then. There were voices, at times. A little girl talking about her garden on the moon. Most of the time, there was nothing.

This time, his eyes could focus. Mostly. One would not quite open. Sad-eyed Libby looked down on him. She smiled.

"I win."

This puzzled Kane, who tried to express it, but his lips seemed stuck together.

"Mama said to do this, so if it hurts blame her."

He felt a moistened finger running over his lips. The water felt good and cool. The pressure of the finger almost hurt. Back and forth.

"Poke your tongue through your lips," she said. "It hurts less if you do it to yourself than if I do it."

He tried.

"I told Mama you would wake up today because yesterday your foot twitched. She said I was silly, but I was right."

Poking his lips apart did hurt, but his mouth was open. Breathing. Oh, breathing! It hurt, but it was delicious.

"Mama took Jeremiah fishing, but she'll be back soon. They never catch anything, but he likes to go. He gets very bored watching you make up your mind whether to die or live. Little kids are like that."

He wanted water. The word he heard sounded like anything but that, but Libby understood. She dribbled it into his mouth. He swallowed, choked, swallowed, choked, and swallowed.

"Mama said that's what happens when you give cowboys water and not coffee," teased the girl.

"How . . ." It sounded like a word. He was sure of it. She frowned, and he repeated it. The light dawned in her face.

"Ol' Seamus Halloran brought you. Uncle Seamus. He's the only man in that place who ever wanted to play with me!"

"He . . . here?"

"No, he went back. I'm pretty sure he'll be back in a few days, but I think he did not want to be missed."

"Help . . . move."

She appeared amused.

"Mr. Kane, you have a busted arm, some busted ribs, two broke fingers, your face is purple and blue and black and green, and a huge bunch of you is all dark, bruised, prune color. The swelling on your eyes has gone down enough so that they kind of open. I don't think you should try to go anywhere right now. Your feet might work, but everything else from there up . . . well, it doesn't!"

He kept trying to move. It hurt.

She reached under his arms. "Mama said you would not listen, and I should have a stick to beat you! Here, try sitting."

He groaned unconsciously as she pulled him up. By now, his eyes were working, except for the big something in the way of the left. He guessed it was something swollen. The first thing he saw were his toes poking out from under a blanket. He wiggled them.

"They work!" giggled Libby. "It is about all of you that does. You got shot in the leg, too, but Mama said that is more like a big bee sting than anything else. She knows a lot about putting people together when they get broken things."

Kane saw a long strip of cloth wrapped tightly around his right arm, with sticks underneath the wrapping. Three fingers on his right hand were tied together and wrapped. Nothing on the left. The blanket had fallen to his lap. More bandage was wrapped around his ribs. As he was waking up, he was realizing how much he hurt.

"Water. More."

Libby held the cup. He drank on his own this time.

"How long?"

"Five days," she said. "Mama thought you would live, I think, but it took a couple of days for her to be sure. She knows when you're hurt and when you're not. I can never fool her when I want to pretend to be sick to get out of chores."

He could hear fast-moving feet, but they stopped suddenly. Turning his head was an effort. Rachel was framed in the doorway. Kane could vaguely see some emotion on her face but could not define it, if it was even there and not a trick of blurry vision. It passed.

Libby turned to her mother.

"Can you watch the patient now so I can feed the calf?"

"Yes, boss," replied Rachel.

"You split anything open that Mama sewed shut, and I am going to be mad because she promised me we are going riding later, and, if she has to sew you again, we can't go!" Libby admonished Kane before leaving.

Rachel sat on the edge of the bed. Kane could see that she was watching Libby as she left. Even with blurry vision, there was a smile on her face.

"You and my daughter. A pair." A hand reached out. Touched

his. "She made herself a bed and has been in here since Seamus brought you." She inspected him briefly. "I did not see the entertainment in that, myself."

Kane said nothing. A less-intense Rachel Wilkins was not something he understood, and his mind was not comprehending much other than being alive.

"Why here?"

"I believe that Seamus thought you were a family friend," she said, mouth twisting as she accented the last word. "He knew Jared was not what the world thought he was, and he was very kind to Libby when the children in town were cruel. He knew you came here because of us, but he did not know why. I did not tell him. I told you I was waiting for the Spirit to tell me what I should do. It was not the message I expected, but I accept it."

Kane could not follow. Halloran? "Why did he . . ."

"Who knows?" admitted Rachel. "Seamus has so many pasts that I don't know if any of them are real. From what he said before he left, and that was not very much, he thought you were trying to do the right thing for those people in Rakeheart without knowing that they were all rotten."

He still did not understand. Perhaps another time.

"Janie?"

"Some woman in town took her. I do not know if she is alive or dead. If she was your friend, I am sorry. I think she always thought Clem would sweep her away some day to some better place." Rachel shook her head. "She never knew him. Another woman who doesn't know her man." Bitter.

Kane recalled what he could remember from the street. It was not pleasant.

"I should leave. This is dangerous. They said . . ."

"No. We have so little to do with the place, no one comes here very often. The last time they came to ask about selling, which was about a week before you arrived, I made it clear who was and was not welcome on my land. They might come back to push me off, but Seamus made it sound as though they have bigger problems right now." She paused. "It is good for you that they will not show their faces. I think Jeremiah could beat you in a fight the way you look right now."

"Can you help me up?"

"You will try, I suppose, if I leave you here alone, and then you would fall and do exactly what Libby told you not to do. I will help you, but you will not like what happens. And if you wonder what you are wearing, it is a nightshirt of Jared's. Your clothes had so much dried blood on them we all but cut them off of you."

She was right. Sitting was bad. Standing, if she was not holding on, would have been impossible. Even with her grabbing him, he thought he would fall over. He was determined to stay standing as long as he could. Revenge was already calling.

"How bad is my arm?"

"A month and you can use it. Maybe less; maybe more. One bone was badly broken, the other cracked. Seamus said they used a piece of lumber to break it. You are lucky the bone was not crushed."

"My hand?"

"One finger broken, but not badly. Others bruised. A week or two and you will be using it. Your ribs will heal in time. I don't know how badly they hurt you inside," she added. "The buckshot in your leg was the least of it, but it was in deep, and I don't dig out tiny shot very well, so you will limp a while. About everything from your hips to your shoulders was a bruise. They beat you pretty good."

"They did."

"Why?"

"Man said it was business that got personal."

"Did you go up against the Riders?"

"Might say so." He pulled her hard as a wave of dizziness came. She put both arms around him to steady him.

"Sit."

But the doorway called. Air and life. It took time, but they finally reached the doorway, where he stood, supporting himself on the door frame as he breathed fresh, clean air that smelled of life. He took a step outside, then leaned against the wall, dizzy.

"Here." She brought a chair from the house, pushed it against the outside wall, and guided him into it. She brought a coat and draped it over him.

"Sit and stay. I have to cook some food, or we will all starve. I assume now that you have rejoined the living, you will make up for lost time eating."

There was that smile again. He wondered what the one he tried to make back at her looked like.

Food. He felt his stomach rumble. He listened to her noises. He smelled the land and felt the air. The sun on his face was warm and healing, not what he had felt face up in the street back in Rakeheart. What to do next would come to him. For now, he was alive and making plans to make someone regret that.

Libby hauled the small wagon. It was heavy for her, but she would not hear of Kane pulling it. He had found a gun. For three days he had been loafing and eating. Enough was enough. Man with work to do had to do it.

Halloran had used Tecumseh to toss him on when he rescued him from Rakeheart. Kane was glad to see the stallion. Men were fools about animals, and he was no different, but he was certain the horse was glad to see him, too. Kane had yet to try to ride. It meant moving more parts than could move.

He had to start with what would take the longest.

Kane realized how hard the chore would be after he barely managed to pry the top off the box of shells Libby had hauled. Then he tried loading the gun. It was something he did without thinking, back when he had two arms and two hands.

"Do you need help?"

He had pride. He had plans. Plans won. He showed Libby how to load the revolver. She knew how to load a rifle and had brought hers along, so it was easy.

"How can you shoot with your arm like that?" she asked.

"Got two arms," he told her.

He held the gun in his left hand. Strange but not unfamiliar. He looked at the hunk of wood Libby had set on a fencepost. Hefted the gun. Went back to a different time.

The farm was a hard place, and 1862 was a hard year, especially after Shiloh. A skinny fourteen-year-old boy who thought he was the family's protector was going to be ready to fight the Yankees when they came. Hours they spent together. Him, that old gun, and Nightmare, a massive, black barn cat who sat on a fence post and watched Kane practice for what seemed like hours.

He was left handed by birth. Shot that way until Uncle Zeb brought home a gun belt with the holster on the right and told him real men shot with their right hands. Worked so well he never went back. Until now.

He tried aiming. Everything felt wrong. He could see from Libby's face after loading the gun for him several times that watching an adult fail miserably at something he was trying hard to get right was as hard on her as it was on him.

"Takes time," he told her. "Learned it once. I'll learn it again."

"Are you going after the men who hurt you?"

Lies were an attractive option when talking to children. Libby would spot it.

"Expect so."

"I don't think you should."

"Why not?"

"Mama was saying you would do that and get killed, and it would be a shame because you were a good man. Mama likes you, you know."

"And she spent all that time sewing me back together." Kane grinned at the girl.

"Well, that, too, of course," she replied. "But she had to. Otherwise you would make such a mess all over."

She handed the loaded gun back.

"Last time," he called. Miss after miss.

Then he could hear Uncle Harry, who was not his uncle but some family friend who lived on the farm while he was hiding from the law.

"Not your hand and your eye. Aim with your soul," he told Kane when first teaching him to shoot.

The piece of wood spun. He had barely nicked it, but for today it gave him hope. It would come. In time. He did not have much. Mid-August would slide into fall quickly. This had to be done before the snow.

"There!" Libby said. "Is there anything else I can teach you today?"

Kane grinned.

For the first time since he had awakened on the Wilkins ranch, Kane felt that he was going to get better—not only to stay alive, but to even the score.

"Guess you won't be dying this day, Friend Badge," Halloran grunted after surveying Kane.

"You seem mighty sober for a drunken fella," Kane observed as they walked to stable Halloran's borrowed horse in the Wilkins barn.

"There is not time for a drop when there is work that must

be done," he said. "Later, I shall talk to you, Friend Badge."

Libby's whooping, unrestrained joy at seeing Halloran stirred an odd pang of jealousy in Kane. The child loved the curmudgeon, for whatever reason. And she was hardly Kane's. For a moment, he realized he was merely passing through all these lives.

Passing through. Was that all his life was? Seemed so.

The children were in bed, although Kane was pretty sure Libby would lie awake and listen, when he, Rachel, and Halloran huddled by the small fire still glowing in the hearth.

Halloran had repeated the full story over and over. No one was really sure who shot who on the night Kane was beaten. Two Riders were injured, that was for sure. One might have died later. Two townspeople were wounded as well.

Janie was shot bad but was not dead. Tillie Witherspoon had taken her in and threatened to shoot anyone who came near, including her father. No one Halloran knew had the courage to broach her defenses.

Pete Haliburton was wounded, but no one knew how badly until they found him the next morning in his stable, where he had passed out on the floor, blood all over. Some people there said Janie had wounded him. The bullet damaged his right shoulder. He would live, but he would most likely never swing a hammer again or work as a blacksmith. Others said the wound was minor, but Haliburton had used it as a pretext now that his daughter was shot so badly she might not live.

Halloran said the Haliburtons were damage from a showdown that grew beyond anyone's control.

"Best I can tell, it all got out of hand," Halloran said, with more anger than usual and minus his usual jovial patter. "They came to use you to teach the town a lesson. Noonan pretty much said so a few days ago. I think Janie thought Wood was sweet on her, and then she figured he was using her, and I think she might have been drunk, too."

Kane tried to focus on the meaning and stared at Halloran closely. The Irishman cleared his throat and then resumed his story.

"Those Riders, they were powerful mad, Friend Badge, when you were gone, but then that Noonan gent came out and talked to that Wood man as though he was somebody that the Riders would listen to. So the tale was told to me, you understand. The Riders took off like bats. I heard the next day or two there were Riders watching like toll-keepers along the road to the fort, should some nosy soul seek to tell the army. No one did, Friend Badge, and Rakeheart has been quiet. No one quite knows where you are or if you are coming back. For your sake, I should hope you do what is right for all."

"Who helped me?" he asked. Halloran didn't answer.

"It was you and Tillie, wasn't it?"

"If she was a man, Friend Badge, she would have cleaned up the town that night."

Kane tried to take it all in. The Riders pulled the trigger, but it was his fault.

"You don't understand what happened, do ye?" asked Halloran.

"I poked my nose where it didn't belong," Kane spoke.

Halloran rolled his eyes.

"He's not as bright as he looks," said Rachel, seeming to enjoy Kane being the target. "It's all those colors he has on his face distracting his thinking."

"Thought it was, dear Rachel, his thinking that led to all those colors on his face," Halloran remarked as they both snickered at Kane's expense.

"Tell me what it was all about," Kane said.

"The Riders work for the town," said Halloran. "They protect the town against the other towns."

"I got that."

"But the price of protection keeps going up, so I hear, which means the good town fathers would like to be rid of the Riders, but they have no one to stop them. They hired you, Friend Badge, hoping that maybe a man good with a gun might be enough to let the town fathers dictate terms to the Riders. The Riders came to send a message that, no matter what the town wants, they are in charge."

"They are vile men," spat Rachel. "Those men, and that Silas Noonan. They are all bad. The rest of them are not much better. The store man, Mr. Conroy, he tries to be nice, but he is old. The rest should burn."

Kane's head hurt. "I don't understand why they didn't just shoot me," he said.

"Ahh, but think, boyo. If the sheriff is killed by a gang, will the army not come to clean out the gang? Why do you think the Riders never killed you? Killing you crosses a line. Telling every man what they get for crossing them only makes them stronger. They have the upper hand, and the town is cowed."

But had they not left him to die? Without Halloran's aid, they would have crossed that line. The room moved. There was a flaw in Halloran's logic, but he could not find it.

Kane felt very stupid. He had been so focused on Sherman's mission he had put himself in a situation where the only real surprise was that he was, in fact, alive. He tried to think of ways he could get revenge on them all. Halloran talked about ways he could get out of Rakeheart unseen.

Tired of listening to such plans, Rachel ordered them both into silence.

"Kane?" Rachel put a hand on his left arm. She had assumed some level of ownership over him in these past days. "I know you are trying to figure this out, but in case you do not understand, because Libby told me what you said, you might want to think twice at some level other than your usual level of thought about ever going back to Rakeheart."

"Why?"

"You don't understand, do you?" Rachel's tone was as gentle as he had ever heard. "You probably suit the town better dead than alive. Now that they know you can't stand up to the Riders alone, that you can't whip them single-handed, they don't need you alive, and they don't want you alive. You so much as walk one step back into that nasty place, there's a target on your back every minute. The only one to stop the Riders is the army, and the only way the army rides in, is if the sheriff gets killed. Seamus was telling me the way it is for you there. You cannot ever go back if you want to stay alive. It is time to look to something else. Seamus has some ideas."

He could see her face monitor his reaction until she was sure he fully understood her meaning.

"You lost, Kane. You can't win. It's over."

Kane wanted to rage; to insist she was wrong.

But she was right.

Kane had gone outside, with the excuse that he felt dizzy and needed air. In truth, he felt the unwelcome approach of defeat. He had come close in Texas. Many times. There was always a way; always a plan; always something.

Not here. Not now.

He saw the brief square of light as the door to the house opened and shut. "Kane?"

"Here."

He did not hear her until she was next to him.

"You cannot help it, Kane. They are bad people. I know what Jared became from being around them. Everything that was good and kind in him was gone. You do not have to go back there. Count yourself lucky."

"Lucky?" He could hear the edge of wild emotion in his words. "I have an arm I can't use. I can't always see right. I can't shoot a gun. I came out here to do one simple job, and I can't do that because I'm not ever telling Sherman the truth—no way, Rachel. Give me one reason I should not ride into that town and take as many of them as I can before they get me."

"I don't want you to."

"Why? You of all people should! Me dead, no one ever learns the secret about Jared's death!"

"I should slap you!"

Kane had regretted the words. "Maybe you should. I am sorry, Rachel. Can't imagine what it was like."

"No, you can't. And you can't imagine what it would be like to explain to Libby how her friend—and she thinks of you as a friend because you act about her age—rode off to get himself shot instead of staying alive to be her friend!"

Kane swallowed. Rachel's intensity was daunting. He never quite thought of Libby as liking him. Or anyone else.

"I can't let this go, Rachel."

"Can't or won't?"

"Man is what a man does. It comes down to my fault. I thought I could face them down, and Janie paid for that. Those other folks who got shot . . . I'm responsible. That gets squared."

"Why? Because Janie was your woman?"

"Because she got herself bad hurt—dead maybe by now for all I know—killed tryin' to do somethin' to save me or some-thin' to help. I can't . . . can't let that ride, Rachel. Won't."

"You are a fool!"

"You think they will wait? They think I'm your friend, Jared's friend. How long before they come sniffing? Or come riding?

Only so many places to hide a wounded sheriff. Me or them, woman."

"Us."

"Huh?"

"Us or them, Kane. You do not have to fight them alone. I . . . Libby . . . oh, men! You have been good and kind and honest, Kane. You could put me in your jail. Your town would hang me and never think twice. You did not. I owe you."

He shook his head. "No. You got it backwards, Rachel. Got more courage in your finger than I got in my body."

A yellow square appeared and vanished. A hinge protested.

"Mama?"

"Libby!"

Mumbling about not being able to see what she was looking for, the girl's voice grew louder as she walked closer. "Where are they?" she finally asked.

"Where are what, Libby?" Kane called.

"Uncle Seamus told me to come outside and find you because he said there might be sparking out here, and I don't see any."

"I will give that man sparks," Rachel muttered. "Telling my daughter . . ."

Kane could not stop laughing.

He reached out his good hand to touch Rachel's arm. "Let it go. Explaining what 'sparking' is about between a man and a woman is only going to make it worse."

"Indeed. That man!"

Libby was up to them.

"Where are the sparks?"

"C'mon Libby," said Kane. "Maybe we can find some out that way." He touched her right hand with his good one. "Bet your mom will find some, too."

"Kane . . ."

"Oh, good. Come on, Mama, let's all go sparking-hunting."

"You two go," she said. "I have to go back inside and have a very firm talk with Uncle Seamus."

They went.

The gun bucked in his hand. Again. Again. Again.

The piece of wood was unmoved by the noise, or his shooting. Some days were good. This one was not.

It still hurt to breathe. His right arm was a purple mass. Touching something the wrong way with his right hand sent a wave of pain to his shoulder, but most days now he could use it to load the gun if he went slow enough. Some days he only dropped half the bullets.

Libby was watching. She had been faithful in going with him to where he practiced. Afterwards, they would find flowers, animals, or enjoy walking in the warm Wyoming sunshine. She would play the wooden flute he gave her. Sometimes well. Always happily.

When evening rolled around, he and Libby would talk about whether she had picked the right place on the moon for her garden, while Rachel watched in wonder as her daughter grew closer to Kane than she ever had to Wilkins.

Rachel insisted the arm would need weeks before she could take the sticks out of the wrappings and weeks more before the arm was usable. It had been two weeks since he awoke on her ranch. Almost three weeks since his beating. It was time.

He noticed Rachel watching. She could smell the scent of decision.

She walked up to him with displeasure on her face. "You are preparing to be a fool," she said directly.

"Yes, ma'am."

"I thought you understood this is not a fight you can win."

"Understandin' and quittin' are different."

"Tell me your plan."

"Don't have one."

"Kane!" She started to rage.

"I'm not Jared," he said.

That silenced her.

"Rakeheart does not mean more than you, than seeing that girl of yours laugh or that boy of yours try to figure how worms move," he said. "This is personal. You tell me to walk away. I don't know how to do that, Rachel. I can't do it. I was ready to let it all go, but not now. I can't look at what comes next until I set this to rights. There was more in that town that was crooked, and I think it cost you your foreman. And them Riders . . . there's an accounting to be made. I know your friend Halloran means well when he keeps telling me to pack up and get out, and to take you folks with me, but I can't do that."

"Kane, I do not want to bury you. I have lost one man that I . . . I don't want to . . ." She stopped. Her eyes looked wet. "Men!"

She was gone.

Libby, who had given the adults space for their conversation, now came over.

"You should take me with you when you clean up Rakeheart," she said.

"Libby, you're too young."

"Am I?" she said archly. She picked up her rifle and, standing fifty yards from the wooden target Kane had been missing as much as hitting, emptied the rifle into the target.

"I didn't know you could shoot that well," Kane said.

"Pa taught me," she said.

"Good shooting."

"Mama can't hit the sky with a gun," she said, laughing. "That's why she carries the shotgun, because she can still hit something. I never saw her ever hit anything with a rifle. I never miss."

Kane saw her face reflect what she saw on his. She had said something that made the scales fall from his eyes. It was almost painful. So close to the truth, but so far.

Now, he knew.

"You lied to me!" he seethed to Rachel as they stood by the fireplace, the roll of blankets she used as a bed since his arrival curled by her feet.

She had food cooking in an iron kettle. The house smelled of fresh bread. Sweat glistened on her forehead from the heat.

"No. I let you believe what you wanted."

"I want the truth."

"Yes," she admitted. "Yes. I . . . I was not sure what you would do when you said you knew. I let you believe a lie, but it was necessary."

"Why?"

"Kane, Libby and I know what you are thinking just from the look on your face. Do you think if I had told you what happened that you could for one minute not let Libby know that you knew she killed Jared? Do you think you could pretend, and it would make no difference? I told you: I will protect Libby until after my body is done breathing. What if you told someone? They would destroy her if she ever set foot in that town. What difference does it make? It is different with me."

"I want the truth."

"Jared was drunk. He and I had a horrible argument. For the first time, Kane, I fought back. I was not going to let him hurt her or me any longer. He laughed, Kane. He knew there was no place for me to go. We both thought Libby and Jeremiah were asleep. He told me he was going to teach me a lesson I would never forget. He dragged me out to the barn. I tried to fight him. I never screamed. I did not want Libby to know my shame. That's what it is, Kane. Shame.

"But Libby was outside in a spot she went for comfort, even though she was forbidden to be out alone at night.

"We reached the barn. She called his name. He told her to go back to bed or she would get what was coming to her. She told him to let me go. He hit me in the face. She fired her gun. I can still hear the echo. It was so loud—louder than I ever heard it before. It sounded like more than one gun, it was so loud. I do not know if she meant to hit him or warn him. She is good, but it was dark, Kane. She was horrified at what she did. He was dead in a moment or two. He never said anything coherent.

"I told Libby we would make up a story. No one seemed to care. I think Clem figured it out, but he would never tell. The army man knew there was something wrong in our story, but no one else knew anything, and he went away. I don't think he really cared as long as there was nothing that would make work for the army. Then you came, and I knew you would not stop. I knew it when I saw you."

"Libby tried to tell me."

"She *what*?"

"She tried to tell me. She wanted me to know you were not the one responsible. Said you were in your room. She wanted to tell me but didn't know how."

It was silent.

Kane moved stiffly to the door.

"Good-bye, Rachel. Once or twice I wondered . . . you and me . . . guess it all don't matter now. I better go."

"You can't go!"

Libby was in the doorway, blocking his path.

"Mama did what she had to. We didn't know you. I was afraid, Mr. Kane."

"Even when you both knew me, sweetheart, you lied to me."

"Mr. Kane!" It was a wail of misery.

"Ride with God, Libby."

He put his hands on her shoulders, set her to the side, and walked out of the Wilkins house.

CHAPTER FIFTEEN

Rakeheart was in sight. If anything had changed in the weeks he had been away, it was not visible at a distance.

Not wanting to ride in to Rakeheart at night, he had ridden to the shack he was now calling home after riding furiously away from the Wilkins ranch. He was spending a sleepless night until he gave it up altogether.

They lied to him. It was that simple. He kept repeating that as his anger ebbed away like flour spilling out of a hole in a sack.

Libby's tear-streaked face appeared in his mind. Did it matter if their reasons were good, and he would probably do the same thing if he had a child? He told himself it did not. He was not very convincing.

He could leave. Maybe he should leave. Rakeheart meant nothing to him. He had ridden away from the only thing that meant much in all of Hall County, and he had no idea how to go back.

He had told himself he had three things to do—make the Riders pay; find out who killed Clem Ferguson and Frank Kruger; and cut the head off whoever was pulling the Riders' strings. Then he would leave and never look back.

Wood was a brute. Someone else was the brains. Noonan? Made sense to start there.

The first bird's song was starting in the pre-dawn dimness when he eventually nodded off. The sun was full up when he woke, and he was stiff and sore. The landscape eased some of the anger in his head as he took his time. Time was all he had.

The horse had wandered a bit in the night to where the grass was tall but came when he saw Kane stagger out of the shack. Kane felt guilty for not tying him to the tree. He stroked the animal's long face as he turned his own battered one to the sun to let it warm him. Once again, he thought of riding on. Once again, he rejected common sense.

He flexed his right hand. Not good for much. He could pretend to use it when he dismounted, but if he put any real weight on it, the game was over.

He took the gun out of the jury-rigged holster on his left hip. Set it back in loose. It was about fifty-fifty he would hit what he aimed at. He didn't think that would stay a secret very long unless he was a whole lot smarter than he felt. There was always someone who wanted to find out. Always.

Preacher Siegel was slack-jawed as Kane looped Tecumseh's reins around the rail.

"Sheriff . . . I thought . . . we heard . . ."

Kane forced his arm up to touch his hat with his right hand. A thousand times in practice made him expect the way it would hurt. It didn't disappoint.

"Riders in town?"

"No . . . um . . . no, Sheriff. They came by last week for some provisions, and they went to Noonan's, but there was no trouble."

Big surprise. No one would dare. That was the point. He could feel hot anger welling up.

"Pete Haliburton still around?"

Siegel looked in the dirt. "Pete drank too much before. I don't think he even tries to work now. I went to see him on account of his wound, and he threw a bottle at me with the arm he was supposedly wounded in."

"I'll talk to him. What about Janie?"

"She is still alive, Kane. Mrs. Witherspoon has refused to let anyone in to see her and made a very un-Christian remark when I said that my attendance could only but help her, but she said the girl was alive. She has not moved since she was shot, Tillie said, but she has not died, either. I do not know what that means."

"I'll see them both."

"Are you . . . I mean . . . how are you?"

"Oh, fine, Preacher. You tell everyone you meet that I am. Hear, Preacher?"

The menace and meaning were clear.

"Yes, sir. I mean, yes, Sheriff."

Kane stopped at the Cartwright house. Mae had no bruises, was looking happy, and made him coffee. She had heard that he was beaten but said as little as possible. Bill was working with Conroy. Their world was so focused on getting through every day, everything else seemed remote. She kept most of her questions to herself and answered all of his. The town had carried on as normal, she said.

"One of the people told Bill, and he told me, but it was all jumbled. Some people said you were dead and others that you only got a little hurt in some fight." She paused. "I am glad you are alive, Sheriff. You were good to Bill and me."

"Glad things are better."

"Some people were nice. Eloise Brewer came by one day with some food. I really could not imagine why."

"I never told her a thing."

"In a town this small, Sheriff, people always talk. The neighbors told their neighbors, and probably everyone knows by now, but no one will say anything. She was so sympathetic and kind. You know, when you see her she is always so quiet and almost aloof, but the way she talked, you would think that she lived through what I had—and worse. It was nice of her to be concerned."

Kane wondered about that. Brewer was the bullying kind of man who pushed everyone around. Was he also a man who used his fists on his wife? Not something he could ask.

He had put it off long enough. He downed the rest of the coffee and walked as slowly as he had ever walked down the main street of Rakeheart.

Soon he was there. Where it happened. No marks. No stain where Janie had bled; where he had bled. Trampled away, washed away. Forgotten.

No.

He took a long look at the doorway of Noonan's. He was aware people were talking. He didn't much care.

He pushed the doors open wide as he entered, letting them bang to announce his entrance.

He walked slowly to the bar, taking his time to look here and there, from side to side—the sheriff way to tell everyone he was watching. There were more than a few stares back, and a lot of buzz as voices began to fill in the gap of noise his entrance had created.

"Beer."

He had put the nickel in his right hand when he entered and tossed it on the bar with his right hand. He used the hand to raise the glass and hold it as he sipped the watery mix, wishing from the taste he could spit it on the floor. But it had to be done. Folks needed to see and spread the word.

Noonan would either be watching or be told every detail. It needed to be a very convincing show.

"Later." He nodded at the bartender and sauntered away as though it were nothing more than another day.

It was not.

"Didn't think you would show your face."

Kane was fully of the opinion that had he let Bud Franklin shoot Kevin Morris the world would have been a better place and his life a simpler life. Most young men outgrew adolescent meanness. Some, like Morris, embraced it their whole lives.

"Kevin. Had to come back, see if you might amount to anything."

Morris, who had been drinking again with a different crowd of hangers-on, rose unsteadily. Kane had been told the young man's father had run a ranch and died, leaving the boy too much money and too much time on his hands.

"Town needs a real man for sheriff," Morris said, puffing up.

"This your interview for the job?"

Morris moved away from the table, becoming briefly entangled in his chair. When he looked up, Kane had the Colt pointed at him in a rock-steady left hand.

"First, Kevin, set the gun on the table so it don't go off and hurt someone."

The young man looked around. No one who had been telling him great things only a moment ago was there now. He did as he was told.

"Outside."

They were at the trough where Wood had dunked Kane. The onlookers were inside, waiting for their entertainment.

"Kevin, I can probably make you dunk your own head in there. Pretty sure I can. What do you think?"

"I . . . I guess so."

"Got no call to humiliate anyone. Know how it feels. You got a ranch, fella, and you got a life, and you been lettin' 'em both slip through your fingers. Look at that doorway. Look!"

Morris shifted his attention from Kane to the crowded doorway of the salon, and the windows packed with customers.

"Nobody there to help, Kevin. Way of the world. On the day you need them, there's nobody to help." Kane stepped closer. "I can kill you easy enough. Strong is not about killin', Kevin. It's about doin' the right thing. Won't tell you that you can't come to town. Hope you figger that maybe there's more to life than what you been doin' with it. If not, fella, we are gonna do this dance again, and it won't be fun for either of us, because I know how it ends.

"Get me the man's gun," Kane called. When someone said they had it, Kane told whoever the man was to toss it to Morris. He did.

"All of you," Kane said. "Go about your business. Kevin, go about yours. No hard feelin's. Way I see it, you've about used up all the warnings you get in this world. Learn from them, or you will wish you did. The rest of you, how many times you got to see a man humiliated before it is enough entertainment?"

The stable door was open. Haliburton was sprawled on the dirt. The man stank. Bottles littered the hay. Whatever wound he had received, if he had been wounded at all, there was no evidence of a bandage. Kane figured this time he might as well act, since words would be pointless.

The water in the trough looked disgusting, but Kane plunged the man's head in anyhow after dragging him one-handed across the stable.

Haliburton came up, sputtering. Down. Up. Down. Up.

After his arm started to hurt, Kane let go.

"What . . . what . . ."

"Tell me what happened the night she got shot."

"Kane? You were dead."

"Tell me." Implacable.

Haliburton told. The Riders always kept their horses at this stable and paid him for information about the town and what it was up to.

"You told them about me."

"They were bound to hear it sooner or later."

"What about that night?"

"You had braced them, and they was fuming about it. I told them that night maybe I could work something out . . . um, so's you and they could talk this out."

"Don't lie to me."

"Didn't know what they planned!"

"You knew enough!"

Haliburton wailed. He had told the Riders Janie was sweet on Kane, and she could get Kane alone in a place he would not expect a trap. Wood told her they wanted Kane to ask about a job. She did not know something else had been in the plan until after Kane was dragged away to his humiliation. He admitted he figured there might be more than talk, but he didn't expect what happened.

"Never seem any of 'em so angry with any one man," he said.

"At least your daughter knew enough to do something about it!"

"She called me names . . . no daughter should call a father that . . . after they took you; she called me Judas and smashed things, and then she went off with my gun. She didn't understand! All I ever did was try to make enough to provide for her . . . she couldn't see that there was no way to fight these people. Thought that Rider Wood she was sweet on would want her, but he didn't, and she never told me."

"Which people, Haliburton?"

"All of 'em. Town created the Riders; now the Riders own the town." His head weaved and sagged and lolled, then came up sharply. "Where is she?"

"A good place. A safe place."

"I want to see her."

"Maybe when you deserve it and climb out of your bottle.

Quit faking and start being a man." Kane spun on his heel and left the pitiful wreck of a man behind. Not evil, but weak, broken, and now shattered.

He turned back. "You want redemption? Go find Halloran. You do whatever that man says. He'll know when it is time to fight back."

"He's a drunk!"

"So are you!"

He left. Stopped cold.

Rachel's wagon was hitched in the street by Conroy's store. He stared at it. He did not plan to walk towards it, but his feet kept moving. He reminded himself to walk there slowly, in the pose of a man with not a care in the world and endless time on his hands. He told himself there was no reason to enter the store.

None at all.

Conroy's smile seemed unaffected.

"They told me you were back," he said, nervous eyes betraying his thoughts. "How . . ."

"Wyoming beatings don't hold a candle to the ones down in Texas," Kane said with a grin he did not feel. He had a sudden inspiration. "Had to go to Fort Laramie a spell. Army business I can't talk about."

He could see Rachel frown as she looked his way. They had politely greeted each other in passing when he entered. He wondered how much his face told her. Hers said nothing to the world, as always.

"You work with the army?"

Kane wondered if it would be one hour or two before the whole town knew the sheriff none of them bothered to help might be working for the army now.

"About what happened . . . I'm not young, Kane . . ."

Kane held up his good hand to stop the words. He didn't

want to hear it. Being afraid of men with guns who could use them wasn't fear—it was also a thing called common sense, which he did not possess. Anyhow, he still had a question to ask and did not want Conroy to have his guard up when it was asked.

"Need a couple things. Still got that Remington? Need a good holster, too, for the other hip. Gonna carry two guns."

"I have just the thing in the back, and, yes, the gun is still here. Oh, I am glad to see it go to good hands!" Conroy bustled, stopping to ask Rachel if she needed assistance as she took an extraordinary amount of time looking at some blue cloth. She smiled politely and silently shook her head.

Kane walked near her and looked at what seemed to be fifty identical shirts.

"Why are you here?"

"Have I broken the law, Sheriff?"

"Rachel, this is no place . . ."

". . . for a woman whose men keep getting shot dead? I think it is exactly the place. And for your understanding, Kane, the lecture I got from my daughter for letting you leave the ranch was worse than any I ever gave her. My choices were very clear— either I could come here and try to knock sense into your head, or she would do it for me."

"Libby?"

"Good. You remember her name. Do not forget it when you are tempted to do something stupid."

"Mr. Conroy?" she called in dulcet tones Kane had never heard before. "I have to see Mr. Brewer at the bank. I will be back in a few minutes when that is over. I want to browse a little more, but I made an appointment when I stopped there first thing this morning, and I dare not be late."

Conroy was bustling and nodding as he emerged.

"Yes, Mrs. Wilkins, I'll be here. Take all the time you want.

Sheriff, give me one minute. I know that gun is there. My new assistant puts everything in order, and now I don't know where anything is," he said as he returned to the back room.

"Frank Brewer has asked me to stop to see him," Rachel said softly. "He seemed very anxious and oily when he saw us drive in this morning. I believe from the way he said it, he wants to make an offer for the ranch."

"You should . . ."

"Tell him what I wish," she finished, giving him a look he had come to recognize.

Kane swallowed. " 'Zackly."

For a second, he was sure Rachel's stern façade registered a smile, but it was gone before he could be sure.

"Rachel, I . . ."

She talked as though what he was saying did not matter. Perhaps it didn't.

"I will have tea with Mrs. Jeffries later. In that time, I shall learn everything I wish to know about everyone since my last trip here and far more I do not wish to know. As a widow, I am watched for any least politeness with a man because you white people are like that—as if I am supposed to live alone forever—so please do not approach me out there. I do not mean to be rude. I assume you are as clueless about gossip as everything else. If there is something I wish to speak to you about, you will find out."

He nodded. "Libby? Where is she?"

"The people who run the Last Chance are fond of her and Jeremiah, and they are there eating far too much."

"Rachel, I . . ." There was an apology somewhere that had unexpectedly demanded to rise to the surface, but she moved to the door before it emerged.

"Do not get shot in front of her, Kane."

Rachel left the shop.

CHAPTER SIXTEEN

Kane was back on the far side of the store when Conroy came out with a black leather gun belt with holsters for two guns. The shop owner pulled out the Remington and gave him a box of shells for the gun, then refused his money.

"Figger we owe you, son."

Kane felt a bit guilty as he loaded the gun and spun the cylinder—then, holding it in his left hand, pointed it at the old man's nose, inches from his face.

"You lied about Tompkins. Place was never a ranch. He never had a wife. My guess, he got himself killed. I want the truth."

"Well, Sheriff, I'm sorry! It . . . we were all . . . you see . . ."

"You were smuggling things that were either stolen from the army or the Indians, and somewhere around here was a way station along the way," Kane said flatly. "If I had to guess, that place was near where the Riders are holed up."

Conroy looked ashamed. Kane felt guilty. Then he thought of Janie.

"Few years back, Ken was hauling things. If we protected him, we made a profit. Store was doing poorly; we thought it might make a few dollars to keep things going, and he was going to go ahead—if not here, it would have been another place. Maybe it wasn't right, Kane, but we didn't really break the law."

"You helped someone else break it."

"When you say it like that . . ."

"What happened to him?"

"He and the Riders had a falling-out. Not sure of the details, but I think they killed him, or ran him off. Most likely, he's dead. That was when it started."

"What started?"

"When all this started, Kane, the Riders worked for Rakeheart. Now, they are asking for more and more. We've got no protection against them, and they know that. We work for them. They don't ask for too much. They know what we can give, as if one of us is telling them what they need to know. This Kruger fella—know you asked about him—some of us thought he was with them. We wondered about Wilkins, because his sudden intrusion into town affairs coincided with the collapse of the relationship between the Riders and the town. Now don't tell Brewer and them what I said, because they think they can manage this. I think it is a fire out of control, but I have no idea how to stop it. I'm too old to fight, Kane. I only want to run a store."

Kane guessed Conroy had given him what he had. He offered the man little mercy and less reassurance. They had made a deal with the devil, and now they were coming to regret it when it was far too late.

Regrets. He looked at Rachel's wagon as he passed it. Yup. Everybody had them.

Kane had put the new Remington in his left holster, his old Colt in the right, and dumped the shells in his saddlebags.

The arm was hurting, but he had to pretend it did not as he walked up one side of the street and down the next. So far, no one had challenged him. As men came and went, he wondered which ones were bound for the Riders' hideout. He was sure someone was.

They would come. Maybe the talk about the army would make them think. Either that or it would make them hurry. Either worked for him.

In the meantime, he needed to see about Janie. Tillie Witherspoon opened the door, upbraiding him for being out and about in his condition. She kept talking and moving in front of Kane as he tried to get past her to the back room. He heard a man's voice. With his good left hand pushing Tillie aside, he moved as fast as he could to the back room.

Chad Washburn, very sober, was standing by Janie's bed with a gun pointed his way.

"Put it down, Chad." He did.

"He's been here almost every minute since she got hurt, Sheriff," Tillie said softly, trying to avoid a shootout in her bedroom.

"She's a nice girl," said Chad. "Didn't deserve to get mixed up with those Riders and shot. She . . . we . . . we kept company a while back, Sheriff. Went our separate ways. I let her go, and I should never have done it, because she made fun of me. But she was right, and I was wrong. She's a good girl, and I ain't gonna lose her."

Janie was as white as the sheet upon which she lay. He looked the question at Tillie as he knelt next to her. He felt her weak breath when he put a hand near her mouth.

"She lost a lot of blood. One shot hit her in the side of the head. I did the best I could. That barber is worthless. She barely breathes, but she breathes. She has not woken up. I think she is dying, but I don't really know. We watch her, and we wait. It is all we can do."

Kane stood up.

"Sheriff, you call me when you go after 'em," Chad said. "Know maybe I made some mistakes, but I'm not what I was. I'll get even for her. I should have been here to protect her. I know Pa said only quitters want it easy."

Kane watched Tillie's face watch the boy. He touched Chad gently on the arm. "Take care of her, son. When it's time, I'll let you know. You got a man's work to care for her. Do that, and you're doing all anyone asks."

Tillie Witherspoon eyed him critically as he went to leave.

"Did Rachel actually let you out in your condition? You look terrible, Sheriff."

"Wilkins family is not a subject I care to talk about, ma'am."

"Harrumph. Don't try to fool me, Sheriff. I know the lay of the land in this town. The poor woman deserves better. So do a lot of others, but do not get me started on that Brewer man again. Now go about your business and finish it this time!"

Kane had a smile as he left. He wondered, if all the men suddenly vanished, if the indomitable women of the West would settle the territory every bit as fast. Maybe faster.

He went back to making his rounds of the town, making sure every last person that could tell the tale knew that Sheriff Kane was back.

He saw Libby and Jeremiah walking ahead. He wanted to talk; he wanted to let it alone. There were words, but he had no idea what they were. He hung back and watched.

Four boys emerged from an alley to block their path. Kane didn't need to wait any longer.

Kids up to trouble always took a while to talk, but he wasn't sure how long a fuse either Wilkins kid had on a day like this.

He was not fast enough. Jeremiah launched himself at one of the boys. Soon two had him, and one was blocking Libby as the other started mocking the boy.

"Two half-breeds," he said. "You got no right to walk on our street."

"Let you go if you crawl," said one boy.

"If you beg nice," said another, squealing as Libby grabbed an ear and twisted it, hard.

"Enough," said Kane, grabbing the boys holding Jeremiah.

The lead talker sneered. "You're that sheriff what got put in his place by the Riders. You're nothing."

"Let 'em go," said Kane.

"Or what? You gonna use that arm the Riders busted?"

Kane's left arm snaked out to grab the big talker by the throat, lift him, and drop him—hard—in a coughing, scared heap. Libby had meanwhile delivered one good kick to the one blocking her from her little brother. Jeremiah was struggling with the two holding him and got in one good punch with a fist that had a rock clenched in it before Kane grabbed one boy who had held him and Libby grabbed the other.

"You do the honors?" Kane asked.

"Hey!" yelled the boy in Libby's grasp before she slammed his head into the horse trough. When he came up sputtering, Kane pushed the other one at her for his turn.

Soon, four pitiful boys, two dripping wet, were on the wooden duckboards. Mary Ellen Pierce had come out of the Last Chance to see the end of it. It was hard to tell if her shock was her way of containing her amusement.

"Ma'am," said Kane. "Know these boys?"

"Too well. That one," she pointed at the big one, "is Harden Jeffries, Enoch's son. The rest are followers."

"Then let's take him home to Papa." Kane turned to Libby, who spoke first.

"I am sorry we did not tell you the truth," she said. "We . . ."

Kane opened his arms. Libby walked in and grabbed tightly enough to remind him of the state of his ribs. His exclamation brought a wicked gleam in her eyes and a smile.

"And that's just the beginning unless you listen to Mama," she said.

"And why would I do that?"

"Because she has a plan," Libby said. "She said because you have the heart of a mountain lion and the head of an oak tree, you need help in the planning department."

"Libby, I would bet your mother said no such thing."

"She used fancier words that I forgot." The girl grinned. "We will be at the church later. Mama said to meet us there."

"How did she . . ."

"Mama knows everything!" She and Jeremiah were led away by Mary Ellen, with the promise of pie.

As for Harden Jeffries, Kane figured it was time to be on the giving end of a show.

He grabbed the boy's ear and, knowing the hotel was not far, dragged the boy through the dusty street until he reached his destination.

"Sheriff!" Jeffries exclaimed when his son was dumped, whining, in the lobby.

"Disturbing the peace, Enoch," Kane said laconically. "Next offense, I'll shoot him."

"Now I know you may have hard feelings . . ."

"Hard feelings, Jeffries? Town hires a man to go up against the toughs that have gotten beyond its control, then stands back and watches them beat him. Hard feelings don't begin to cover it, Jeffries. Town lets toughs shoot the Haliburton girl, town has no right to tell me what to do. Your son tries to push around Libby Wilkins and her brother, you got no right to lecture me."

Before he had returned to the town, he was focused on proving that no one could keep him down. The more he walked its street, the more he grew angry not only at the Riders, but the town itself. They were all guilty. They corrupted Jared Wilkins, and, with their support for the Riders, they were even dirtier than the outlaw gangs he had broken up in Texas.

He wanted to take off the badge and throw it in the man's face, but he checked that impulse. Whatever came next—and his ideas were walking on the far side of the line between right and wrong—it might be his saving grace to say he was the law.

"Your boy, your responsibility," Kane said. "Leash him, muzzle him, do whatever you want, but let me catch him saying one cross word to any member of the Wilkins family, and he won't ever say another one."

He turned and left before his anger took him to a place he did not want to go, hearing an irate father begin demanding why a child he had allowed to roam around the town all day had somehow gone astray.

"Friend Badge!" Halloran said as they met while Kane continued his rounds. "Lost your mind to be here, lad?"

Kane was not in any mood for jovial banter.

"You got any fight left?"

"For what, lad? Against all of them? You cannot beat them, lad. You cannot. You surprised them today; they will not stay surprised long. Chance has given you the hope of a life with Rachel; she is a fine woman and with a fine family. Take what you can get, Kane, or you might end up losing all of it. If you do not leave, I cannot help for what befalls."

"Rachel's a fine lady, Halloran, but we'll walk our own ways, I reckon," Kane said. His thoughts went down a road he wanted to leave. "Never was patient, Halloran. Rather get it done than spend days lookin' over my shoulder. If this Noonan is the brains, he ought to tip his hand. If you want to help me, follow him; watch him. They are more used to seeing you wander than they are me."

Halloran sighed. "Rachel and her daughter would not look kindly on anyone who helps you to your grave."

"Lost once because I was too cocky," Kane admitted. "This time, I fight my way. Get me some information, Halloran."

The man hesitated.

"With me, Halloran, or with them?"

Halloran thought about that for a moment.

"Friend Badge, you will be the death of me, and Sunday supper with Rachel may be a thing of the past if you end up dead, but a grand adventure it will be."

"If you got a gun that fires, find it. Watch Noonan. I will see you later."

Kane had sauntered down to the church after walking through the rows of headstones. If the dead could only talk.

In time, Rachel and the children entered. It was all very simple now. Funny thing how seeing her made it so clear.

"Rachel . . ." He held out his hands. Libby was smiling, Jeremiah, too.

She let him enfold her, then pushed him gently away.

"You are forgiven, and I hope you understand, Kane, that we have learned too well that people we think we can trust do not always pay us back. I should have told you. We will have time later, Kane, to talk about all that. We will. Although I think neither of us are very good at talking about things we wish to be silent about, Kane."

A soft, brief smile.

"There is not much time now. From what you said and what Jared said, and what rumors I am hearing today, I think that I understand much I did not before. The banker will be coming to the ranch next Monday. He said he will make an offer so I can leave before the snow but wants to see the ranch."

"Monday. Five days away?"

"You have five days, Kane. I do not yet know who is connected to whom, but if you assume that the Riders are connected to the town's council—and I think we can be certain there is some connection—none of them will want to do anything for the next five days, because it might upset their plans. After that, I do not know." She stepped closer.

"You told me you were ready to ride away. We can still do that, Kane. The children, you, and I. Whatever they want for the ranch will be fine with me. You do not need to try to even some score that only you know exists. The Haliburton girl played with fire and was burned, Kane. You and I both know that."

"Rachel, would you want a man who ran?" She was silent. "Give you an answer in five days. I will see you then."

"I will prepare." She turned. "Kane?"

He waited.

"Awinita."

He gave her the baffled look she had come to know well.

"It is a Cherokee word my mother loved. It means fawn. That is what she called me until I was taken. I wanted you to know who I really was."

"Fawn. Awinita."

"Kiowa had another word for me after they took me. Hoo-coo."

"Devil," he replied. A wicked grin looked back at him as she nodded.

"Five days, Kane."

They exchanged one look that lingered, then she and the children were gone.

Five days. A lot could change. A lot needed to. He felt like a man trying to climb a sheer rock face, needing one handhold to find his way. Only one.

The saddle shop was open. Gallagher was not surprised to see Kane, and, after some polite conversation about his injuries, Kane got to the point.

"Why is Silas Noonan not part of your group? He owns a business. He has a lot to gain or lose. Like or dislike all the day long, but, if growing the town is a business, I don't understand why he is frozen out."

"It is more the other way around, Kane," said Gallagher. "Noonan said he wanted a wide-open town, all the gambling and drinking there could be. When the rest of the town council was not with him, he refused to do anything else with us. That was three or four years ago."

"When did the Riders first form?"

"Around the same time. There came a time when we really had to decide what kind of town we wanted Rakeheart to be. Other towns were starting to grow, and it was a competition of the fittest to see who would win. I can shoot a gun, Kane, but who knows what I would hit? If we were going to face towns that had toughs, we had to have the toughest toughs. I can't say that it did not get out of hand, but we always thought we were in control. Other towns have sent riders through the streets at night. They do not cause a lot of damage, but they scare everyone. One day, we will not be lucky."

Kane noted again that other towns seemed to do very little damage to Rakeheart.

Gallagher looked down. "I guess we were wrong. I still think there will be a way to resolve this, Sheriff, but I don't know what it is. There was a council meeting about making peace with the Riders, but with you here, I don't know."

"You figure I should leave?"

"I do not want any more violence in town," Gallagher said. "The violence makes Silas Noonan richer, but it leaves the town poorer."

"Yes, it does," said Kane thoughtfully. "Yes, it does."

Noonan oozed deceit. Kane had never caught the man in a lie, but, as he sat across from the saloon owner, he was certain every third word was either false or truth warped out of shape.

He said he knew nothing of any Rakeheart connection to the Riders other than what Kane already knew, and that his conversations with Wood were simply part of his determination not to allow things to go from bad to worse.

"I do not pretend, as some of the others do, that I am somehow superior to anyone else," Noonan said. "My establishment makes money off the fact that men want to drink, gamble, and carouse. I make no secret of this. A town where the only excitement is old women knitting is a town getting ready to die, Sheriff. I do not pretend that I do not abhor some of the things men do, but this is not my fault; it is only business. When men are out shooting at men, they are not in here drinking. And so, in my own fashion, I am a peacemaker as well as a man of business." He was smirking at Kane.

Everybody's words, thought Kane. *Just business.*

Kane knew there was a lie in there but lacked the way to prove it. Noonan's connections with Wilkins were business. Everything was business.

"Think them Riders are in it for just business?" Kane mused.

"Hardly."

"Everybody else is. Everybody else knows exactly what makes 'em money." Kane had half a thought and was trying not to let it drift off.

"What are you trying to say?"

Kane wasn't quite sure but said it anyway.

"Town gets too safe, town gets its way, town gets so big nobody needs to hire the Riders because there's nobody to protect against. But if the town is always at risk, the Riders can pretty much demand whatever they want, because the town knows it always needs them, regardless of how little the Riders actually do. What do you think about that, Noonan?"

"I cannot speculate about the inner workings of the Riders, Sheriff Kane."

"Killing me would have changed the game so much that Rakeheart would have been behind—with the army coming in. But getting rid of me would have meant no one was getting in the way, so the game the way it has been played continues, and they make money."

"An intriguing speculation."

"But those Riders are about as subtle as a punch," said Kane. "So, maybe they are working for someone who wants everything to stay the way it is for a little while longer, knowing that this kind of game never goes on forever."

"You are talking about an extremely clever man."

"And somebody who might act like he's making more money than he really is," said Kane. "Take this place. Empty more than not. Wonder where the money comes from. Drinks can only cost so much and have so much water in them."

"I believe, Sheriff, if you have nothing else to say, I have a business to run."

Kane rose.

"I'll be back. Don't you worry on that, Silas Noonan. I will be back."

Kane was tired and sore as he reached the shack. Almost too tired.

The rifle barked; the slug close enough for him to hear something.

He rode with the pistol in his left hand. The Remington fired where the muzzle flash for the rifle had been.

Hoofbeats told him he missed.

He dismounted, not caring about the pain. He waited. Waited.

A foot. Clear a sound as could be. He lined the gun on the noise. Heard the branch rustle and saw the solid shape against the sky of a deer pulling leaves from the tree near the shack. Kane replaced the gun and went inside. His belongings were sparse. A bedroll, sack of flour, sack of coffee. Yet he was certain they had been moved.

He was upsetting somebody. He wished he knew who it was.

Riding in to Rakeheart the next morning, he knew something was wrong. Conroy, Brewer, Jeffries, and Gallagher were all waiting by Conroy's store.

For him.

"You and Silas Noonan had an argument yesterday." Brewer. Accusing.

"Conversation."

"What about?"

"Riders and such."

"Sheriff, we employ you," said Jeffries. "We want an answer."

"You got it," said Kane. "He complaining?"

"Hardly," said Gallagher, speaking as Conroy tried to cut him off. "He's dead."

"How?"

"Shot behind his saloon," said Conroy. "Where were you last night, Sheriff?"

"Old Tompkins shack," he said. He was intrigued. Had Noonan let something slip he should not? If a Rider killed him, it was not the gang, because he would have heard them. Someone in town. One of the town council? But they were enemies. No. They said they were enemies. Interesting. He wanted to tell Rachel. Let her sort this out through their lies. She saw this better than he did.

"Sheriff?" It was Conroy. "You had nothing to do with this?"

"If I shot everyone in Rakeheart that deserved it, I can think of quite a few folks that would be dead," he said, glaring at Jeffries. "I'll look into it."

"No." It was Brewer. The others began to nod as they moved behind the banker.

"We thought Rakeheart needed a sheriff; we thought you were the man for the job. Since you started working for us, we have had more killings and more violence. We know that you have suffered greatly, but we have decided that we no longer need you in your position, Sheriff," Brewer said. "Our town was better without a sheriff."

Brewer held out his hand.

Kane took off the badge and handed it over. Oddly, he felt free more than he did fired.

"Can I get one last breakfast on the town?"

"Of course," said Conroy. "No hard feelings, Sheriff. I think we both know things did not work out the way we would have liked. The town wants you to pack up whatever we can give you when you go."

"I know," replied Kane. "Just business."

Then he had a thought.

"Who said I was going?"

The looks they gave him back were beyond priceless. Now all he needed to do was understand why they wanted him gone.

Tillie Witherspoon bristled about petitions and elections, but Kane patiently waited until the storm blew itself out. Janie lingered. Kane wondered how long a body would live without really living.

"Not really such a bad thing that they fired me," he said at last. "Got a free hand. Going to Laramie to let the army know. Then Rachel's. If Janie wakes up, don't let that girl think this is over. It ain't."

Halloran, who did not seem surprised Kane was fired, said he had watched Noonan until the saloon closed.

"When the lamps were extinguished, I gave up," he said. "He has rooms upstairs, and he usually stays there after the place closes. Sorry, it is that I am, Friend Badge."

"Last thing I expected. Somebody always seems a step ahead. At least we know whatever he was, he wasn't their boss." Kane did not share the fact that, with Noonan gone, he now had no idea who the Riders' contact was. "Gone a day. Then Rachel's. Likely back here after. You get wind of something, meet me there."

"Where is it you plan to go, Friend Badge, with no badge?"

"Fort Laramie," he said. "Want the army to know I'm leaving."

That was not the full story, but Kane was concerned about saying too much to anyone.

"What does it matter now, Friend Badge? They fired you. The Wilkins lady is a rare prize, and I can see you make her daughter smile. Take what life gives you, Friend Badge, or you will lose everything."

"No woman wants a quitter, Halloran. Army might want to know what I think, too. Won't hurt to talk," he said, thinking that he might try to see if Sherman could be of any use—a question he had been debating with himself, coming to no conclusion.

"You should let all of it go, Friend Badge," said Halloran. "Take what you can get, go find a better life, and do not grab for what you cannot."

Kane merely smiled. After he left, he thought over and over about Halloran's comment. Was the man helping Kane or himself? Kane knew he was probably seeing ghosts, but he was convinced that one of the people whom he spoke to regularly was relaying information to the Riders or whoever controlled them. Halloran was an unlikely spy, but, then again, so was he. He thought of Libby. She and Rachel liked Halloran, so he should as well. He did not want to think that the gang controlling Rakeheart had somehow or other gotten to Halloran, but very little of what he wanted had happened since the day he set foot in Wyoming, and there was not much chance of it happening now.

CHAPTER SEVENTEEN

Lt. August Greene had been frowning and making dubious faces throughout the tale.

"Keep hearing how all these towns keep toughs that need to be held in check by the Riders. Army's good at ignoring problems it can't solve, when it wants to, but the army also knows how to hear things it doesn't know about. About these towns fighting with Rakeheart. Everybody tells me about it, and I guess there were men riding through shooting out windows before I got here, but I ain't seen any evidence of that, and I want the low-down," Kane said.

Greene shook his head emphatically. "Someone making something very strong to drink down Rakeheart way," he said. "Seems a lot of folks are drinking it."

"This don't happen?"

"Kid stuff," Greene said, waving his hands in a deprecating manner. "Somebody sent a wagon to take people getting off the train at Rakeheart down to their town. Drunks shoot out windows now and then in every town I've ever known. Ranchers would claim they had ranches out by one town and go into all the saloons and talk about the water bein' awful so folks would move to another one. For a while they were knocking down the signs they had at the edge of town. This is a whole different kind of violence that you are talking about. No, no. If Rakeheart wanted to out-tough every town along the railroad it would need about five hard men. Maybe six. That's all it would take."

"But you knew about the Company Riders!"

"Of course. Men up to no good. Men who know guns. You know ranchers, Kane. Can't hit the sky if they aim all day. They hire men to do rough work. What's the word? Mercenaries. That's them. A few toughs. Not some private army."

"You sure? I got some evidence they're a bit more than that. Maybe thirty men. Organized."

"Not sayin' they don't exist, Kane. Way you look is proof they do. They don't have running fights with other towns like some kind of range war. That is not so. Can't say I'd mind if three or four of those towns dried up and blew away. Make the world quieter, because they all want the army to protect them from something that usually doesn't exist, mostly Indians. Except for Rakeheart. The only one that never asked. They want the army to let them alone. Arrogant; told you that once. Think they got the answers."

And that, Kane wondered, might be the key to unlocking the mystery of Rakeheart.

It was not home, but the Wilkins ranch triggered a smile on his face as soon as it came into view. He could smell dinner while he was a long ways off. Rachel would have food. Better yet, she would also have answers. Best yet, she would simply be there, and he could let go the breath he always kept in when he was out there alone.

Dinner had been the best moment Kane could recall in days. He didn't feel that he hurt. Much.

But now the food was gone, and he and Rachel had to talk about how two people could face up to everything the town and the Riders could throw against them.

Libby had been asked to leave the table but issued a one-word response that was also good enough for Jeremiah. Kane was uncertain about talking about real life in front of children. No one needed to know how ugly adults could really be until they had to be one. Rachel told him that the children would either sit and listen or listen in hiding.

He asked her about the extent she had seen damage to Rakeheart from other towns' gangs of toughs.

"Never."

"You sure?"

"I did not go often, but everything I ever heard that the other towns did came second-hand. I think it was an article of faith to Jared and the others. Why?"

"I'm starting to think it was all a fraud, Rachel. A game. A swindle, I guess, but I can't figure out the why of it."

He related what Greene told him.

"No real rivalry, no need for a private army, means they are up to something—the lot of them—that they need a private army for. Bet they go off and vandalize from time to time if they need to intimidate someone, but the rest of the time it is all for some other reason."

"What reason?"

"I wish I knew. Conroy admitted to me that they used to smuggle things—stuff stolen from the army; things stolen that were supposed to go to the Indians, smuggled into the reservations—but that hardly seems enough to need the Riders."

"Stop."

He did.

"You can close your mouth, Kane. If I wish you to catch flies, I shall tell you."

Libby giggled.

He obeyed. Her fingers danced as she molded the words she needed.

"Plain works fine, Rachel. Figger this: I suspected you of killing your husband; let you go; you stuck me back together after that and fed me still, in spite of myself. Don't know that all that polite manners stuff matters no more, if it ever did. None of us here are much good at it except Jeremiah, and he's turning out like his sister."

Rachel looked at him for a moment as though there was not a thing wrong in the world, as though sitting in her house talking about armed gangs and dead people was what life was all about. For them, it was.

"They have fooled you, Kane. They told you a story. They made you believe it. Forget everything they said. They fooled everyone. I never really listened, because whatever they did in their world was not important to me. If you take away what they told you, maybe you can figure out what is really happening. Think about what you know, and only what you know. Not how they explained things away, only what you are sure has actually happened. Let me ask you this: they say gangs rode into the town. Who can prove these were not the Riders who did the damage to make the town think the Riders needed to be hired? Most of the people who live there, or come to town, are more interested in their lives than anything else. If Brewer and the rest say so, it is good enough for them. Forget them and their lies. What do you know?"

"The Riders do something that requires guns. It makes the leading citizens of Rakeheart rich, because there has to be a connection, and people only make connections like that when there is money to be had. It can't be legal, or they would not hide so much of what they do and make up stories to scare little children."

"And Texans."

He let that go.

"That story about Tompkins had truth in it. The best lies all do."

"How do you mean that, Kane?"

"Conroy talked about smuggling Indians liquor or stolen army property. Didn't think when he said it. Reservations are too far for your ranch to be the shortest route, or to be the first place the army would come looking. Nobody ever said the army kills itself out here, so they probably look in a few places and give up quick. If you steal from the fort, coming this way makes no sense. It's too far, unless this is a route they've been using for years to transport things around Laramie without anyone being the wiser. And you told me about that level spot on your land. Travel over your land might save a lot of time through a lot of hill country."

"So what are they doing, Kane?"

"I don't know. It pays good. Too good, I think. Town has a lot of stores, men seem to have a lot of money for a place this small. Rakeheart is big as Wyoming towns go, but not that many people ride in. Wondered a time or two when I was sheriff what they were worried about when they talked about fights."

"They were worried about the Riders."

"About that. That's what they said. They ever really act worried? Jared ever hint they were not partners? Town and Riders are partners. Forget this 'other towns' pack of nonsense. They had a falling out. Riders and the town council. Over what? Why do thieves usually fall out? Somebody wants more; the other somebody doesn't want to give it. They were partners a while. Maybe they started small, and then something big came their way. That's usually why thieves have a falling out. Town sends a message to the Riders—me—and the Riders send one back. They get rid of me. Could mean they resolved whatever it was. They got rid of Noonan. Somebody did. Does that play in? This Kruger. Pinkerton, sure. Hunting a baby? Not likely. Out here, everybody is so busy surviving nobody's gonna look years later for . . . what he was looking for."

Jeremiah did not seem to notice, but Kane was still glad he heeded the warning in Rachel's eyes.

"And, if they do, no one is gonna find him. He might have seen the family, heard about it, decided that was a way to get what he wanted without coming out in the open. Everybody's always glad to talk about someone else."

"You mean we acted guilty because we were?"

"Somethin' like that. Probably an open secret in the town." He paused. Neither child asked anything. He wondered if that was good or bad, then kept talking.

"What is there in Wyoming worth stealing? Folks rustle stock; they push each other to seize prime land; they rob each other. That's too small for something that seems this organized," he said. "There ain't no gold to dig here in Hall County!"

It was quiet.

"Paha Sapa," she breathed, a look of wonder falling over her face. For a second, he wondered what had happened. The look on her face was one he had never seen, as though she was given a revelation that came from somewhere outside the room.

"Jeremiah, cut me a good stick," she said. He darted outside. Libby followed.

Kane missed his reply, which was followed by an interjection from Libby.

"No, Jeremiah, it is not for your sister!" Rachel said, laughter filling her usually serious tones.

She was smiling; Kane could tell she had arrived at a conclusion he had been blindly stumbling for, and now he must wait until she was ready. Smirking should be outlawed, he thought.

When Jeremiah brought the stick, they went outside, Rachel leading Kane by the hand.

Stick in hand, she set out north and the other directions in the dirt, then drew a small circle for Rakeheart and a tiny X for her ranch. She drew a square for Fort Laramie and a line for the railroad, narrating this all to Kane as though he were a small child.

She then drew a large irregular circle to the right of the fort and above it.

"There! Clear now?"

It was not.

"You don't know the land, Kane. This"—she pointed to the irregular circle she had drawn—"is the Black Hills. The Sioux call it *'Paha Sapa.'* It is very sacred ground to all Sioux. For the Minnesota Sioux, there was a pilgrimage to see them that many went on. It is also where gold was found."

"And it is in Dakota. I know the Black Hills are in Dakota, Rachel. You can't move them."

"The gold is in western Dakota, Kane, not far away. I had to learn the territory boundaries, and I know Jared told me, years ago when it would not have made a difference, that the Black Hills spilled outside of Dakota. Now do you understand?"

He did not.

"Jared told me more than once about the thefts that took place as gold was moved from those mining towns to be shipped east. One of the main routes out of the mines runs from the Black Hills past the fort and down to Cheyenne, which is in Wyoming and is somewhere down here." She made a mark.

Something came back to him. When he had met with him prior to coming to Wyoming, Sherman had been raving about gold and robberies and the army never doing anything. Kane had not paid the conversation much notice, because Sherman raved zestfully about anything that drew his attention.

"What if some of that gold is stolen? No. We know gold gets stolen. Risky to take it past the fort. I see that. That's here. Everyone in Dakota and along the Wyoming border is looking for it. Out in the middle of Wyoming? No one cares," he said.

"You have ridden to the fort," she interrupted. "As you ride, the land to the north and east is flat, more broken to the south. If you were driving a wagon, it would be easier to manage if you went from the Black Hills west, keeping well away from the fort, and then turned back south around my east pasture, or maybe east of there, and then went to the railroad at Rakeheart. All you need is no one to ever look, because you have men patrolling the roads. If you think about it, this is the shortest easy path around the fort, and the closest that connects to the railroad, while being far enough away that no one would look for robbers."

She paused to draw breath and add one last conclusion.

"That's how they can be rich in a small town when no one should be making any money."

Kane knew nothing of the Black Hills gold rush other than everyone said there was a lot of it. Rachel's theory explained everything they knew except who was doing some of the shooting. There was one other problem. The biggest one.

"We do not have any proof to show this is really what is going on," he said. "I can't take this to the army and tell them to wait until spring when the gold will start moving again, now that it is August and there might not be more shipments."

"I think we might," she said. "Since last fall, I entered some numbers for Jared that made no sense on the back pages of the ledger. He would never tell me what it was for. I think he kept track of what was passing through Rakeheart. The only thing he ever said was that it would guarantee he got his share. I thought it was something with the town, but that was before I got suspicious."

She brought the ledger. Dates and numbers. Could be anything. Anyhow, this was Wyoming. Not Texas, where there were juries and judges. Here, a man was judge and jury—and executioner. Unless that man could find a way to equalize things.

"Saturday night now. One more day and that banker shows

up on Monday?"

"That's right."

"Barely time." He roughly grabbed Rachel by the shoulders and kissed her on the mouth as she protested in wide-eyed surprise, kissing him back before he released her. Both children were squealing.

"Had to be done, Rachel. Never know. He shows up before me, stall him. If we can get him alone, we might have a chance."

"I must commend you, Mrs. Wilkins," Brewer said. "You have kept this place operating wonderfully well."

She wanted to tell him she had been working her hardest to drive it into the ground, but Kane had not yet returned. She needed to be polite. She hoped Kane knew what he was doing. The ride to the fort and back should not have taken this long. Something had happened. Or he had left. She thought of his leaving. No, Kane would not leave her. This was his fight as much as hers. More. She would play her part, hoping to stall Brewer as long as possible.

They went inside, where Brewer gushed insincerely but loudly over Jeremiah's carving and Libby's sewing. Libby played the longest song she knew. Twice, winking at her mother the second time around, in case Rachel didn't get it. Rachel enjoyed seeing Libby this way. The girl and Kane were cut from the same cloth.

Then came the business part. Brewer threw what seemed to be ever-changing numbers and phrases at Rachel until she was thoroughly confused about exactly what numbers meant what. The longer he talked, becoming more complicated when she asked him to make things simple, the more he convinced her that this was not a kind man sharing information, but a wily man trying to bury her under pointless talk so he could get what he wanted.

By the third time she asked him to repeat his spiel, she was certain he was getting suspicious. For her part, she had come to the decision that she needed to tell him her mind was so full of so many numbers that she needed a day to think it over.

Hoofbeats. At last. She turned hopefully to the door and saw a nightmare.

"Wood?" said Brewer.

The lead Company Rider, holding a gun pointed at her, stepped into the Wilkins home. Rachel saw his eyes stray to the spot where Ferguson's body had lain. They lingered there a telltale moment before turning back to her.

"The Devil is loose, Brewer."

"Fool! We are not supposed to be seen."

"You're the fool, Brewer. Slick man got fooled by a dumb Texas cowboy and an Indian squaw. Time to get rid of 'em."

"What do you mean?"

"I heard from our friend at the fort. Kane knows. He sent word that Kane got there late yesterday and was asking about the gold thefts. Kane has the dates. Wilkins must have kept track. Something was sent to the army. Kane's been working for the army the whole time, Brewer."

Wood glared at Rachel. "Only one way Kane could have got 'em. Dunno how, but she knows, too. We've got to get rid of her, all of 'em."

Brewer seemed nonplussed.

"Then we shall deal with this since we are conveniently here. There are children in the house, or somewhere nearby. Find them and bring them. We shall conclude our business here and depart."

He turned to Rachel and, grabbing her by the arm, pulled her out of the house to the yard in front.

"So many accidents happen here, Mrs. Wilkins. Your poor foreman walked into a bullet when he thought he was going to talk about something he should have kept to himself. Jared should have minded his own business. He thought we would let him into the business when he connected all the clues, even with that Kruger business, but he was too unreliable. It was such a good stroke of luck that his death was so quickly forgotten, but, then again, you would hardly have wanted it differently, would you? All that guilt wasted!"

Rachel frowned.

"You never guessed?" Brewer threw his head back and roared a full-throated laugh. "The joke is so truly and terribly on you."

"Jared's death was a tragic accident," she said.

"Oh, no, it was not! You and your daughter should have talked. Someone you'll never guess was there watching. He told me about your argument. Of course we knew your husband was drinking too much. His abusiveness was part of his weakness, so he had to die. Some said it would even be a blessing for you. Hardly! Extraordinary luck the way it turned out. Our man was here the same night that you fought with your husband, although we now understand that may have been more often than we thought at the time.

"We all know what happened. Your daughter fired her rifle, but she was not the only one shooting at targets that night. You were all too caught up in your argument to see and hear it clearly. After the shooting, the rest was easy. You were both so guilty, nobody said a word. You protected us better than we ever thought. They only found one hole in your husband, so no one asked any questions, and no one was any wiser to what really happened."

Brewer shook his head and mumbled about luck.

"When he told me what happened, I knew we were clear. Then Kane arrived. He would not listen and refused even the common-sense alternative of riding away when we made it clear he was not wanted."

Noises.

"Hurry up with those children, Wood! How much trouble can they be?"

A gunshot answered his question. Rachel hoped it was Kane, firing while still out of range. She craned her neck to see.

Brewer looked around as well. A gun fired from near the barn. Loud, angry voices. Now Rachel could see Kane trying to guide the horse with his legs while firing with his left hand. She figured the shots were going wide, but Brewer would not know how terrible a shot Kane really was these days.

Brewer made a quick decision. He started running for his horse. Rachel moved to follow. Brewer started to turn. He pulled a small revolver from the pocket of his coat and pointed it at her.

"Mama!"

Rachel stopped, more from Libby's cry than the wavering gun in Brewer's hand. Brewer now ran away beyond her reach, sure of his escape, but he no longer mattered. Rachel started running toward Libby and Jeremiah, who were trying to wrestle Wood's gun out of his hands. A shot kicked up dirt at Wood's feet.

Don't hit the children, Kane, she thought as she ran toward them.

The shot scared the children more than Wood. Their holds on him weakened, and he threw them off. He ran past Rachel and was in the saddle and at full gallop before she could do a thing. Soon Wood was heading west after firing two quick shots in Kane's direction.

Kane let them go. He had realized that, while he could sometimes hit a target with a gun left-handed while standing, on the back of a horse, it would only happen through chance. If Wood had fired back or turned to brace him, he would have had no hope of coming out of it alive. His bluff was the best card he had.

"What kept you?" she said, after she told him what passed between Brewer and Wood.

He had asked about gold thefts. Greene had downplayed it and tried to tell Kane they were nothing, but then the fort's commander overheard, by chance. By the time the commander was done talking to Kane, the day was well gone.

"Greene wasn't in on it. Some fella—name I didn't get—lit out while I was there. Greene was tired, discouraged, and lazy. Only saw what he felt like seeing. He passed off everything he heard as just talk. Fort tried to cover its tracks, but Sherman is not going to be a happy man."

To make matters worse, Kane missed a sign on the trail, which delayed him almost too much.

"I found the trail they used for the gold," he said. "I think. Saw a marker, then another. Followed them a bit; then I realized time was getting away from me."

Libby and Jeremiah seized upon their status as rescued heroes. They recounted at least five times in succession the way they defended their mother until they had received about all the gratitude they were likely to get with the promise of extra dessert tiding them over until then.

"What do we do now, Kane?" Rachel asked. "By my count, we have a wounded sheriff, a woman, and two children against about—what did you say? thirty Riders and their friends in the town and whatever other friends they have that we do not yet know about."

"How many men you got left?"

"About a dozen. Some of the hands that Jared signed last fall left when he died. The men who are left are cowboys, Kane, not gunfighters. I don't want them hurt. I don't think they are an army."

"Get a bunch of them together. Get to Rakeheart. Wait at the church. Not sure how this plays out, but I want you near, and I don't want you alone."

"Kane?"

"Time to end it, Rachel. We wait, and one fine day they all show up here, and the kids can't get away. Not sure you can run far enough and fast enough. Settle it now. If we act fast enough, they won't expect it. If we don't, we don't stand a chance."

Kane looked down one more time upon Rakeheart.

He had galloped most of the way from Rachel's ranch but wanted to have one look to plan what he was going to do next.

He thought of how much had changed since the first time he and Tecumseh had stood upon the hill overlooking the town. Then it was nothing more than a collection of buildings. Meaningless. Never again.

Rachel had a point that he could not win a showdown or a battle. There were enough dead people already, and he did not want to add to the list. Folks like Pete Haliburton might be willing to take revenge, but what could they really do?

If it came right down to it, he had no idea who in Rakeheart would side with him and who with the town leaders who had been fooling them all so well. He needed to think straight more than shoot straight and be ready for the final piece of the puzzle he knew was out there but knew he had not yet found.

Eloise Brewer was agitated at her unexpected company.

"Frank will not be home for some time," she said. "I am not sure it is proper for a married woman to host a man without the presence of her husband."

Part of Kane hated to do what came next.

"Because he will hurt you again?"

She recoiled. "How can you . . ."

"Do not tire me with lies, Mrs. Brewer," he said. "Mae

mentioned your visit. I added up what it meant; she believes you only came from kindness and not from experience. Tillie Weatherspoon saw another piece of the puzzle. I know you are being beaten. I am not here to continue your misery but end it."

"How can you do that?" she challenged. "I heard them talking. You are not even the sheriff any longer."

"Where are they meeting? I know they are. I can end this. This place, this Wyoming place, don't give a man power to hurt someone else because she's a woman. Man doesn't have the courage to face up to it."

"Noonan's—or whatever they will call it. How do you know?"

"Little pieces. Don't know who guessed. Not my business except for what I need to do. Doin' what I can."

"I do not ask for easy, Mr. Kane. I ask for a day when I do not hurt to be alive. Mae said you were good to her. What else do you want?"

"Your husband has a desk here. Where? I need what's in it. Is it locked?"

"No," she replied. "He is very regular in his habits. He told me that it would never be locked, because I was never to look, and I never have."

"Then I will."

Kane rifled the drawers until he found a small book. Dates and amounts. Best of all, names. A banker kept track of money. Everyone's money, even in banks that were in Denver. The book went into the pocket of his jacket.

"When is he home?"

"An hour."

"Then you have one hour to decide if you want to be here when he finds his desk has been touched, if, in fact, he comes home. I do not think you do. I think this thing I'm going to do sets you free, but I know if you don't have a husband, you don't

243

have money, so I don't know if what I'm going to do is a good thing or bad, but it's the only thing I know how to do. If your husband has cash stashed away any place in the house, if I were you I'd find it before I leave."

She was trying to think.

"I would bet Tillie Witherspoon would help you," he said. "She is giving shelter to a young woman who may be dead by now for all I know. I think you could get cubs away from a bear easier than anyone could get to you inside of her shop."

"Oh, the girl from the stable. Frank does not like her, or either of them." She thought. "Frank does not like Tillie, either. He calls her a meddler who always has to have her opinion heard."

Kane felt the press of time.

"I shall leave you to decide, Mrs. Brewer. I hope the choice you make will lead you to someplace that is happier and safer."

Kane walked to the church. Afternoon was fading as the August day drew to a close. He noted with satisfaction as he waited outside that Eloise Brewer had gone down the street in the direction of Tillie Witherspoon's shop.

He went in. The church was empty. The preacher was with somebody, he guessed. The man's horse had been tied outside earlier. He shrugged. Somebody needed Siegel.

Kane had never been what he called a religious man, but there were too many lives bound up in the next few hours for a man to want all that weight on himself.

He thought about what to say and how to say it. Then he recalled a phrase from the days when Aunt Amelia read the Bible at dinner.

"I never had to worry about nobody before, God, and, whatever it is, I don't want to lose none of 'em I am trying to protect, so keep them safe somehow. I don't know how, but You do, and let them kids grow up in some better world and some better place. And those I'm responsible for, maybe they can know I tried to help 'em and tried to do right, and I guess we better get it done, God, 'cuz nobody else can or, if they can, they won't."

He paused.

"And if it's time, it's time. Don't matter. Much. Keep Rachel safe and them kids. 'Specially Libby."

In the time he had been inside, dimness had begun to spread. They would gather at Noonan's. He undid the bandage on his right arm. It would hurt more, but he could use it a bit easier. After tonight, it wouldn't matter.

Wasn't a snake in the world could live long when you cut off the head. Tonight, he was the knife.

Rachel and her men had not yet arrived, but it did not matter. They would soon. She would know what to do. She was smarter than all of them.

The Last Chance smelled good as he walked past. Coffee would have been nice.

Later.

He could see the early traces of the sunset's colors reflected in the window of Conroy's shop. The street was empty. Were they at Noonan's? Had Eloise Brewer tipped them off? He would find out in a minute.

Dozens of times in his weary weeks in Rakeheart, he had felt that he did not know what he was supposed to do, or where he was supposed to turn. Not tonight.

How many times had all the fine words in the books come down to a man with a gun and the will to use it? He wondered, if Sherman knew it all, what he would say. Smoke and cuss and cuss and smoke and make them quiver at the sound of his hacksaw voice. Sherman would outlast them all.

The piano was audible now. Be a mercy to shoot the thing. He looked up toward the east, where the growing darkness gathered behind the curve of the street, where he had ridden in and met a young woman who would never be young again, unless she died that way.

He had unconsciously come to stand where the Riders had delivered their beating. He'd like to settle that score. Business first. Personal would have to wait.

He looked behind, around. No one. Touched his hat. "Sleep gentle, Rachel. Best this way."

He turned to the doorway and the lamps beyond it.

"God bless, Libby."

He touched the butt of the Colt in his right holster with a hand that had been useless far too long. It hurt, but it felt like a man becoming whole. Tapped the Remington with the fingertips of his left. Both loaded. Both ready.

A round of male laughter emerged from the saloon.

Time.

Chapter Eighteen

They were there. Brewer, Gallagher, Jeffries, Conroy.

Kane's slow footsteps across the warped, bare wood of the rough pine planks were drowned in conversation and music when he started his walk to the far end of the bar but became audible as the talk and music faded and died.

Jeffries reached in his jacket. Kane did not care for the formalities of life. No waiting to find out if a man meant well or not. Not today. Not these four. Not ever.

The Remington fired. Jeffries went down with a bullet in his leg as the small pistol he was reaching for clattered along the floor. A miracle. Kane had aimed for the man, although it had been the other leg. The smile that mocked his own shooting flared and passed.

He walked. Red faces. Gallagher and Conroy radiated shame; Brewer, defiance. Fear? None. Instinct said he was missing something. No Riders.

He had walked the town enough to know.

Amid men trying to move out of the way of the gunfire, a figure by the door caught Kane's attention and held it. If trumpets blow when fools see the truth, they were drowning out the wind right now.

Kane glanced at the floor, where misshapen circles radiating out from the bar marked the places liquid had slopped from the glass the man by the doorway had taken to the table. Now he sat, almost beyond notice, clearly waiting for the drama to take its course before he took a role. He would get his chance.

Play it out.

"Gentlemen." Kane was fifteen feet from them. Nobody could miss at this distance.

"I can explain everything," Brewer began.

"Kane, all of this is a misunderstanding," blustered Conroy.

Gallagher looked down. Jeffries, stung more than injured, glared back from the floor, where the bullet to his left calf had sent him.

Now was the gamble. He would take it.

"I know it all, gentlemen," Kane said. "All of it. The gold, all of it. Funny thing, when Sherman sent me out here because Wilkins got killed—man dotes on those fellas who marched to the sea—he was raving about gold and such, and I half ignored it. Man's gonna be real happy when I tell him how you corrupted someone at the fort. Real happy. Hear you eat every day or so in federal prison. Hope that's not true."

Kane watched their eyes. They were waiting. It wasn't over yet.

"This is what we are going to do. Any of you with a weapon, set it on the bar. You got one chance to do this. You put a hand in a pocket, I will assume you are going for a gun, and I will shoot you the way I did Jeffries."

The hands complied; their eyes braced for the next step. Kane walked closer. Closer. He had to be close. It had to look right. Their faces mingled fear and tension. They were watching the Remington in his hand. Eight feet away.

Then Gallagher's eyes showed hope. They flicked to his left. Brewer's, too, but faster. Back quickly.

Kane turned. The first bullet shattered a window as Halloran's first shot hit one of the men behind Kane. The second bullet hit Halloran in the right shoulder. He drew the Colt as Halloran's second shot went wide. Kane fired both guns, almost not caring where the lead went, as everything he was seeing was filtered in a white haze of pain. Men were diving from tables to the floor. More windows shattered.

Halloran staggered. The gun in his hand was waving in the direction of Kane as it wobbled. Halloran put a second hand to steady the wobbly arm.

Kane looked over his left shoulder to see what was behind him. Gallagher was down. Brewer had grasped a pistol on the bar. He was waving it in Kane's direction, then jerked it toward the doorway, then back toward Kane. Kane turned toward him, then saw Halloran moving as well.

The guns all went off together as an explosion sounded behind Kane. A hot blast rushed past his face. Something stung. Glass flew across the saloon as what seemed like every bottle behind the bar shattered. Brewer was thrown hard against the bar, then slipped down with a gaping wound in his chest.

Kane wiped the blood off of his right cheek as he glanced at the doorway, where Rachel stood holding her shotgun. Wisps of smoke came from both barrels. Her face was drawn and tense as her eyes met his.

"Jared gave me solid slugs, not just buckshot, in case I needed them. I thought we needed them now." She was staring at the smashed glass and bleeding wreckage that were the results of her blast.

Kane nodded in acknowledgement, then looked over at Brewer. The banker was already dead. Halloran's shot at Kane had gone wide. Kane's shot at Halloran put the man on the floor. He wondered whether a bullet or a fragment of a bottle had cut his face. No matter. Still alive was all that counted when the guns stopped.

Conroy, unharmed, was pale. He raised his shaking hands as he got up from the floor, where Jeffries was bleeding and whining. "Don't shoot. Please. Please. Please," he whimpered.

Kane walked quickly to Halloran. Three bullets. One in the shoulder, one in the chest, one in the guts. He took the gun from Halloran's hand as he knelt.

The man was gasping. A red-toothed grin. "Friend Badge. Smarter than ye look. When did ye know?"

"For sure? Tonight. I knew none of them were smart enough, and Noonan was so contemptuous of them all that they could not have been his boss, and he was not clever enough to be the leader—he only acted the part. When Noonan was killed, I suspected. No. Sooner. You were a town drunk with the most sober eyes I ever saw. Wondered then. You kept leading me to Noonan. Then you fooled me. Fooled Rachel. Why? Why did you rescue me and not leave town? Why do this at all?"

"If a gun had been to hand to shoot them all that night, I would have used it, Friend Badge. They failed to follow orders. Yon Wood is a hothead. The job I gave him was to intimidate you, rough you up, make it unpleasant to continue. Get ye to leave, ye fool! Gettin' old and soft. I liked you, lad. Could see ye and Rachel . . . her children. My soft spot, that lady and that wee girl of hers. A dead sheriff meant the army, but he could only see you as the one man who would stand up to him." Halloran coughed. It was bright red. Eyes met.

"The money was so easy, Friend Badge." Even dying, the thought made Halloran smile. "The smuggling paid; the army never knew what it lost, and the Indians never knew what they never got. Then the gold came. It was too big a hand to let ride. Rakeheart was perfect. Too far for them to see. Ah, the army, sitting on its brains all day. Perfect."

Kane looked down at the dying man. A game. The winner lived; the loser died. The game of the West.

"Friend Badge! My share is in the bank in Denver. The rest gave it to Brewer, but I did na trust the man. I . . . I had to kill Wilkins . . . because I knew what he was. Foul. Cruel. That was personal. That night . . . I hated the killing, Friend Badge. Necessity. Libby told me once how they fought night after night by their barn, the man and sweet Rachel. Wilkins was getting to be a liability . . . going to ruin everything. I went to their ranch. Three times . . . perhaps I was afraid to kill him myself. Rachel would be close by him when they talked. Argued. Then that night, I had him. She was clear; he was in me sights. I pulled that trigger, Friend Badge. It was a good thing I was doing. I smiled at my own righteousness."

Halloran coughed blood. He gasped but was not done telling the tale.

"Then little Libby's gun went off . . . too late to explain. I know . . . I know I hit him, and the little girl must have missed. Never meant her . . . guilt. Rachel did not deserve that . . . Couldn't tell. The only thing I regret. The rest . . ."

"Just business," Kane finished in a tone of disgust. Even dying, Halloran was stung.

"The little girl . . . sad-eyed Libby . . . was real, Friend Badge. The wee lass. She was a sad, lost soul cast adrift out here. Never had . . . daughter. Wanted you . . . Take them and go. Could ye na ha taken the hint? Someplace that was cleaner . . . better. Too late now . . . fool."

"You do not deserve to have my daughter's name in your mouth!" Rachel came into view, stared down at a man she had welcomed as a friend. Halloran's eyes widened. He became agitated and moaned, blood fouling his words. "You kept your mouth shut to save your own skin and left Libby to believe for sure that she was guilty."

She turned away, the boots she wore for riding loud in the saloon's silence.

Kane bent to hear; Halloran grabbed his arm to pull him lower as he whispered.

"Run. Ye fools. They're coming! Run n—"

Whatever else his lips were forming to say was choked off by a rush of blood and then lost forever as his head slumped to the floor.

Kane, gun still in his left hand, turned to Conroy.

"What did he mean?"

Kane thought Conroy was going to faint or drop dead.

"You can join them," Kane snarled.

"They sent Siegel to fetch the Riders."

"The preacher?"

"Halloran had something on him. No idea what. Siegel didn't want to go. Someone saw you ride in. They had been waiting because everyone knew you would be coming. We told everyone we knew to be on the lookout. We were supposed to get you to talk to stall until they showed up. He left a while ago; the Riders are already on their way, Kane. I don't know how far you can get, but there's about thirty men coming to get rid of you for good, son. We never wanted this. We wanted the money."

Kane only thought briefly of shooting the man. There was no time. He turned away after telling one of Rachel's hands to get Jeffries patched, if anyone had the time or inclination.

Conroy, however, was not done talking.

"We wanted to end it, Kane. We wanted it to end."

"How's that, Conroy?"

"There was one more gold shipment next month—the last big one before the snows. We were going to take that one and get out of this. It was getting too risky. The army is sending more men out here next year to control the Indians. More patrols would mean that they might find out. Wood did not want to quit. We thought if we had a sheriff, the Riders might decide not to fight back, and they might move on. We never meant for all of this to happen."

"What about Kruger?"

"Halloran thought he was hired by the Pinkertons. He was afraid of him. He had Wilkins so scared of the man that Wilkins was willing to kill him to join the group. I didn't think he would do it, but he did. He was never the same man after. Starting hating us as much as he hated himself. Then the snow came, and everyone forgot. We wanted one more haul, and then we thought we could end it. All we wanted was this one last shipment, and that would have been the end of it."

Rachel and Kane exchanged glances.

"Don't look like that!" Conroy fumed. "How many men are there out here who have done what we did and worse, but no one knows because it happened back East? We all know men who broke the law back there but helped build communities out here. Wilkins was going to betray us; Halloran was sure of it. He sent letters to William Sherman all the time. We opened and read them. Nothing in them, but we could never be sure. The man could not be trusted."

He looked at Rachel.

"Killing your husband was not something I knew about. We knew Wilkins was unreliable, but Halloran went off by himself. No idea why he let something personal influence his judgment. It created suspicion. That foreman knew enough to cause trouble. It kept getting worse when we wanted it to end! You must have been glad to be rid of him."

Kane put out a restraining arm. Her hand had drifted to the knife she wore at her waist.

"You are not worth it!" she spat, walking to the doorway of the saloon.

Kane soon followed her.

"Are Libby and Jeremiah at home?"

She nodded. "Five men with 'em. Best I had. I brought six men with me."

Kane nodded absently and looked out the doorway. The sun

was taking its time in setting this day in a sunset that was filling the sky with an orange hue that looked tinged with blood. It might be dark by the time the Riders arrived, but darkness would not delay them.

"We end it here."

Rachel had moved next to him, her left shoulder touching his bicep. She also looked to the west. "Got a plan?"

"Kill 'em."

"Good. My arm would have been tired from spanking them all."

He looked at her. When you plan to shoot and die with someone, words don't matter.

She read his face. "Kids need me, Kane, so maybe come up with a plan we all live through. No coffee, otherwise."

"Nag, nag nag." They were like that for a moment that seemed like it would never end. Then she let go with a deep sigh.

"Squaw go round up boom sticks," she deadpanned. She waved her arms wide. "Make big, big booms."

When she looked back to see his expression, Kane was looking back with a grin that spread the longer he looked as he slowly nodded to himself.

" 'Zackly." He walked away. "Conroy, your place locked?"

"Of course."

"Open it. We got shopping to do."

Kane moved back to her. Hard hands clutched her shoulders.

"Put the man of yours with the best eyes and the fastest horse on that east road. Might only be a few minutes, but it beats no warning at all. If there are any innocent people in this place, get them indoors. Don't want anyone else gettin' hurt like Janie, if she's even still alive. Anyone wants to join the party, they can, but don't want folks who can't tell which end to shoot to get killed. Meet me at Conroy's."

He was gone.

The smooth white circle of the moon was clearing the jagged rocks to the east as Kane waited. Leading out of Rakeheart, the hard-packed road of dust gleamed white in the glow. Kane had watched as the moon inched its way over the hill, as it had before men disturbed its presence with their schemes and would long after men and dreams were dust. The plan was mostly patchwork. He had seen worse ones succeed and better ones fail. He could neither hear nor see the Riders, but he knew they had to be approaching. He gave the moon another look. His last one? Time would tell.

Rakeheart might live. It might die. But after tonight, it would never be the same.

All of Rachel's men were waiting at the stable. Kane made sure they knew what to do and when to do it.

Kane had wondered if the Riders would try to ride around the town, take it in reverse. He rejected that. This was not merely a scrap. They needed to regain control of a town that was slipping from their grasp. It had to be public.

Conroy's store supplied the spare rifles and ammunition. In fact, every gun Conroy had was gone along with everything else Kane thought would be necessary. Kane looked down Rakeheart's street. At what the darkness held.

"I got the right," Chad had demanded. He was in Tillie Weatherspoon's shop. Janie might have breathed better, or there was a rush of optimism. But she still never moved a muscle. Tillie had no illusion her windows would survive, or that anything else would. She had her shotgun and Chad.

"One of them—one of them—gets this close, Sheriff, and I will blow him to Kingdom Come, and I don't care if you arrest me. I have had enough of these Riders and cowards." Kane wondered how brave a man would need to be to try.

Pete Haliburton, sober now, and a few of the other townspeople took positions at the far end of town in the church. Kane had no illusions that his ragtag army would stand and fight or be effective when and if it did. They needed to slow the rush of the Riders when they hit. It didn't matter if they won their fight. The Riders needed to think a big ambush was brewing and get off their horses.

Rachel was waiting in Conroy's shop. He had no idea if it was logic or not, but they were going to end this together. Rachel still had some shotgun slugs. She also took a rifle in case she ran out.

"I might not hit anything, but I can scare them."

"You with a rifle scares me, too," he replied.

"A bit rusty on scalping, Kane, but I might get it right if I practice on you long enough."

Eyes met. Then hands. They waited.

One horse, loud in the night. Drake Phillips was back.

"They might be five minutes behind me, Kane. No more."

"Tell the rest. Shoot straight."

He walked down to the church, told the volunteers to stay down when they weren't shooting, refrained from observing that the dead would not have far to go to be buried, and walked back to Conroy's store.

The store was set slightly apart from the rest of the block by an alley that ran along the right side of the building as it was seen from the street. Beyond the building there was a space of a few yards before Brewer's bank.

Rachel had everything ready.

"Time."

She took the butt end of her shotgun and smashed out the windows in front of her.

"Them depredations and them Indians," Kane remarked. "Got to get me the army out here to deal with 'em proper."

"Do your own side, then, and quit whining," she shot back. He did.

The white of the moon was now shining straight down the street in front of them, leaving both sides in darkness. Most of Rakeheart was dark except for Noonan's.

Death was coming to Rakeheart. He was sure he could hear the Riders. He leaned as far as he could through the glassless window.

Near.

Near.

Rakeheart exploded.

Rachel's cowboys would get one good chance, and they were making the most of it. Two volleys of fire were directed at the mass of men riding past. Kane had ordered them to wait until the front of the pack had passed.

Guns opened from Tillie's shop. There were now horses milling in the street. The Riders never got to Conroy's.

"Kane!"

He leaped through the shards as Rachel bellowed at him.

"Get back here."

He stood in the middle of the street, where the moonlight was so bright they could not help but see him. The Remington was emptied as he fired as fast as he could. One of the Riders saw him. A bullet thunked into the wood. Rachel's voice kept calling until the gunfire grew too loud to hear her.

Soon bullets were sailing into the shelves and displays, landing in the ceiling. They came closer as Kane ducked into the shadows.

Rachel fired her shotgun into the moonglow-drenched street, where men could not have been better targets. Kane heard windows shatter and men yell. The shotgun blasts stopped them from charging the store, then they fell back to the shadows across the street.

"Rush them, you cowards! They're in the store!"

Kane knew Wood's voice.

As Rachel kept shooting, he ran in the alley. The flame from his gun would give his location away.

He hoped.

He moved back deeper. Reloading in the dark with stiff fingers was a challenge, but it got done faster than he expected. Facing death does make a man hurry.

He fired fast. They had to follow.

They did. He holstered the guns and hugged the wall of the alley as he ran to the back of Conroy's store. He made as much noise as he could running through the back door, which he left swinging open behind him.

Heading into a dark place after a man who had a gun was enough to make anyone pause. The Riders were no different, until Wood started cursing at them to move.

Kane had cleared a path that was barely visible in the dark. Rachel was firing intermittently. She had switched to the rifle. From the noise, Riders must be firing back from across the street. They had seen their comrades run down the alley and must have figured it was a matter of time.

He moved the barrels. It would happen fast. He could see the trail of darkness. He hoped they could not.

One breath. Now!

He fired the gun from behind one barrel and moved as quietly as he could toward the window he had left open. Gunfire—six or eight guns—smashed the barrel as he fired enough extra shots to keep their attention. The foul liquid stung his eyes and face, but he wiped it and ducked down. More bullets hit the barrel. He was splashed as he crawled on all fours but did not dare stop.

Now for the big risk. He heaved himself up to the window. He was sure something Rachel sewed shut popped open, but, if they lived after this, he would have all the tomorrows in the world to heal.

Pull. Up. Air! Out.

The bottle was there. The rag was wet. He lit the match. The rag flared. He knew they would soon see the light outside the window. He threw it as the flame caught, hearing the glass crash against something—or from the exclamation of pain, someone.

"Fire!"

The flaming kerosene caught the pools and drips Kane had spread across Conroy's back room. Men well into the store had an irresolute moment as they debated whether to run out the way they came or face Rachel and the front door.

It was their last moment.

The kerosene hit the black powder Kane had left after he and Rachel pried apart as many bullets as they could to add to the sacks Conroy found for them.

As Kane raced around to the front of the store, the explosion deafened him. The force of the blast knocked him sideways, and he slammed into the brick of the bank, bouncing forward and falling until he caught himself to emerge from the space by the front of the store to see Rachel on the duckboards, prone.

Too much powder, he told himself, as though there would be a next time.

Flames were licking toward the front of the store. Gunfire erupted up the street. A wave of shooting came from the far side of Rakeheart's main street.

Ignoring it all, he ran for Rachel.

"Ow!"

He had grabbed her arm where, by the glow of the flames, he could see a patch of skin was burned away.

"You sure you didn't blow up and burn down Texas, Kane?"

"Got to run, Rachel. Think we maybe used a mite too much."

She could be angry later. If they lived.

"Men can never read recipes," she grumped, giving him her good arm for him to pull.

Kane turned to fire at the Riders across the street. After sending several shots blindly toward them, he realized they were not attacking but walking slowly in the glow of the moonlight, hands upraised. Four men, maybe six. Pete Haliburton was yelling something. Tillie Witherspoon was demanding he watch his language.

Kane pulled Rachel's uninjured arm before they, too, became victims. Together they moved as fast as two half-dead people could. They arrived, gasping, behind the bank, where Kane feared the Riders were regrouping.

Other than the inferno that had been Conroy's store, where small explosions took place as flames reached the ammunition Conroy would never sell, there was silence. The flames showed two charred bodies that made it out from the store. If any of the Riders who chased him into the building ever escaped alive and fled, there was no sign.

Rachel looked her question. Kane shook his head. It could not be over.

Kane and Rachel slowly walked back up Rakeheart's moonlit main street in disbelief. Eight Riders were lying dead by Tillie Witherspoon's shop. Seven lay by the stable. Seven others had surrendered. None rode away. The rest left the world of men in the flash and fury of the explosion.

It was over.

By Noonan's he came to the form of Conroy, lying face up in the street with a Colt in his hand.

"He got away from me," said Zeke Hughes, one of the hands who rode in with Rachel. "Yelled something about redemption, and he was out that door. Think he got one of them before they got him. Not sure; it was all noise, and then it was over."

Hughes cleared his throat and said a stray shot finished

Jeffries. Kane did not ask. He did not care.

"Just bury them. Families want them, they can have them."

The wind gusted; smoke billowed and swirled. Kane moved down the street.

"Haliburton! You know the town and the men. Fire brigade before the whole place goes up," Kane called out. "Got to be somebody left to save the place for."

CHAPTER NINETEEN

By dawn, Rakeheart was a sight to behold. What used to be Conroy's store was a skeleton of blackened wood, where anything stood at all. The bank remained standing, but its windows were shattered, and much of the wood inside was damaged. Gallagher's saddle shop, which had been across the alley from the store, was a complete loss. Scorch marks from windblown flames marked a few other buildings, but everything else had been saved.

The smells of the charred wood, wet from the water that had been thrown upon it, and the burned leather from the saddle shop made the town smell of death.

As the sun replaced the moon's glow along Rakeheart's main street, dead men still lay in the dirt next to jaded men and women who had thrown buckets of water at the flames all night until their arms could move no more.

Rakeheart was scarred, but it was alive.

Soon, Tom and Mary Ellen Pierce, who had spent the night fighting Riders and fires, were walking through the knots of survivors, doling out coffee, bread, and whatever was left over from the day before. Others were soon helping.

Siegel, who confessed to Kane that he had killed a man in Chicago and let it slip once to Halloran, was contrite.

"No time for that," said Kane. "Got people to feed, dead to bury. Past don't matter no more, Preacher. Not nobody's past. Too much work to waste the time looking back. Everybody out there, Preacher, their real lives begin today."

Wood and Karl were both pulled from the wreckage of Conroy's store, along with six others. Kane had wanted them dead. Now they were. He felt nothing. It was long over, and all he wanted was to rest. Soon.

Kane talked to the assembled Riders who had survived.

"You are done riding rough over the law. Wood and Halloran hired you to steal whatever you were told, whenever you were told, as though the law did not apply to you. That's over. I want answers, or none of you get out of here alive. Who killed Clem Ferguson?"

"None of us," called out one voice. "Someone from the town hired Clem to watch ol' Wilkins 'cuz they didn't trust him. We'd act in town like we wasn't friends, because it was supposed to be a secret or somethin'. One of them town people—that town council."

"I think Wood did it," Rachel whispered. "He gave himself away at the ranch."

"Who ordered it?" Kane called.

"Wood talked with them folks," the man said. "The town council. Never wanted to kill nobody, Sheriff. Idea was always to scare people but not kill 'em. That night he went crazy was nothin' any of us signed on for. Wood liked killin'. He liked hurtin'. Some of us was plannin' on pullin' out come the snow because he was gettin' worse."

"Who killed that Kruger man last fall?"

"Wilkins," the man replied. "Don't know more, but Wood said that he had to test him, had to be sure of him. Might have been something else. Dunno. They didn't tell us everything, Sheriff."

Kane was certain Conroy had been lying. Perhaps not about this.

"Who took potshots at me?"

"We got told to see if we could scare you off," the Rider said. "Wood didn't want no sheriff here. Nobody hit you. If they'd'a said to kill you we'd'a done it, but they never did. Didn't mean no harm . . ."

"Just business," Kane snapped.

Kane wanted to argue and claim the Riders knew more than the man was letting on. He wanted answers. But the man had the ring of truth in his voice. At least more truth than was common in Rakeheart. Kane could keep it going. He could end it. No choice.

"She's dead!"

Chad Washburn emerged, wet-faced and bareheaded, from Tillie Witherspoon's store.

"She gasped once deep, and I thought she was coming back, and then she went," he told Kane. He looked at the Riders huddled together. "And one of them did it!"

He drew his gun and was in the act of aiming it when Kane shoved the boy hard with his left arm, his right by now having screamed at him that he had gone beyond its limits.

Chad stumbled and then looked down the barrel of Kane's Remington as Kane moved between Chad and the Riders.

"Can't let you kill them, boy," he said. "They might deserve it. Might be the best thing you ever did, but it ain't right. You can't kill a man who gave himself up, no matter how much you want to."

"They killed her!"

"Never gonna know who did, Chad. Might have been them. Maybe the ones that are dead done it. Wood was a killer, Chad. You kill a man without a gun in front of all these people, and it is murder, Chad. Throwin' your life away."

Tillie Witherspoon had been trying to catch Chad. She now came next to him and touched the arm that held the gun.

"Chad? I need you to help me prepare her. I can't do it alone."

Chad wavered.

"I'm sorry, Chad."

Rachel Wilkins walked into the circle of spectators. She put a hand on Chad's right shoulder.

"Too many people are already dead, Chad. You cannot bring her back. Please?"

Chad looked daggers at the Riders, spared a glance of disgust at Kane, jammed the gun hard into its holster, and went with Tillie as she took him by the arm and led him to her shop, holding him firmly, Kane noted.

He told the Riders they could ride out with one pistol each and some food. No rifles, nothing else.

"I see any one of you back here, I will kill you without asking," he said, ordering Rachel's cowhands to be sure the men left one by one to avoid any of them thinking they could return as a group.

Racing horses sparked a panic, but it was two children who did not seem to know the meaning of obedience, flanked by every Wilkins ranch hand that wasn't already in town.

"I told you to stay!" Rachel scolded as Libby and Jeremiah eventually managed to stop after scattering more than a few townspeople.

"Mama, there was all this smoke in the sky, and we had to come," said Jeremiah.

"It was his idea," Libby agreed. "I came along to keep him out of trouble, because I am a good big sister."

She grinned at Kane, who grinned back.

Lefty Sullivan, whom Rachel had put in charge at the ranch when the rest rode into town, explained the situation.

"You want them critters not to run off, we got to get back out there. Those kids were either gonna ride here with us or without us, Miz Rachel. Got sand, them two. Figgered it was safer this way, even if it left the ranch open. Had to watch 'em every minute last night to keep 'em from coming here in the dark. Could not hold them off no longer once the sun came up. Pistols, both of 'em. Rather watch cows, ma'am."

"You 'figgered' right," she said. "But don't tell them. It might make them more headstrong than they already are."

"Not my place to say, Miz Rachel, but I don't think that can be did."

Rachel laughed as she watched Libby happily jabbering at Kane. Jeremiah looked around at the burned buildings, holding Kane's hand. Kane dropped his hat on the boy's head, making him laugh. She smiled at Sullivan.

"I think, Lefty, there might be someone who will give that a try!"

Rakeheart was quiet. The army, stung by the fact that someone within Fort Laramie had been working with the thieves to frustrate its efforts to prevent robberies or catch the thieves, had descended upon the town in reprisal, but there was nothing left for the army to do.

Kane felt a twinge of pity for Conroy, whom he knew was less evil than some of them, but even good men pay the price when they build their dreams on the bones of the innocent, he mused. The rest, he would have gladly shot.

Janie was buried in the churchyard. The stone gave her last name as Washburn. Kane doubted there was much of a legal wedding, but if it helped Chad survive, it was fine with him. Most of the town turned out, although Eloise Brewer had managed to disappear without anyone noticing.

Tom Pierce, a quiet man who left the talking to others, was trying to help the town survive. He hung the Last Chance sign on Noonan's, which still gave cowboys a place to be young and stupid, but the food was much better. Townspeople admitted one by one to Kane that the town's leaders had insisted that the

Riders were important, but since they never asked for money from the citizens to support them and paid the bill for the Riders themselves as the leading town citizens, it did not really matter much.

Tillie Witherspoon's name was tossed about as the person who ought to be the town mayor. She blushed, giggled, and said it was about time someone with sense was in charge. No one bothered with an election. There was no time for such things when there was work to be done.

Bill Cartwright had started working on a new building for a general store. The army had agreed to share some of its stocks of food and clothes with the town. Since Cartwright was building the new place, everybody figured he might as well run it. Kane liked the way Mae Cartwright smiled when she heard.

But laying ghosts to rest would only go so far.

"No," Rachel hissed at Kane as they sat on the stone fence watching the sun dip down toward the distant hills. They had returned to the ranch earlier that day.

"Rachel, you heard what Halloran said. If we tell Libby that Halloran shot Jared, she can stop thinking she did it."

"Kane, you don't understand."

"I don't want Libby living her life under that shadow," Kane insisted. "She ought to know she might not have done it!"

"Is it better to have her know she told the man who killed her father, if he was telling the truth, how to find him? Is that better? Do you even believe him? Kane, that was a horrible, terrible night. You were not here. You cannot understand." Rachel's voice began to rise as she recalled the anguish of the boiled-over emotions that raged on the night Jared was killed. She balled her hands into fists.

"Libby is just starting to come back to life. Do you really want to keep her trapped in that night and have her picture what happened over and over again by telling her something that could be a lie? You do not know what happened—truly know. We never will! What do you want to do? Dig up Jared to find out which gun killed him? Think! This is her life we are talking about!" she exclaimed heatedly.

"Are you two fighting?" Libby's face and tone reflected her fears. She had lived through one family where fights took place every day. She knew how that ended.

"No," said Rachel, at the same time Kane said, "Yes."

Kane was quiet a moment as Rachel glared, and Libby turned perplexed, fearful eyes upon him. Life and death. Today and tomorrow. Guilt and feeling guilty. He realized as something like an answer came into his head at last that Libby would shake her feelings over the past about the same day he would convince himself that he bore no share of blame for getting Janie into the predicament that got her killed.

"Folks say to forget the past, Libby. All the bad things. Doesn't work. You can pretend it's gone, but one day it all comes back. We all got to live with it. Ain't always easy. But justice comes around. Them that deserve it get punished. The Riders. The rest of 'em that got dead. They got retribution for what they done." Kane was sweating trying to make himself clear, aware how much he was failing. "When bad men start doing bad things, even good people get caught up in it all, and bad things happen."

Libby looked puzzled more than comforted.

"Mr. Kane is trying to say that we need to look ahead, Libby. The bad times are over."

"Then why didn't you say so?" Libby asked Kane.

Kane struggled with an answer until Rachel rescued him again.

"Come here, child," she said as she patted the still-warm stones from where the sun had shone upon them. "We can watch the sun set, and Mr. Kane can talk more sense by keeping his mouth shut than he ever does when he speaks."

Libby looked from one adult to the other, laughed, and hopped up between Rachel and Kane as the day drew to a close, and the Wyoming prairie slowly wrapped itself in the velvet darkness of night.

The September wind had veered and was now strong from the north, Kane noted, as he looked at the weathervane on the barn. These past days, the wind and Rachel had much in common. Some days she wanted to live on the ranch forever. Other days she wanted to leave it far behind.

Kane tried to talk about Wilkins. Once. After days of finding the right words. He explained that what pushed Wilkins over his own edge was killing a man just to get into the town's inner circle. It was not Rachel's fault that he changed.

Rachel had let her hair blow loose in the wind that day. They were sitting on the fence by the horse barn, and the fading sun was in her face.

"Kane, anybody ever tell you that you handle words about as well as Jeremiah does an axe?" She did not give him time to respond. "Perhaps someday, Jared will not be a raw, hurting hole in me. It may be then that I can understand what you are saying. That day is not now, and it may not be ever. You mean well, Kane, but do not speak to me about him again." She got down from the fence. "Ever." She walked back to the house alone.

Halloran's Denver bank account amounted to more profits than the ranch could have made in ten years. As the sheriff of Rakeheart, with the weight of the army at his back, Kane ordered the bank to pay her. Rachel at first said it was evil money, but then she decided to keep it. She had no idea how to give back what was stolen to the rightful owners. She made a gift to Tillie Witherspoon and the town to buy some lumber to help repair the damage she and Kane caused, but the rest she set aside because, sooner or later, her family would need it. Kane had buried the money Sherman wanted him to give Rachel under a floorboard of the Tompkins shack. He gave it to her, entertaining Libby along the way with a stammering explanation of why it was not delivered immediately in the days when he suspected Rachel of killing Wilkins. With that and Halloran's money, they could mismanage the ranch and still eat.

Kane found out the depth of Halloran's game when he visited Frost Springs and Gray Flats. Each of them had been visited by toughs allegedly from Rakeheart. Each knew Wood as the leader of a group one town knew as the Protectors and another as the Regulators. Each knew Halloran as a man who helped them arrange for their protection. Kane made sure they understood it was all over.

Kane had been fired but put the badge back on to help give the town some sense of order. He had wanted to toss the badge back at Rakeheart and leave it far behind but now felt an odd reluctance to leave the place to itself now that there was even less need of a sheriff than there was before. Ranch chores kept his hands distracted, but there was no sense of purpose in his movements. He figured one day he might turn over the badge to Chad Washburn, who had grown into a man. Maybe soon.

Then the rider came.

Kane lived in the bunkhouse at the Wilkins ranch. There was room, with the hands out. He liked it there, but he knew that the day would come when the crew would return. He would have to decide if he stayed or if he left.

He was gazing south across the flat lands. He saw the man while the rider was a ways off. The rider was not hurried and seemed stiff in his movements. Kane did not perceive a threat. Still, he picked up a rifle. He could shoot one now. Hitting what he shot at was another story. His arm was healing, and he could more than not hit what he aimed at with a pistol, but with a rifle, his shooting might never be what it was.

"Rachel. Company."

She emerged from the house with her shotgun. Kane was as unclear about his future as she was about hers. There were thoughts that made him wonder if he could handle responsibility; there were days he knew he could not. There were days when he knew there was no other place he belonged. That Libby had very clear opinions on his future was easy to see; to Jeremiah he was a cross between father and big brother. He wished his life was as clear to him as it was to them.

The rider was taking his time. The man had lots of gold braid, even on the coat he wore over his uniform. He was not young and looked fatigued from travel. He announced his intentions from about as far away as a man could yell.

"Got a letter for a man named Kane they told me in town was staying here."

"Who from?" Rachel called.

"General William Sherman, U.S. Army headquarters in St. Louis," the man called back. "I'm only delivering it."

Kane set the gun by the fence. Rachel kept hers ready.

"What's Sherman want?" Kane called out to the man, who said his name was Col. Roland Jones, that he had come from Denver and then to the ranch by way of Fort Laramie.

"Never open the general's mail, myself," said the man with a grin. He stood expectantly. "I have to wait for a reply."

"Come in then," Rachel called.

The letter was in fact a telegram to Kane: "Coming Rakeheart 12th. Special train. Meet me."

"He always like that?" Rachel asked.

"This is him being polite," Kane replied.

Kane looked at the messenger.

"You don't know anything about this?"

"I know the fur has been flying since the men from Fort Laramie came to get what they could of that nest of snakes you cleaned out of Rakeheart," the man said. "General was a mite angry that his soldiers were outsmarted. Some folks got sent other places they will regret ever seeing. He sent this to me because I don't think he trusts them to do anything right."

It was the fifth of September. Sherman would be leaving in a day or so. He was not asking. He was telling. Kane thought back. It was barely three months since he had sat in Sherman's office wondering what Wyoming might hold. He had found out.

"Rachel?" Kane had drifted off and missed what she said.

"Pay attention for once." Jones almost stifled a snicker. Kane saw two heads in the doorway listening.

"We might as well see him, Kane. Otherwise, we will be waiting for him to show up here, if I understand him correctly, and I do not want the army paying a visit."

The special train puffed almost as much as the man it carried.

General William Tecumseh Sherman inspected Kane while holding a fat envelope Kane had managed to slip him. Pulled his coat tighter. Puffed. Mid-September winds get cold in Wyoming, especially when a man not accustomed to being told what he must do is being lectured.

Tillie Witherspoon, as mayor of Rakeheart or whatever she decided to call herself, was welcoming the general while demanding the army pay for every last bit of damage that took place. She had a list. A long one. She was gesticulating with energy. Kane enjoyed the show. Nothing set Sherman aback like an angry woman. Kane figured Sherman would promise enough wood to build three towns if it got him away from her.

Kane had used the time between knowing Sherman was coming and the train's arrival to write a report explaining everything he had done and why. He knew Sherman was itching to open the envelope and read.

"Won't that make him angry?" Rachel had asked Kane.

"Had enough lies," he had told her.

After telling something that made Tillie Witherspoon respond, "Well I should think so!" and leave the train platform with her head held high, Sherman walked over to where Kane, Rachel, and the children were waiting.

He began to read every word of the report while he sent forth a volley of words about the punishments meted out to the guilty and the inattentive.

In between gulps of reading and puffs of noxious smoke he examined Rachel intently and not very discreetly over the top of the papers.

"Can I tell him it's not polite to stare?" she said in one whispered aside to Kane.

"You can tell him. Won't matter, but you can tell him."

Sherman eyed them as though they were disobedient privates.

"Last thing we need out here is war," he said to them while scanning. "Army has to keep order. Sounds like you two waged your own war without informing anyone. Told you to stay in communication."

"I could have sent a smoke signal," Rachel loudly muttered in a tone the wind fortunately swallowed along with her words. Sherman caught some of it and looked at her sharply.

"It worked, General; wasn't that what you told him to do?" she said, refusing to back down. "And if you told him how to do it, you know he would have disobeyed you, because that's how the man is."

Sherman's eyes—as best they were visible behind more clouds of cigar smoke—reflected both mirth and respect after her outburst.

Rachel had been uncertain about meeting the general, but he

was charm itself. Kane was certain there was a giggle he had never heard before after one Sherman remark about handwriting aimed at Kane, whose early departure from school was reflected every time he put words on paper.

Jeremiah, whom the general kept calling "Sherman," and Libby, who found that the general wanted to hear all about how she made her dress and said she should have a metal flute that he would send her from St. Louis, were delighted with the man who had decided—no, demanded—they should call him "Uncle Billy," the words by which thousands of soldiers knew him.

Sherman and Jeremiah drew a horse together in the dirt with sticks the boy had sharpened and argued over the name until Jeremiah won. Sherman told the boy and his sister to see if there was anything in the train they might want to eat. Rachel left with them, casting a look over her shoulder at Kane as she stepped into the general's private car.

The men were left alone on the windswept platform.

"Now what?" barked Sherman.

"Not sure," replied Kane. "Not goin' back to Texas. Might stay here a while."

Sherman handed him a piece of paper.

"Good. Hired. Territory has no law. Montana, Dakota. No different. Army should be the law. Hear rumblings about the Sioux. Black Hills. Fools started a gold rush. Looks bad. Powder keg. Need stability. You do, also."

Sherman. Always the optimist.

"Army needs a detective. Not a Pinkerton man. Useless. Always want more money. Always. Someone I trust. You. Got a family; I see that. Married when?"

"We haven't . . ."

"Life doesn't wait. Good woman. Comanche? Good choice. Stood by a man who wasn't worthy of her. Don't like being fooled, Kane. General has to have faith in his men. Not all of them deserve it. Wedding present." Sherman handed him a thick envelope. "Back pay since the war. Tired of hanging on to it. Not sure why I had to deal with it, but since you were not going to . . . well, it had to be done. Army will pay you to be sheriff as well as whatever I need you to do. And keep that Witherspoon woman happy! I don't want to hear from her again. She don't like something, fix it until she does. They will know at the fort. Order out here. Order. Must have order. The army has to uphold order. Hear that? Now take this. Tired of carrying it across the country."

Sherman could never do a good deed without grumbling to prevent any accidental eruption of thanks and refused to let Kane even try to say the word, changing subjects and firing off orders.

"Got to get telegraph strung here. Stay in touch. No more private wars. Black Hills are trouble. No trouble here, Kane. Fix it." He bellowed to an aide and barked out that the telegraph line must be extended to Rakeheart before the snow fell.

Rachel and the children left the car, the children still chewing something. Sherman took his hat off to her. She could see the men were talking and waited by the depot.

"Keep me informed." Sherman turned to leave.

"General. What if I don't want the job?"

A full belch of smoke emerged at that remark. Sherman moved to within inches of Kane's face.

"Want it? Kane, none of us want this job. It's the job we have to do. A world full of fools and drunks. That's the real West, Kane! Look who comes out here, Kane, along with all the decent people who want to grow a family. Every card sharp, robber, thief, murderer, and loafer hoping for an easy way out. Don't take 'em long to turn wild like wolves. Then the army has to save them when the Indians could do the world a favor and rid the world of a few of them. Sometimes, Kane, and say it I will deny it, I wish there had been an ocean no one could cross to protect the Indians. Great fighters. Men try to rob them blind and kill them when they get caught. Wish we could pack them off to some safe place or enlist them, but it don't hold. It don't work. Most of 'em would rather die than lose the land, even if they don't know what to do with it. Sad. Dregs of the East drift out here. Someone has to control it. My job." Multiple puffs. "Your job, now."

The cigar wagged as Sherman talked.

"Sioux. Comanche. Had them in the army, we would have whipped Lee in a month. Their day is done, though. Can't expect them to accept it. But we need order. Red, white, they break the law, shoot 'em. Whatever disturbs the peace, fix it, stop it, fight it, kill it if you have to." He looked at the raw wood of the new store under construction. "Guess you know that already."

Sherman looked out at the hills. Puffed a cloud.

"Settlers killing each other, whatever it is, we have to stop it before it gets out of hand, like this did. A territory without the law is not good, Kane. Report to me. Job is what it is, Kane. West needs law. Indians and whites alike. Justice. Job is yours. Pay's better than you were getting, so no more objections. Think that girl wants a piano? Boy's a little small, but when he's ready for a good horse tell me."

Kane was quiet so long that Sherman eventually stopped watching Rachel and the children and looked at him. "Well? What is it, Kane? Pay is what it is, Kane."

"Wonderin'. Does this mean I have to salute?"

The lines in Sherman's craggy face erupted in wrinkles as he grinned.

"Why start now?" Sherman gripped Kane's hand hard enough to break it, pumped it as though drawing water from the deepest well in creation, reminded Kane to tell him when he should send a wedding gift, and then turned away, calling to an aide for coffee and cigars. He darted past Kane to tip his hat to Rachel and talk to the children one last time. Soon the special train—two locomotives sandwiching one car—was gone.

Rachel waited for it to puff its way out of sight, then came over to Kane. She laid her left hand on his right arm.

"What did your general say?"

"I get to stay here and work for him," Kane said flatly.

"No."

Kane frowned. "No?"

"Do you think a general in St. Louis is the boss you will listen to or a Comanche in Wyoming who makes you coffee?" she said with a laugh. "That is, if you have come to realize that Comanches are very particular about being married, and terrible things happen to men who take advantage of poor, defenseless young women. Anyhow, with winter coming on, the crew needs the bunkhouse, and I hear you are the king of slobs, and there would not be room enough for them and you. And as for the barn . . ."

"Horse never complains."

"To you. The rest of us hear it all day long."

"So that leaves the house, and that means . . ."

She mimicked him perfectly.

" 'Zackly."

Even Kane had to laugh.

"Your general has given you a gift, Kane," she said. "The gift of a new life. Think about it."

He was. He watched the train puff until its smoke was a distant tiny wisp of a cloud. He could feel Sherman taking the old life with him. Might not have been much of one, but he knew the rules. It fit him like an old boot. This new life? It was the life at which Wilkins failed. Most men failed. He probably would, too.

Then a small hand touched his. Libby.

"Mama says it is time to go home, Kane. Aren't you coming?"

The past was now out of sight. The future was in the eyes of a girl who could look past the dust of her yesterdays and find hope in tomorrow, a boy with no father, a woman who defied the world every day, and a rock-hard frontier where only the strong could survive.

It was time. He squeezed her hand.

"Let's go."

ABOUT THE AUTHOR

Rusty Davis is a Spur Award–nominated writer who writes about the rugged individualists of the West as they fight for freedom against the corrupting influences of power and wealth. He draws his inspiration from the conflicts that raged across the towns and ranches of the High Plains in a time when men and women who wanted to fight for what was theirs needed to pick up a gun—and risk their lives—to do so. Davis is the author of two other westerns, *Wyoming Showdown* and *Black Wind Pass,* both published by Five Star. His next book, *Spirit Walker: A Cheyenne Saga,* which looks at the Cheyenne exodus from a different perspective, will also be published by Five Star. Davis can be reached by email at rustywork777@gmail.com.

The employees of Five Star Publishing hope you have enjoyed this book.

Our Five Star novels explore little-known chapters from America's history, stories told from unique perspectives that will entertain a broad range of readers.

Other Five Star books are available at your local library, bookstore, all major book distributors, and directly from Five Star/Gale.

Connect with Five Star Publishing

Visit us on Facebook:
  https://www.facebook.com/FiveStarCengage

Email:
  FiveStar@cengage.com

For information about titles and placing orders:
  (800) 223-1244
  gale.orders@cengage.com

To share your comments, write to us:
  Five Star Publishing
  Attn: Publisher
  10 Water St., Suite 310
  Waterville, ME 04901